CHRONOS
AND THE
NEW CIRCLE

EDWARD ECK

YEAR
of the
BOOK

Year of the Book
135 Glen Avenue
Glen Rock, Pennsylvania

ISBN 13: 978-1-942430-53-7
ISBN 10: 1-942430-53-1

Library of Congress Control Number: 2016931698

To Mom and Dad

PROLOGUE

Bright stars shone in the clear night sky above Cairo. Moonlight cast dark shadows in the bazaar where vendor carts normally lined the busy street. But this evening, carts were left unattended as if abandoned in a hurry. A solitary figure crept through barren streets and melted into shadows as he neared his destination. His eyes darted and his nerves were on edge. He sensed he was being followed, but the message had been urgent.

He passed a shop with dark windows and caught a glimpse of his reflection in his black trench coat as he attempted to avoid detection. He was Egyptian with black hair that was greying at the edges and wore a gold ankh on a chain around his neck.

A light was on in a quaint shop that sold trinkets to tourists. Shadows in the window indicated someone was present, but he had no idea if it was his mysterious emissary or an enemy. Time was running short so he took a chance.

Upon entering the little shop, he was surprised when a frail elderly gentleman stepped from behind a stack of shelves filled with Sphinx and Pyramid souvenirs. The old man's simple green robe did nothing to indicate his status. Mass-produced and overpriced tourist items ate up every inch of shelf space. After assessing the man for a brief moment, the shopkeeper motioned silently for him to follow to a curtain-covered backroom.

Crates upon crates of tourist bait lined the room except in the back where a single bare bulb provided the meager illumination. Beneath the light, a young man in his late teens was fast asleep on a ragged old cot. His hair was unkempt and dirt streaked his face. The front of his tunic was ripped and stained with dried blood though his breathing remained regular.

When a ring of others stepped out from the shadows, the solitary figure feared he had walked into a trap. He started to speak, *"Alecto..."*

"No!" The older man held up his hands, fear etching his face. The others shifted back into hiding. "The use of any magic and they will find us."

The man in the black trench coat stayed silent, fear gripping his heart. A bead of perspiration ran down the side of his face as he scanned each set of eyes upon him. He waited for someone to explain the reason for his mysterious summons and the obligatory secrecy of their meeting.

The elderly man lowered his hands. "Hankun Mala, I presume," he said in just above a whisper.

"Call me Hank. You are?" Still being cautious, Hank realized he was outnumbered. He backed into a nearby corner, fists clenched, keeping everyone visible before him.

"You are among friends," the elderly man spoke softly as if to calm Hank. "We need your help. You must take the boy to America." The older man extended an open hand toward the young man on the ragged cot.

"Why? Who is he?" Hank took a few steps toward the unconscious person to get a better look at him, but gave no indication of recognition.

Stepping forward, the old man knelt down next to the boy as he placed a hand on his head. "His name is Chronos," the old man said, but when Hank continued to look perplexed he continued. "He is the Titan Chronos, from Greek mythology. He is one of the three immortals—and possibly the most powerful sorcerer on the planet."

"He's just a kid. How can he be Chronos? The guy would have to be thousands of years old."

"He was near death when I found him and has been in a coma ever since. Each day as his injuries mend, he's getting younger. Soon his wounds will be healed and he will wake. You must take him to the New Circle in America."

"What makes you think I know how to find this New Circle?"

"You are friends with Gollnick Strom of the Old Circle, are you not?"

Hank didn't respond right away. He wasn't sure how they knew about the Circle, new or old, but he needed to remain cautious. "Maybe, but why bring him to me?"

"Only you have the knowledge to find the New Circle in time. Please, you must take him. The ancient seal is weakening and the portal between our world and the Nightmare Realm may soon be breached. Even now, the spells protecting the prisons around the world are beginning to weaken. Dark sorcerers will try to free the creatures of myth and build an army. They will rip open the seal and cover the world in darkness."

"How do you know all of this?"

"I know what I must know in order to deliver the power you need to save the world."

"What?"

Hank was still trying to comprehend the response when another man rushed into the room and whispered something into the old man's ear. The alarm on his face alerted Hank to trouble. Maybe he really had been followed? Hank's heart sank as he looked around the room, but didn't see another exit.

The old man addressed the room. "It's time. Dark sorcerers have arrived. We must defend the shop until Hank can make his escape with the boy."

Twelve people, men and women, rushed out through the curtain into the shop. Within seconds, an explosion rocked the building. As dust fell from the ceiling, the old man rolled back a carpet on the floor to reveal a trap door.

"You must take the passage to the river. There is a small boat waiting there. I'm sorry I don't have time to tell you more. Please, you must make sure Chronos finds his way to the New Circle. They will need his power if they are to keep the portal closed. If they don't, then all is lost. We will protect your escape to the last man. Good luck, my friend."

No sooner did the man say his farewell than he ran from the back room to join the fight.

Hank could hear spells being cast and more explosions. Trinkets from the shop were falling to the floor each time the building rocked. Screams of pain from injured sorcerers on both sides echoed through the devastation. Hank wanted to join the battle, but knew his task was the reason the others were defending the shop with their lives. He wasn't willing to let their deaths be for nothing.

Hank opened the trap door to find stairs leading down. He hefted the boy over his right shoulder then descended with great care. Still hearing spells flying and explosions rocking the building, he made his way out through the passageway.

The ancient tunnel ran for over a mile before they encountered a metal gate covered in thick vegetation. As Hank cleared the moss-covered gate, he paused to notice the sounds of battle that previously echoed through the sandstone tunnel had been silenced. A new fear struck as he sensed their protectors had been overrun. It would not take long for the enemy to discover their escape route. Working more diligently, he cleared the remaining vegetation. The rusty gate creaked loudly, too loudly, as it swung open to reveal a small rowboat secured to a mooring stone a mere ten feet from the exit.

Hank lowered the limp body of Chronos into the rickety old boat. The chipped paint and small puddle of water in the bottom of the craft did not infuse Hank with confidence. But with the sounds of battle gone, he knew the adversary had surely penetrated the defenders' ranks.

Hank cast a spell. *"Destra assor rectu."* An explosion caved in the tunnel exit while Hank leaped into the rowboat and grabbed the oars. He began to maneuver them downstream with as much urgency as he could muster.

1 AWAKENING

Just enough light emanated from beneath the door to give objects in the room a vague definition of shape. Heavy eyelids resisted, but surrendered to the desire for consciousness. Through hazy vision, the boy could tell the room was small with almost no furniture. Beside the bed was a nightstand with a chair next to it. The blinds were shut, but the slightest hint of sunlight crept through the cracks and cast little lines of daylight on the floor. The room had the stench of ammonia. The scent triggered thoughts of cleaning, but he couldn't quite put his finger on when or where.

He felt groggy and disoriented after being roused from a long deep sleep. His tired eyes peered around the room again, attempting to get his bearings. The boy spotted a mirror on the opposite wall. Though he had no idea how bad he looked, he was certain how bad he felt. Each endeavor to sit up in bed caused a wave of nausea to wash over him, forcing him backward onto his pillow.

Though unsure of his objective, his hands discovered a small object with a button connected to a cord. With tired fingers, he grabbed it and pushed the button.

A moment later, a lady in white rushed into the room. She seemed frantic to make sure he was all right and that he remained reclined in his bed. She was dressed in a nurse's smock with her hair up in a bun, though a little overweight. She snapped on the light and rushed back to the door. "Call the doctor, he's awake," she yelled down the hall.

The lights were bright for someone who had just awoken from a lengthy sleep. Again the boy attempted to sit up, but slower. He could only barely see his reflection in the mirror through squinted eyes. The patient he saw reflected was in his late teens with olive-colored skin and dark frazzled hair. He was slender with a muscular build though he didn't feel strong at the moment. As with most hospital patients, he wore the standard-issue gown that was open in the back. He was covered in layers of sterile blankets.

"Where am I?" was all he could think to say in his dry scratchy voice, still squinting to adapt to the bright light. His mind was trying to kick-start like an outdated computer with too little memory. The excessive light improved neither his sense of perception nor his mood.

The nurse waited by the door until a doctor sprinted into the room. A tall man with thinning grey hair bent to examine his patient, stethoscope dangling. From inside his white lab coat, he pulled a penlight from the pocket of his striped shirt.

"Where am I?" asked the boy once again, barely able to focus on anyone or anything. His mind continued to try and sort through cloudy images just beyond his reach. The penlight further aggravated his vision, causing him to now see spots where it had flashed in his eyes.

"You're in a hospital in Baltimore, Maryland," the doctor replied, continuing his examination. He seemed more concerned about his patient's vital signs than bedside manner. After a few moments, he stepped back and crossed his arms over his chest.

"What is your name?" he asked the boy.

The patient looked up from the flat of his back and just stared at him. "I don't know."

With sudden concern, the boy scanned the room for something or someone familiar. A rush of adrenaline at the shock energized him into action—action for which his body was not yet ready—and nausea set in once again. But he needed to get up. He needed to get out of there. But go where? He couldn't think, he needed to remember, but it wasn't there.

"Just take it easy," instructed the doctor who attempted to restrain the boy. The patient's eyes darted around as he continued his attempts to sit up and get out of bed again and again.

"Take it easy?" the boy cried in disbelief. "I don't know who or where I am, and you want me to take it easy?" His mind raced as anxiety amplified. *Why can't I remember who I am? Why don't I know anyone?*

He strained to remember anyone or anything familiar to him, but each attempt left him more frightened and alone. Agitated, he tried to force his way up and out of bed yet again.

The doctor had to use more strength to restrain the boy. "Nurse, a sedative!"

She grabbed a needle off the cart just inside the door and ran to the other side of his bed. The patient, fighting harder now, turned and pushed upward into the doctor's chest. She plunged the needle into the boy's bare bottom, revealed by his open-backed gown, and pumped in the sedative.

After a few seconds, he became groggy and fell back onto the bed. Before fading from consciousness, he heard the doctor ask the nurse, "The man who comes to see our amnesiac friend, when is he expected again?"

"Tomorrow afternoon, if he keeps to his normal routine," responded the breathless nurse.

The doctor sighed. "Good. Keep the boy under until then. Hopefully a familiar face might help to calm him."

* * *

The next afternoon, the patient woke again. This time, there was a middle-aged man seated in the chair next to the nightstand with a book in his right hand. He gave no indication of noticing the boy's consciousness as he continued to flip pages. Dark eyes stared at the pages as if in search of something hidden within. The book appeared to be very old with a soft leather cover that had seen better days, its spine repaired more than once, and the scent of old leather hanging in the air.

The mysterious man looked up from his book and made eye contact. He had short, salt and pepper hair with considerable stubble for a beard. His black button-down shirt and pants were barely visible beneath a brown trench coat. He appeared in good physical shape for someone of his age, but the boy had no idea who or why the man was seated at his bedside.

"Hello, my friend," said the stranger. "I see you've finally awakened... and not a moment too soon. How much do you remember?"

The patient frowned in concentration. His eyes dropped to the sterile bed linens then darted in panic around the room. He attempted to sit up and this time found his nausea was tolerable, not nearly as bad as the day before.

"Nothing." He took a few deep breaths while he studied the older man's face. "Who are you?" he asked, wondering if this person before him was a friend, family member or something else.

"Not to worry." The man stood up and stretched. He had obviously been seated too long. "Based on the doctor's report, I expected as much. We have to get you up to speed as quickly as possible. But not here," he said, moving to the boy's bedside. "I've arranged to have clothes brought for you. The doctor has already signed your release papers. Once you're cleaned up and dressed, we can get out of here." He spoke and moved with confidence.

The boy had little choice or reason to argue. At least he was about to get out of this place which made him happy, but his lack of memory kept him anxious.

Everything about the place and the people seemed confusing. How was it he knew how to walk and speak, but could not remember anything else?

"Who are you? For that matter *who am I?* And why should I go anywhere with you?" Fear and uncertainty gripped his heart as he tried desperately to remember anything about this mysterious person.

The older man gave him a quizzical look, as if it should be obvious why the patient should go with him, but then he conceded, "I guess you have a point. My name is Gollnick Strom." The gentleman bowed slightly. "You are... Well, for now, we're just gonna call you Max. I'll explain later. Right now, we need to get you out of here. If the wrong people find out you're awake, you could be in some serious trouble."

Max had a sudden sense that maybe he had been better off unconscious. *I just woke up yesterday and already I have enemies?* Questions were heavy on his mind, but the man seemed anxious to leave.

Max forgot his list of questions when a teenage girl walked in carrying a bundle of clothes. She was thin and attractive with tight blue jeans and a white t-shirt covered by a trench coat similar to Gollnick. She gave him a pleasant smile, but her expression turned more urgent as she addressed Gollnick.

"Nick, we have a problem. I saw two men in dark clothes asking about our friend here at the front desk. We've got to move fast." She waited at the foot of the bed for a response.

Gollnick checked his watch, concern obvious on his face. "They got here faster than I expected." He slipped the leather book into a coat pocket and faced the door expectantly.

"Who got here faster than you expected?" Max looked from the girl to Gollnick in an attempt to follow the conversation. He had no idea what was upsetting them, but based on their reaction, he too was concerned about these unknown men in dark clothes.

Gollnick peeked out the door then looked up and down the hallway as the girl walked closer to Max.

"Hi, I'm Meagan Strom." Her blue eyes sparkled as she handed him the bundle. "Now get dressed. We don't have much time." Long curly blond hair stretched down to the middle of her back. Max had trouble thinking.

With the bundle of clothes in hand, he slid out of bed to get dressed. A slight breeze up his backside caused his face to redden. "Um, could I get a little privacy?" he said, trying to hold the back of his gown shut with one hand.

"Oh! Right, I'll be in the hallway. Yell if you need any help." The smile on her face turned to mortification as she realized how awkward her comment must have sounded. She fled to the hallway and closed the door behind her and Gollnick.

"If I need help with what? Putting on clothes?" Max said once she was out of the room.

Max undid the bundle Meagan provided, but the clothes looked somehow strange, as if they were not his normal attire. He pulled on the blue jeans and black t-shirt. The shoes seemed even odder than the clothes, but he put on the white sneakers anyway. Finally he looked at the trench coat and thought, *Unusual robes*, but put it on as well. The clothes fit, but he couldn't shake the odd sensations.

Max was examining his new clothes when he heard a noise in the small bathroom. He took a few steps toward it, but moved cautiously, listening for the noise again. The door flew open and out stepped a man in a black suit and black trench coat. Taller than Max, his slicked-back black hair, goatee and sunglasses gave him a striking dark appearance.

"You will come with me or die. Choose now." The man's straight face indicated this was no joke.

Max had no idea who this new stranger was, but at least Gollnick hadn't threatened to kill him. When the stranger raised his right hand and pointed a clenched fist, Max decided he really didn't need to know who this guy was. He just wanted to escape.

The ring on the dark figure's finger began to glow as he muttered something in a strange language. Max began to back away when he realized he didn't have anywhere to go.

Before the stranger could finish his incantation, Gollnick burst into the room. His right hand was engulfed in flames. He dove toward Max and pointed that hand at the man in black, a ball of fire shooting forth.

The stranger adjusted his aim and a beam of light shot from the ring, just missing Gollnick. A scorch mark marred the center of the door where the beam had hit. The flames Gollnick threw had engulfed the stranger's right arm in fire.

Max stood there dumbfounded, unable to move or react. He had just witnessed one person shoot a light beam from a ring and another throw a fireball from his hand. *Is this a weird dream?*

Gollnick hit the floor hard, but rolled into a crouched position in front of Max then faced the stranger. He shot his left hand forward this time and threw yet another ball of fire at the stranger.

The man in black turned and let out a grunt as the sphere slammed into his back. He stared at his arm still engulfed in flames then fell to his knees. Once again, he began to mutter something to himself.

Gollnick seemed to understand the stranger's words and unexpectedly sprang to his feet, grabbing Max and diving over the bed. Just as they crashed to the floor on the other side, the room burst into brilliant light.

Max pulled away from Gollnick and stood. Much of the room now bore the same blackened marks as the door. The only thing left of the stranger was a big black circle on the floor covered by a puddle of water where he had previously knelt.

Backing away, Max turned to Gollnick and opened his mouth to speak, but Gollnick held up a hand to stop his questions before they started. Max didn't know how to process what he had just witnessed. Had the world gone mad? Or had he gone crazy?

"Now is not the time for questions. All will be answered. For now, we need to get you out of here." He ran to the door and called, "Meagan! It's time to go." Gollnick grabbed Max by the arm and headed for the bathroom.

Max shrugged off Gollnick's grip and started to back away. "I'm not going anywhere with you. You're as crazy as he is... I mean was... whatever," Max said, pointing to the puddle.

"Max, you don't understand, they're after you because you're a powerful sorcerer. We need to keep you safe."

The world really had gone mad while he was unconscious! Who was this Gollnick and why should he go anywhere with someone who throws fire from his hands? Max couldn't process the questions in his mind fast enough. He turned and ran for the door, but Meagan barreled in and the collision sent them both sprawling to the floor.

Meagan quickly stood, obviously surprised. "Do we have a problem?"

"Our friend here is panicking." Gollnick moved closer to Max again and grabbed him with a firmer grip.

Max was puzzled by the direction Gollnick had chosen for their escape. Why were they heading to the small bathroom? He had to wonder if these two even knew what they were doing. Or worse, maybe they were escapees from the psych ward.

"Hurry, the other ones are on their way!" Meagan yanked the hall door shut and her curly blond hair whipped around, dazzling Max.

Gollnick entered the bathroom first. It was just a small room with a toilet, sink and handrails for the disabled. It definitely looked like a hospital bathroom, and smelled like one too.

Meagan pushed Max inside as Gollnick started to mutter something just as incomprehensible as the stranger had done a minute before. When he finished, the mirror's surface began to swirl like a whirlpool with a myriad of colors.

"Stick your hand into the mirror," ordered Gollnick as he looked to Max with expectation.

"What? What is that?" Max staggered backward in surprise. *This is not normal*, thought Max, staring in wonderment at the swirling mirror.

"No time to explain." With a firm grip on Max's arm, Gollnick stuck his own free hand into the mirror. Gollnick's hand appeared to stretch as it passed into the whirlpool image. First the hand, then the arm, followed by the rest of Gollnick, and then Max.

Passing through the mirror, Max felt a wave of cold rush over him followed by a blinding light.

2 The Sanctum

A flood of dazzling light enveloped him. The rush of cold overwhelmed his senses as if life itself had been wrenched from his body. There was a sense of movement, but direction held no meaning and all sides were the same.

In a split second it was over.

Max stood in a large, poorly lit room, Gollnick's grasp holding him steady. His eyes needed to focus while he regained his equilibrium. A wave of nausea hit when he noticed the whirlpool image in a bronze-trimmed, oval-shaped, full height mirror hovering in midair with no visible supports. The image shifted and a shape stretched out from the mirror. As the figure reformed before his eyes, Meagan, the girl he'd met just a few moments ago, stepped through.

Once she completed her reformation, Gollnick uttered a command and the mirror's surface returned to normal. No more swirling image, just Meagan's curly blond reflection.

Max pulled his arm free of Gollnick's grasp. The scent of incense was thick in the air. There were many unlit candles throughout the room, though a few burned in a three-tiered candelabrum dripping wax onto a nearby table. The table was only three feet square, except one corner had been singed off. Other furnishings included four large overstuffed chairs, chests of various shapes and sizes, shelves full of old scrolls and stacks upon stacks of oversized books two feet high and six inches thick. He tried to estimate the sheer number of volumes. *Haven't these people ever heard of organization?* The scant sections of visible wall consisted of large grey stones. The old wooden double doors off to the side had black wrought iron metal hinges, reminiscent of an old English castle. The two doors formed a half circle which opened in the middle.

Next to the mirror stood an old wrought iron coat rack. Gollnick and Meagan removed their trench coats and handed them to the rack. Max's jaw dropped as it promptly moved to accept the coats. Max walked over to the rack and it stretched out a knobby arm in anticipation. He removed his own trench coat then handed it to the arm which took it and retracted back to normal.

Max just stared at it for a few seconds. *This should seem weird to me. Objects like coat racks don't just move on their own. People don't just step through a mirror and end up somewhere else. I should be really freaked out by all of this... but I'm not. And that alone has me even more confused.*

In another part of the room, Gollnick and Meagan studied Max's reactions.

"Meagan, why don't you make something for our guest to eat," instructed Gollnick in a calm tone, but never averted his gaze. "He's probably starving."

Meagan moved toward the wooden doors which opened without a sound at her approach and closed just as quietly with her departure.

Max's emotional state was twisted in so many directions. He felt confused, angry, anxious and a little helpless. Some strange things had just happened to him, but yet he was not surprised. He had been pulled through a mirror to an unfamiliar place all because some guy in black had fired light beams from a ring. Things just did not add up.

Once they were alone, Max whipped around and fixed his attention on Gollnick. "Okay, old man, where are we? How did we get here? Where is *here*? Who just attacked us? And most importantly, who am I?" Max's voice rose in volume with each successive question.

Avoiding eye contact, Gollnick walked to the table and picked up a book. He began to flip through the pages before responding with a calm demeanor. "We are in our sanctum, we got here through that mirror, this is our library and that was an agent of one of our enemies. Not sure which one as of yet, but I'm sure we'll find out soon enough."

Gollnick acted as if these were simple questions, requiring simple answers, and of not much concern.

"WHAT???"

The older man looked up from his book with an expression of surprise. "I was just answering your questions."

Max tilted his head, eyes bulging as frustration continued to build. "None of what you just said answered any of my questions. Everything was either too vague or has no meaning to me! And you missed the most important question of all! *Who am I?*"

The anger and desperation in Max was evident. Gollnick set down the book and leaned back against the table, crossing his arms in front of him.

"We are in what sorcerers call a sanctum. It is our safe house, training area, the place where we keep our secrets and our home." Gollnick decided a better explanation might help to calm Max down a bit. "Our sanctum is a castle in Baltimore, Maryland, called Ravenicon Castle. Applying my powers of magic, I used the mirror in the bathroom at the hospital to open a portal to this mirror in order to escape your attacker. As for your attacker, I don't know his identity. Since he was firing energy beams from his ring, I thought it best not to stick around to ask questions."

"Magic!" Max had a blank look on his face and disbelief in his eyes. "You expect me to believe everything that just happened was because of magic?"

"Yes. Can you think of any other way to explain the events that just transpired?" Gollnick's mouth curled into a slight grin.

Max sat down on a nearby chair with an absolutely deflated look and just hung his head. How could this all be because of magic, and why didn't it seem like a surprise to him? It almost made sense, but he knew magic wasn't real, or was it? Once again, things didn't add up.

"You can't seriously tell me this is all because of magic." Max tried to convince himself there was another explanation. "Magic isn't real, it's just a bunch of tricks performers use for entertainment."

"Ah, don't confuse us with the magicians you might see in some place like Las Vegas. What we do uses real magic. Magic is all around us, it's part of the world in which we live. And it's a powerful tool, for those of us who know how to access that magic."

Max looked up at Gollnick with a bewildered expression. In a softer voice he asked, "Okay, just for argument's sake let's say magic is real. Why was that guy after me? And why does everyone keep avoiding my main question, who am I?"

Gollnick sighed deeply. He put his hands on the table to either side of himself and hung his head to ponder the question. "Actually, I had hoped you could fill in the blanks."

Gollnick looked up into Max's eyes, but no response was forthcoming.

"An associate of mine, Hank, put you into my custody about a week ago. He knew he was in danger and wanted to make sure you were safe," continued Gollnick. "I felt it best to keep you in the hospital in case there were any medical issues. His last message indicated your identity must remain a secret for now and admitted you under the name of Max. Though he did neglect to mention your amnesia. He gave me no other information about you. Apparently he hadn't planned on disappearing."

The desperation in Max's eyes was evident. What he needed right now was to not feel so alone and cut off. He needed a friend, but he wasn't sure about this Gollnick quite yet.

Max stood and walked to the mirror. He stared at his own reflection for a few minutes then turned to Gollnick with a look of depression. "I don't even recognize my own face." His saddened gaze returned to the mirror.

The wooden doors opened and Meagan carried a serving tray with a plate of fruit and raw vegetables and a glass of water. She placed the tray on the table and regarded Gollnick, noticing the lack of conversation.

He merely glanced at her and then shifted his gaze to Max. She understood his signal and approached, placing her hand on Max's shoulder.

He saw her behind him in the mirror, but returned to his own reflection. *Why can't I remember who I am?*

Meagan gently turned him around. "Come eat something." She led him back to the table.

Max stared at the food then shot a sideways look at Meagan.

Gollnick gave a little chuckle. "Sorry about that, Meagan is vegetarian. If you'd like something else..."

"No, that's fine." Max didn't wish to offend her. He picked up a piece of pineapple. When he crunched into the juicy fruit, he realized just how hungry he really was. Within a few minutes, he had cleared the plate and emptied the glass. "Thank you, that was great."

Meagan gathered up the tray and once again, the door quietly closed behind her.

"Let's see if we can restore your memory." Gollnick approached Max with eagerness. He faced the boy and held out his hands on either side of Max's head, then muttered some strange words. Max felt a rush of energy flow through him, but it subsided as fast as it had begun.

"Do you remember anything?" Gollnick inquired with hopeful expectation.

Max thought for a minute as he attempted to remember anything about his past, but to no avail. Whatever Gollnick had tried didn't work.

Max shook his head slightly. "No, still nothing."

Gollnick too looked depressed as he sighed. "Well, then there's one of two answers. Either your amnesia is due to normal medical or psychological reasons or..." He paused for a few seconds to consider the alternative. "...Or the sorcerer who wiped your memory is more powerful than me, which would mean we would need a more powerful sorcerer to remove the spell—if it is indeed a spell causing your amnesia. Perhaps your memory will come back in time."

Gollnick sat down in an old wooden chair that had seen better days and motioned for Max to sit in a similar chair opposite him.

Max felt deflated and alone as he took his seat. "So what happens now?"

"That's a good question. Since neither one of us knows anything about you, I guess we should start by discovering what you do know."

"We've already decided I don't know anything."

"I mean how much magic you know," Gollnick clarified.

"I don't know any magic." Max raised his eyebrows in surprise. He studied Gollnick as he tried to understand the insinuation.

Gollnick placed an unlit candle in a bronze candelabra on the table between them. "Without the use of matches or a lighter, light this candle," Gollnick instructed.

Max tilted his head to look at Gollnick, but the older man just smiled and nodded toward the candelabra. "Concentrate," he encouraged. "Think about lighting it and say *alecto orona na-see*."

Max stared at the wick and thought 'light' then mumbled, "*Alecto orona na-see*."

Nothing happened.

Max closed his eyes and once again repeated the phrase, "*Alecto orona na-see*."

He opened his eyes to confirm what he already knew.

"I told you, old man, there is no such thing as magic."

"It's not working because you don't want it to," Gollnick said patiently. "You need to believe in what you are saying and thinking."

With some reluctance, Max made one more attempt. "*Alecto orona na-see*." He waited a few seconds then stood up from the table. "This isn't getting us anywhere. I need to remember who I am, not waste time on some mind game with a stupid candle. I need to get *out* of here!"

At the mention of the word 'out,' the candle flew at the door and splattered into a bunch of waxy goo on impact.

Gollnick grimaced as the remains dropped to the floor. "A little too much force behind that thought. You need to be careful with both what you think and how strongly you think it. Your mind can grant you powerful magic, but you need to be able to control it. Without control, you can be a danger to yourself and those around you."

A few seconds after the wax glob hit the door, it swung open and Meagan rushed in. "What happened? Is everything all right?"

"No problem." Gollnick tried to calm her concerns. "Just a little too overzealous with some practice."

Meagan noticed the wax globs on the floor then looked at the young man standing next to the table.

Max had not yet grasped that he had destroyed a candle with a mere thought. *Is there really such a thing as magic, or is this guy just messing with my head?* He wasn't sure what to believe at this point.

"Don't worry, it gets easier with practice." Meagan turned to exit the room, then looked back over her shoulder, smiled and winked at him. Automatically, the door closed behind her.

Max felt his doubts fade as his face reddened.

Gollnick spoke in an even, but firm tone. "Meagan is my niece. Need I say more?"

"Nope." Max realized that meant Meagan was off limits unless he wanted to incur the wrath of an uncle who seemed to know a lot more about magic than he did.

Though a spattered candle didn't prove magic was real, the idea of it began to hold some interest for Max.

Gollnick placed another candle into the bronze candelabra and moved it between them. "Try again, gently."

Max still wasn't convinced. "Look, old man, I don't know how you did that with the candle, but..."

Gollnick showed the first signs of losing patience as he raised his voice. "I didn't do it, you did. Now sit down!"

Max was a little stunned by Gollnick's reaction, but reluctantly took a seat opposite him.

Max closed his eyes and thought 'light,' this time with the slightest hint that it might actually be possible. Then he spoke the phrase, *"Alecto orona na-see."*

He opened his eyes and once again the candle was not lit. He was about to complain when he noticed Gollnick's attention was elsewhere. Max followed his gaze... only to realize all of the candles in the room were lit—except the one in front of him.

"'Not exactly what I had in mind, but good nevertheless." Gollnick regarded Max. "Maybe we're just starting too small. Come with me."

3 First Attempts

Gollnick rose and made his way to the door. Max yawned and followed close behind. He could still feel the effects of the medication from the hospital. The doors swung open at their approach with barely a whisper. They left the room and hastened down a wide stone hallway. Candles floated in midair on either side of the spacious corridor, but the space appeared to be more illuminated than what the few candles should have been able to provide.

When they reached a four-way intersection, they turned left and continued down another wide hallway. Before them stood another set of huge old wooden double doors with black wrought iron hinges that formed a half circle just like in the library. Gollnick leaned into the doors and used his weight to push them open. This time, the hinges creaked under the strain.

The room was dark, damp and musty. There was not a single light source to be seen. Max followed Gollnick inside. Gollnick then instructed Max to help close the doors. The room became darker and darker until there was no light at all.

Max's nerves were already frayed, but the endless darkness heightened his anxiety. "Gollnick? Where are you? I can't see a thing in here."

There was no response. Max couldn't remember much from his past, but he started to suspect he didn't like the dark... or at least not knowing what was in the dark.

He knew they had entered the room together, but he hadn't gotten a good look at the contents of the room before the doors closed. He had no idea where the old man had now gone, much less what was in the room or what to expect from someone he'd met less than an hour ago.

After a minute in the disorienting darkness, Max cleared his mind and thought 'light.' *"Alecto orona na-see."*

A burst of fire sparked in four huge cauldrons, one in each corner of the room, enough to light the entire space. Each cauldron measured three feet high and five feet in width with flames dancing just above their rim. Next to each cauldron sat a ten-gallon water basin. Large grey stones flagged the wall fifty feet in every direction, even up.

Max examined the room and noted no other furnishings beyond the cauldrons, not even windows. Gollnick just stood in the center of the room with his back to Max. His feet were spaced apart, hands crossed behind his back, gazing toward the ceiling as if in search of something.

Max looked around and up and down the walls in an attempt to figure out the object of Gollnick's attention until his curiosity got the better of him.

"What are we doing in here?" Max whispered, but the bare stone walls made his whisper echo louder than expected.

Gollnick made no response. As Max walked around to face the older man, he realized Gollnick's eyes were closed. Max couldn't decide if the old man was meditating or just ignoring him.

Max stood beside Gollnick, mimicking his stance and posture. Minutes passed and Max grew bored and frustrated. The older man made no attempt to communicate.

Gollnick peeked out the corner of his left eye to see Max next to him with crossed arms. The boy's anger and frustration were evident. After fifteen minutes, Gollnick broke the silence. "You must learn to control your emotions."

"What?" Max startled.

"When you lit the cauldrons, the flame was barely above the rim," said Gollnick. "As your frustration builds, the flames have grown."

Max now looked around the room to realize the once tiny flames blazed five feet high. Frustration turned to surprise and the flames subsided slightly.

"Your anger and frustration were feeding the fire. Control your emotions and you will control the flames. Bring them back down to where they started," Gollnick instructed.

Max closed his eyes and concentrated on his breathing. After a few minutes, the flames were back to just above the rim of the cauldrons.

"Good. Remember that your emotions and feelings impact your magical powers. Sometimes this can be a good thing if you really need to unleash powerful magic. But usually it's not so good, especially for more delicate magic. Be cautious with your thoughts and feelings and you will maintain better control."

"So this was just a test to see if I could control my feelings?"

"That plus I wanted to see how high the flames would go. An indication of your power," the older man continued. "Interestingly enough, had I not stopped you, I'm certain the flames would have reached the ceiling..." He concluded in a quieter voice, "...and probably cooked us in the process."

"So what does that mean?" Max asked expectantly.

Gollnick thought for a second. "Either you have the potential for some very powerful magic," he began, "or you've got real psychological issues."

Max wasn't sure whether to laugh or flee.

"Look, Max," Gollnick softened. "Normally I'd sit down with you and go over every bit of magic step by step, but we don't have the luxury of time right now. The great seal is weakening and so are all of the world's magical prisons. If we don't act soon, many powerful mythological creatures will be released on humanity and few will survive. We need a new group of sorcerers to take up the defense of mankind, and they'll need your power. That's why the dark sorcerers want you dead. If Hank is right, you could be the key to saving this world."

"And they can't wait until morning to destroy the world?" Max didn't have the energy to get excited about the destruction of the world tonight.

"They've already set plans in motion. They're preparing for a war on humanity. We have to be ready, and that means getting you up to speed, quickly."

Max could hear the concern in Gollnick's voice. He wanted to help, but his hardest battle right now was keeping his eyes open.

"This is our training room." Gollnick waved his hand and the wall in front of him moved away at a rapid pace. The room that was once a cube was now a very long hall. A heavy mist hung in the air fifty feet in front of them. The mist slowly swirled round and round until a solid iron disc formed in midair, ten feet in diameter with a red and black bull's-eye painted on it.

"Let's see what you've got. Destroy the disc," Gollnick ordered.

Max yawned and his eyelids felt heavy. "And exactly how do I do that?"

"However you like. You have the magic within you. I need to see how you'll use it."

"What I have within me is a desire to sleep." Max yawned again and bent over, resting his hands on his knees. "I don't think the medication has worn off yet. I'm still weak, I have a headache and I'm tired. All I want to do is rest."

"You can rest later." Gollnick appeared determined to press on. "Right now I need to know what you're capable of. If the dark sorcerers find us before we're ready, we'll all be dead."

"If I don't get some rest, *I'll* drop over dead."

Gollnick considered Max for a few seconds then spoke in a softer voice. "I know you're tired and you want to sleep, but I need to know what you can do. Please just stay awake for a little while longer." Gollnick pointed at the target once more.

Max still had no idea what to do so he held out his right hand and pointed his finger at the disk. He concentrated on its destruction. After a few seconds, a tiny energy bolt shot a few inches from his finger and fizzled, but nothing more.

Gollnick raised an eyebrow. "That's it? I had hoped for more, but perhaps with practice things will improve."

"I'm tired, what did you expect?" Max's anger and frustration returned as he held his hands out to either side. "We've already decided I don't know any magic and I don't know any spells."

Gollnick waved his hand and the room returned to its normal dimensions. He then turned to face Max. "One last test." Closing his eyes and extending his arms out to the sides, he mumbled a spell beneath his breath.

"Okay, so what will I fail to do this time?" Max's frustration was getting the better of him. He had destroyed a helpless candle, lit up a room, and fizzled on target practice. One more failure and he was ready to walk out the door. That is, if he could find it.

"There are many forms of magic. This is a test to see if you possess any elemental powers," replied Gollnick patiently. "There are four cauldrons of fire in the room. Next to each cauldron is a basin of water. There is earth beneath our feet and air all around us. These represent the four elemental magics. Close your eyes and relax. Let your mind touch each of the objects I just mentioned, but don't focus on any one item."

Tired, Max gladly closed his eyes and just stood there in the middle of the room, thinking vaguely about each of the objects Gollnick had mentioned: cauldrons burning hot, cool water gently lapping the basins, the soft dirt beneath their feet and the gentle breeze.

After a minute, Gollnick whispered, "Interesting."

Max opened his eyes to see four water tentacles hovering in midair from each of the basins. The liquid reached toward him and fluctuated with gentle ripples. "What does that mean?"

Gollnick appeared pleased. "Only one in ten sorcerers possesses any elemental magic. It seems you have a predisposition to water, though from the way the cauldrons reacted earlier, I would have guessed you were a fire elemental sorcerer."

Max looked at the waving tentacles of water then began to move his hand around one of them. As he did, the water reacted to his movements and floated around his hand in a tandem dance. Max clenched his fist tight and a section of the appendage instantly froze into a solid chunk of ice.

He turned to look at Gollnick and realized the sorcerer's mouth was agape, staring at the ball of ice.

Max quickly motioned toward one of the cauldrons and without hesitation, the tiny sphere flew toward it at incredible speed, shattering on impact. The fire from the cauldron burst forth in a huge fireball that soon dissipated into thin air.

"I could get used to this," Max breathed. All of his anger and frustration began to fade as he considered the possibilities. It made him think about what else he could accomplish with magic. He was hit with a sudden desire to learn everything he could. The desire was so strong, like taking a bite of the best piece of chocolate ever.

"Perhaps you're more of a water elemental sorcerer than I had anticipated. This could prove interesting." Gollnick seemed pleased with the results of the test.

"I need to learn more about this water magic." Max wore a big smile. Frustration gone, all he could think about was this new desire to learn. He still had no idea who he was, but he had found something to fill the void in his life until his memory returned.

Max's excitement ended when the brief rush of adrenaline was overcome by his overwhelming tiredness.

"I'll have Meagan pull some tomes on water elemental magic for you to look through."

"Tombs?" Max asked.

Gollnick refocused. "*Tomes* are ancient books of magic. They contain instructions on how to use magic as well as spells and other useful information. All sorcerers can cast spells, but only elemental sorcerers can affect their element naturally through thought and movement. It's easier than memorizing spells and gives you more control over your element. I think you'll find it very interesting."

Gollnick headed toward the door with Max close behind. The older man snapped his fingers and the doors slowly opened on their own.

As they passed through, Max asked, "Why didn't you do that earlier?"

Gollnick cracked a smile. "It made the whole thing seem more imposing my way."

Max just rolled his eyes and yawned.

They exited and headed left down another wide hallway ending at yet another wooden door. This one was more of a standard size. The door was old and had seen better days. Gollnick open it and went in, but indicated for Max to wait outside.

Max peered in and saw the room was a complete circle. Every few feet held another door, each identical to the next with one exception. Inscribed at the top of each door frame was a name.

Some had been scratched out, but three still remained. Max could see the names of Gollnick, Elisa and Hank.

In the center of the room floated a large crystal, three feet high. A warm light emanated from it, but dim like a light bulb that was about to burn out. Within the crystal floated three symbols. Max tried to inch his way inside to get a better look, but as he did so, bolts of energy spat out from the crystal toward him.

"Only members of my circle are permitted into this room," cautioned Gollnick, motioning Max back outside.

Max did as instructed and backed out of the doorway.

Gollnick walked to the door with his own name at the top. "This is my room. Once accepted to a door, your name will magically appear and only you will ever be able to enter that room. Unless invited into another's room, of course."

"Why are there only three doors with names? And why are the other names scratched out?" Max counted eight other doors.

A look of sadness filled the old man's eyes. "They were members of my circle." Gollnick gazed off into the distance. "Every generation, a new circle of sorcerers is formed to take up the protection of this world. I am one of the last of my circle."

Max noted the absence of Meagan's name. "What about your niece?"

Gollnick looked at Max suspiciously. "What about her?"

"I don't see her name on any of the doors. If she's not in your circle, then where is her room?"

"Why do you want to know?" Gollnick asked defensively.

Max realized the protective uncle role had kicked in again and he didn't want to cause any additional discord.

"Look, old man... I'm tired, I don't know who I am, you haven't provided any real answers and I just want to lie down and get some sleep. If her room isn't here, then I assume there are other rooms somewhere else. I'd just like to find someplace where I can get some rest."

Gollnick released the breath he'd been holding. "Sorry, I'm just a little protective of Meagan."

"You don't say," Max hissed.

Gollnick left the circular room and led Max down yet another wide hallway to another wooden door. This one was about the same size and style as the last door, but it appeared newer and hardly used. Gollnick open it and allowed Max to enter another circular room, but did not himself enter.

In the center of the room floated another large crystal three feet high, just like in the previous room, but the light that emanated from this crystal was much brighter, almost difficult to look upon. This crystal held only two symbols. The first was the sign of the Taurus, but the second was constantly morphing. Max scanned the room and noticed two doors. One bore Meagan's name carved into the frame, but the other was blank. The crystal started to crackle with sparks.

"That's strange." Gollnick's attention was drawn by the activity. "It's almost like the crystal doesn't know who you are either. Normally when someone new is encountered who is destined to join the circle, it glows bright like now, but without the sparks. You seem to have confused it. It's not even sure about your zodiac symbol."

"Great, even the crystal doesn't know anything about me," Max said sarcastically.

"Go ahead and open the door. Just like many things in the sanctum, these doors are enchanted to only allow access to the person destined for that room."

Max attempted to open the unnamed door, but it would not budge. "Apparently the door doesn't like me either."

"You're a sorcerer and possibly a powerful sorcerer. I'm sure you belong in the new circle. Try again." Gollnick sounded confident about his assertion.

"And what if I don't want to be part of your new circle?" Max now took a step back.

Gollnick just shrugged his shoulders. "I don't know, but where else are you going to go? You have no memory, no identity, no money," he paused, "and there are people trying to kill you."

Max considered Gollnick's words.

"I know in my gut you belong here, Max. Call it sorcerer's intuition."

Max tried the door again and it opened on his second attempt. The sign in the crystal settled on the image of a scorpion.

"Ah," said Gollnick, "it looks like you are the Scorpio of the group. The crystal uses zodiac magic to select members of the circle. There will never be more than twelve."

As Max pulled the door toward him, his name appeared with a strange pattern above. "What's that?"

"Another symbol of some kind," Gollnick answered, "though I'm not sure what it means. I'll see what I can find out about it. In the meantime, get some rest. Dinner will be around six o'clock in the kitchen. We'll get started with training right after that." Gollnick turned and closed the door to the circular room.

Max was tired and wanted to lie down. As he entered his new space, a few candles around the room lit. It was a spacious chamber of thirty feet by thirty feet flanked with the same grey stone as the rest of the castle.

Around the room he noticed a bed, a new wooden desk with a chair, an empty bookcase and an empty chest. There were also two doors at the back of the room. Upon closer inspection, he found one led to a large walk-in closet and the other to a private bathroom. Nothing fancy, but at least it appeared to have modern fixtures. The bed had a wooden frame with clean white sheets that appealed to his tired state.

Max flopped indelicately down on the bed and stared up at the ceiling. Questions once again began to flood his mind. *What the heck am I doing here? For that matter, where in the world is Baltimore? Are all buildings here made out of huge grey stones? I just wish I could remember something about myself.*

"Oh, well. Nothing I can do about it now," he murmured. And with that he fell asleep.

4 A Little Excursion

Max awoke to a knock at the door. He rolled over to realize he was still within his chamber in Ravenicon castle. The light in the room was dim, but it brightened a bit as he stirred. He heard another knock and looked to the door with displeasure.

"Come in." Max sat up in bed and rubbed his eyes. When he looked to the door again, he saw Meagan enter with a tray of food.

"You didn't show up at dinner, so I brought you something to eat." She spoke in a polite yet quiet voice.

Max smiled as she placed the tray on the desk. He noticed she had traded her blue jeans and white t-shirt for grey sweatpants and a sweatshirt, with her hair pulled back in a ponytail. Her new hairstyle revealed the tips of her ears were pointed. *What baggy clothes,* he thought, *but they look comfortable.* She turned to face Max and caught his stare.

"Do you need anything else?" Meagan smiled.

"No, you're fine. I mean... I'm... I'm fine. Thanks." Max stumbled over his own words as his face reddened.

"Good," Meagan grinned. "I'll be in the training room if you need anything." She turned and closed the door behind her.

Max collapsed back into his bed. *You idiot,* he thought.

A minute later, he got up and crossed the room to eat, sautéed rice with steamed vegetables and a banana. *I guess if I want something other than vegetarian, I'll have to find it myself.* He considered it for a minute then decided. *Maybe it's time for a little walk into town. Hopefully this Baltimore place isn't too far away.*

Max grabbed his trench coat from the knobby little rack and started for the door. With one arm in, he realized he'd actually left the coat on an animated stand in the library. *Weird,* he shrugged and walked out.

Max cracked the door and peeked out to make sure no one was around then slipped out and made his way to the hall. Once there, he remembered he had no idea how to get out of the castle. *Everywhere Gollnick has taken me so far has been a left turn.* He took a hopeful left and walked down the corridor, praying he wouldn't run into anyone.

He found a set of upward spiral stairs on his left and another hallway on the right. *Well that's some progress, I guess.* Max decided to stick with left turns. He climbed the stairs made of large stone slabs then came to a landing where another set of stairs led up. Next to the stairs was an old wooden door and a rusty suit of medieval armor. The armor stood on a foot-high raised platform. As he gazed at his reflection in the shield, he thought, *Even after a few hours' sleep, I still don't know who I am.* He examined the armor to find it was empty. A quick listen at the locked door revealed only a sound like a cat's purr.

Max continued his ascent eager to find the exit. At the top of the stairs he opened the latch to a door and stepped out onto a balcony the same size as his room. With blue sky above, he looked around to see clusters of trees below. Beyond the trees were large buildings. He staggered backward when he realized the size of this place called Baltimore. This was no mere village, but a much larger city.

Upon further inspection, he noted the balcony was on one of the lower levels. Numerous spires and towers reached much higher into the sky. The enormity of Ravenicon Castle meant he had yet to even see a small portion of the inside. The castle reminded him of... of... *Camelot?* Except the exterior was black not white—it couldn't be Camelot. But how could he remember what Camelot looked like? That must have been hundreds of years ago.

Max stood in awe for a minute before he regained his senses and decided to search for a way down. He looked over the edge to see a moat three stories below.

A noise behind him revealed the suit of armor had followed him out onto the balcony and was lurching its way toward him. It was shiny and looked like an old English suit of armor with a little rust around the edges. It was six feet high and made of steel. He recognized the armor from the previous landing. It made a loud clank with each step as it approached with outstretched arms. But it didn't appear to be on the attack. It acted like it didn't want him to leave.

Max kept his distance as it approached. Without knowledge of its intentions, Max climbed up on the edge of the balcony. The armor tried to grab for him and he jumped, holding his breath as he fell in expectation of a splash into the water below.

Moments passed in eternities. He then realized his fall had ceased. He looked up to see the armor as it leaned over the edge, but it was too far away to reach him. He then looked down to see the water had risen to meet his feet and he now stood on a column of water from the moat. *Well that's new*, he thought. The water had swirled around like a spout and shot up from the moat to catch him.

As Max concentrated, the column sank back down then moved to the side and allowed him to step off onto dry ground across from the castle. As he did, the water splashed back into the moat. The spray was cool on his skin and Max avoided an unexpected swim.

He walked twenty feet from the moat before turning to view the castle and see if the armor had raised an alarm. When he did, he was shocked to find Ravenicon Castle wasn't there at all. *Okay, that's not good. No idea how I'm getting back in, but I'll worry about that later. Where's the food?*

He made a quick inspection of the area. It looked like a small lake in a big open lot sparsely populated with trees and small structures. It was late on a warm spring evening and Max could see lights in the distance. The scent of saltwater was on the air. There had to be a larger body of water nearby. He walked a short distance when he came upon a sign that read, "Patterson Park."

"Well, now at least I know where I am. The big question is where am I going?" Max pondered what to do next.

There was a small pavilion nearby where he noticed a couple walking. As he approached, they picked up their pace to avoid him. "I guess they don't want to be interrupted."

From the smell in the air, Max could tell the water was to the southwest. With his hands in his pockets be began a stroll through the park. At the southwest corner, he turned west onto Eastern Avenue. It sounded like a contradiction, but he needed to choose a direction or he'd end up walking in circles. This way he need only remember to head east on Eastern Avenue for his return.

After an hour-long aimless walk, Max realized he had been so caught up in everything around him, he'd forgotten to look for a place to eat. He finally spotted water to the south, but continued in his westerly direction. He crossed three bridges and passed a sizeable ship near a building named the National Aquarium. There he encountered some people who gave him directions to a place where he could get food.

Within five minutes, he arrived at Inner Harbor. Two large structures were set back from the water of the bay with an amphitheater between them. Various signs announced stores and restaurants on two levels.

Night had fallen, but for some reason, his closeness to water gave him comfort. Before he entered a restaurant, he walked over to the edge of the water near the amphitheater and just stood there. He took a deep breath to enjoy the smell of the saltwater in the bay.

Out of the corner of his left eye, he noticed two people. As he turned to look at them, they ducked around a corner. He moved to see where they went, but felt a strange sensation from behind. He spun around to now see two figures in black trench coats, still a hundred feet away, headed in his direction.

He stood in the middle of a circle of fire, twenty feet in diameter with flames just over three feet high. Beyond the flames was a void of darkness, even above him was pitch black. He wore a white robe marred with the signs of battle. Burn marks and soot covered him. Situated in the center of the flames he stood with arms extended to either side. He raised his hands and the flames grew higher. His attention was fixed on the figure just beyond the fire. It was human size, but had large fiery wings. He tried to make out who or what it was, but the memory changed.

Now he stood atop a mountain. The clank of chainmail was muffled by layers of warm furs. Leather boots, a horned helmet and battle axe rounded out his possessions. He remembered being the rear guard for a group of Vikings headed home. The weather was wicked. Snow blew sideways making visibility poor. But he could make out someone below him on the mountain headed in his direction. This bothered him, but he wasn't sure why. He clenched his left fist and raised his arm. A new mountain peak rose to block the way of his pursuer. The person attempted an alternate route. Max clenched his fist once again and another rock formation shot forth, but his pursuer would not relent. Max tried to focus on the person, but his memory changed again.

This time he was in the desert with a group of travelers headed to a nearby settlement. The sheet he wore had a hole for his head and a rope around his waist. His sandals were worn and the dull blade of his short sword posed little threat. During their trek to the settlement, he turned to find a group of twenty-five horse-drawn chariots approach his position rapidly. They had gold detailing and the riders carried bows and arrows. Max knew these were Egyptians. A quick assessment of the travelers' haste told him the pursuers would overtake them before the safety of the settlement. He spun around and raised his hands above his head. The desert winds picked up and a sudden sand storm slammed into the enemy. Their horses reared and stumbled until all but one of the group was forced to flee. The single pursuer dismounted and the horse and chariot fled. This single individual stood his ground against the sand storm by placing his forearms together to create a red orb of energy to shield him and then braced himself against the howling winds.

Without warning, the memory flashes ended and he once again found himself at the harbor as the two figures clad in black approached.

Once they realized they had been spotted, the figures broke into a sprint. The first raised his clenched fist and Max knew what was coming. A light ray shot from the man's ring. Max dove and the beam scorched the light post beside him. *Not this again.* He stood up and started to concentrate on casting a fireball, until he realized he didn't know how. A second shot flew past him and broke his concentration.

Okay, plan B. Run! Max started in the opposite direction of the men but one of the light beams caught him in the calf muscle of his left leg. Excruciating pain sent him to the ground hard and he bit his lip. Max rolled to face the two men who still approached at a brisk pace.

From out of nowhere, a brick slammed into one guy's face. It landed him flat on his back. Max looked behind to see the two figures from earlier, now only thirty paces behind him. He couldn't make them out too well because of the poor lighting, but he could tell one was a boy and the other a girl. The guy continued to mutter in the strange language everyone knew but Max.

As he worked on his spell, the girl stretched out her hand toward the second attacker. The man knelt as he raised both arms and placed his forearms together. A faint grey orb appeared around him. The wind grew in strength until it created a mini tornado centered on the attacker. Though the winds blew hard against him, he appeared unaffected so long as he kept his arms up, but the winds continued to increase.

Within seconds, the boy finished his spell and the bricks beneath the attackers' feet started to shift, sink and spin. The man had to release his forearms in order to balance himself, then the mini tornado had him. It pulled him off his feet and sent him into the harbor. At the same time, it knocked Max down, overturned a couple of benches and bent a light post. Even with the attacker gone, the winds continued to grow in strength.

The man who had been flattened by the brick sat up groggily. Three additional men dressed in black dashed out of a restaurant and headed in their direction. The man on the ground pointed his closed fist at the two strangers and fired a light beam. It struck the boy in the left shoulder and spun him to the ground.

Max stood up and did his best to hobble to the two strangers. As Max approached, the girl focused her attention on him and the once-mini tornado moved in his direction, still growing. He stopped and raised his hands to his sides to show he was no threat.

"Wait, I'm a friend. I hope." The girl redirected her attention back to their attackers. Max went to check on the boy. He was conscious, but in pain. Max noticed they were around his age. The guy had a muscular build and black hair. The blue jeans, white sneakers and black t-shirt appeared to be a common theme, but he also wore a black leather jacket. The girl was shorter than Max with brown hair down to just below her shoulders and a slender build. Her black jeans and dark brown jacket made it easy for her to blend into the shadows.

Another man dressed in black with a black trench coat stepped out of the shadows. "Stop. Join us or die. Those are your only two options. I will not make this offer a second time." The man had a very stern and straight face. It was obvious he was not joking.

After he issued the demand, a fireball slammed into the ground at his feet. He jumped back in surprise and searched for the source of the unwelcome attack.

Two other figures approached from the direction of the aquarium—Gollnick and Meagan! Max was relieved to have them join the fight as he realized the three of them were severely outnumbered and outmatched. Gollnick hastened to cast a spell and held his hands out to his sides at shoulder height. A giant wall of energy appeared between them and their attackers.

"Get behind me, all of you!" Gollnick shouted his instructions and appeared disposed to overlook the two newcomers for the moment. "Girl, shut down that tornado!"

"I... I can't... I can't control it." The girl's voice quivered and she dropped to her knees. She was terrified of her power and had no idea how to use it.

"Great. Meagan help her out." Gollnick attempted to give instructions and hold the enemy at bay at the same time. The other sorcerers sent fireball after fireball against the energy shield.

The boy was still in pain, but noticed a man in a black outfit climbing out of the water, drenched and angry. "Look out! At the water's edge!"

They all turned to look, but froze in panic.

"Max, use your elemental powers. Focus on the water. You can do it." Gollnick did his best to encourage Max.

There was nothing Gollnick could do without dropping the shield between them and the multitude of other sorcerers. Max had no idea what powers the others possessed and decided it was up to him to deal with the soaked survivor. He reached out to the water, but nothing happened.

The sorcerer had climbed onto dry land and pointed his clenched fist at the group. Max disregarded the pain in his calf and ran straight at the sorcerer. The action surprised everyone, even the enemy. Max tackled the sorcerer over the edge and into the bay.

"Not exactly what I had in mind," said Gollnick.

Meagan arrived at the girl's side. "You need to calm down. Focus. Look at me and listen to my voice." She spoke in a soft, gentle tone as she tried to calm the unknown girl.

"Meagan, wait." Max had already climbed the ladder from the bay and rested at the water's edge. "Don't stop her, unleash the tornado on the dark sorcerers."

"Max, she can't control it. She'll do more damage than good."

Max scrambled from the ladder to where Meagan knelt beside the girl. "What's your name?"

The terrified girl whimpered as tears streaked down her face. "Amber."

"Amber, I need you to trust me. Can you do that?"

Amber nodded her head.

"Close your eyes and focus the tornado on the dark sorcerers. See them get sucked up by the wind storm in your mind." Max tried to paint a mental picture for Amber. He spoke in a confident tone and gave no hesitation in his instructions.

"Max." Meagan had concerns for the damage a tornado, even a small one, could cause in downtown Baltimore.

Max merely held up his hand to forestall her comments. He kept his focus on the girl.

The tornado commenced its movement toward the dark sorcerers. The fireball barrage stopped and the dark sorcerers scattered in an attempt to find cover. All but their leader ran for shelter. He alone stood against the wind storm. He placed his forearms together and brought them up in front of him as a shield. A dark grey orb of energy formed around him as the violent storm broke against his defenses.

Gollnick dropped his energy wall and threw a fireball at the sorcerer's feet. The explosion from the fire disrupted his concentration and the winds had him. Within seconds the unknown dark sorcerer was hundreds of feet in the air.

The tornado ripped panels from the roof and signs and grabbed outdoor furniture from nearby restaurants.

"Semo nigh free." Max cast a spell and Amber relaxed and went to sleep in his arms. His eyes open wide. *Where'd that come from?* As she lost consciousness, the destructive winds quickly died to a gentle breeze. He then hoisted the girl up on his shoulder and stood.

"Get the guy to his feet. We need to move," Max instructed Meagan and Gollnick then started for the aquarium.

"Wait," Gollnick called to him before he had gone two steps. "Go into one of the clothing stores. They'll have mirrors."

Max understood Gollnick's escape plan in an instant and turned toward the nearest building while Gollnick and Meagan helped the boy along. When they reached the nearest building they went in and turned to search for any pursuers.

"Thanks for the help. Are you sorcerers, too?" Max was curious about their two new allies. He waved a hand over Amber's face and she awoke, but still a little groggy.

"Keep your voice down, you fool. We don't need the entire city of Baltimore to know who we are." The boy continued to scan the area for other possible threats.

"What happened, and who are you?" Amber asked.

"My name is Max. This is Gollnick and Meagan."

"I'm Cyrus," the boy said, eyeing all three strangers. "Nice to meet you, Max, now let's get out of here before the cops arrive."

"The who?"

Everyone just looked at one another then back to Max.

"Are you serious? The police? The local law enforcement?" Cyrus paused after each name waiting for Max to acknowledge a description.

Finally Max understood the need for secrecy. "Come on, we need to move." As Max spoke, he noticed two additional men dressed in black uniforms coming out of one of the buildings toward them.

"More bad guys!"

"Not bad guys—police," corrected Gollnick as everyone turned to look.

"We really don't want to be here right now," said Cyrus.

The group moved in among the shops until Gollnick spotted a clothing store and indicated the way in as a clerk was preparing to lock up.

"I'm sorry, but we're closed for the evening," said the clerk.

"That's okay, we were just leaving." Gollnick led the way in as the shopkeeper looked on in confusion. The five of them ducked into a changing room.

The clerk just stood there. "What the heck? Why are they all going into the same changing room together? Wait a minute, I don't want to know."

Once they were all squeezed in, Gollnick muttered his spell and the mirror began to swirl. Gollnick looked to Cyrus and Amber. "Are you coming?"

"Where?" Cyrus and Amber spoke in unison.

"Home."

"That's kind of vague." Cyrus looked a little uncertain, but with the police less than a minute behind them, they had few options.

5 NEW FRIENDS

Max noticed Gollnick at the doorway, his arms crossed in anger. He had given Max instructions not to leave the castle yet that was exactly what Max had done. Fortunately, they'd discovered two new friends.

At least Max hoped they were friends.

"What did you think you were doing?" Gollnick ranted. "You barely know how to defend yourself. Had these two been agents of the dark sorcerers, you would've been in real trouble. Possibly even dead."

Max hesitated as he realized Gollnick was right. "I wasn't aware I was a prisoner. I wanted something other than vegetarian food, so I decided to go for a walk. You never said they could track me."

"I have no idea how they found you. The point is, they did."

"Not necessarily." Cyrus drew their attention as he interrupted the argument. "Actually, I think they might have been after us. At least at first. Two of them had been following Amber and me for about ten blocks before we came across Max. Once they spotted him, they shifted their attention."

Gollnick turned his attention to Max's new friends. "As for you two, who are you? And what were you doing at Inner Harbor?"

Cyrus and Amber edged back toward the mirror in anticipation of a quick escape. Max could see the uncertainty in their eyes and guessed Gollnick's tongue lashing did nothing to inspire confidence.

"I wasn't aware it was a crime to walk around." Cyrus mirrored Max's defiance.

"Perhaps not, but I saw your girlfriend there attack Max with that tornado of hers before redirecting it to the dark sorcerers." Gollnick had grown noticeably angry.

"My name is Cyrus Marx and this is my *sister,* Amber. And before we answer any more questions, I'd like to know where we are. And who *you* are!" Cyrus' response came with a sense of authority in his voice.

"This is my castle, I'll ask the questions. What were you doing at Inner Harbor?" Gollnick had grown tired of the disrespect. Max, as well as everyone else, could see things were not going well.

"Whoa! Everyone just calm down and let me explain." Max noticed Gollnick and Cyrus each open their mouths to say something. He held up a hand to stall them. "Questions later."

As Max started his story, Cyrus and Amber kept close to the mirror in the event things went bad. Gollnick and Meagan stood close to the door with the same thought in mind. Max stayed beside the table in the center of the room to keep everyone's focus on him.

"Okay, short version." Max hoped to ease the tensions. He figured he could always fill in the details later. The priority was to defuse the situation first. He proceeded to retell the evening's altercation with special attention on Cyrus and Amber's heroism. "After the dark sorcerer issued his threats was when you and Meagan showed up."

"So she moved the tornado your way because she thought you were attacking Cyrus." Gollnick appeared satisfied with Max's explanation and the tension in his face eased a little. "It still doesn't explain why they were there in the first place."

"They spotted us in an antique shop nears Fells Point," Amber responded before Cyrus could raise the tension level again. "We were told it's a good place to find magical items. Once they spotted us though, we went to Inner Harbor in the hope they would not attack in public."

"Cyrus and Amber have only provided help to me so far," Max continued. "Besides, my gut tells me they're *supposed* to be here." Max knew this was a little bit risky, but he needed to find common ground to quiet both sides. Gollnick wanted to form the new circle as quickly as possible, but would he be able to accept the two new strangers so easily?

"What makes you think that? Have you remembered something?" Gollnick appeared surprised, but still cautious.

"What do you mean 'remembered something'?" inquired Cyrus as Max shook his head no. Gollnick was about to answer when Max spoke first.

"I have no memory of my past before this morning."

Amber's eyes went wide.

Max proceeded to recount his memory flashes as best he could. Gollnick made no reply, but considered Max's story. "It's not unheard of for a powerful sorcerer to learn more than one elemental power, but to learn all four would either take an enormous amount of power or... more than one lifetime. The question is, how could someone so young and inexperienced as you have memories of using all four elemental powers?"

"You speak English without any accent." Amber drew Max's attention with the question. "So you must be from around here. Or at least somewhere in the United States, right?"

Max was seeing her for the first time in the light and realized just how beautiful she was. He hesitated for a second until Cyrus cleared his throat to get Max's attention back on topic. Amber blushed.

"Look, I have no idea who I am or where I'm from." Max tried to fill in the blanks to get everyone on the same page. "I was placed in Gollnick's care until I awoke. He has no more knowledge of my identity or where I'm from than I do. Now that I'm awake though, I've had two attempts on my life. Personally I'm content to stay here, at least until I know what's going on."

Meagan had been quiet until this point. "Perhaps their arrival here was predestined."

Gollnick shot her an angry look. He knew what she was about to suggest, but that did not stop her. He knew he would have no say in who joined the new circle, yet he was reluctant to want Cyrus as a member.

Meagan continued, ignoring Gollnick's look of disapproval. "The crystal in the circle room can tell if their hearts are pure and if they truly belong here. We need to form the new circle quickly. Maybe they are the next part."

Max was relieved to see calmer heads prevail, at least for the moment.

"We know of the circle of sorcerers." Amber continued to speak for her and her brother. "The last circle died off ten, fifteen years ago."

"They're not all dead yet," Gollnick spoke up. "I'm one of the last from the former circle. Meagan and Max were to be the start of the new circle, but perhaps Meagan is right. Regardless of my personal feelings, if they trust you two, then I must support them."

Everyone could see it took an effort for Gollnick to admit it was not his decision to make.

Cyrus lowered his voice and pulled close to his sister. "We've gotten by on our own. We don't need them," he said. "We can continue as we always have."

"No," Amber answered. "We've been running long enough. Besides, when we thought the circle was dead, we talked about starting our own group. Now we have a chance to join the real circle. I'm willing to give it a try if you are."

Max could see Amber trusted her brother. If he said no, she would follow his lead. "Cyrus, you said the dark sorcerers were following you. At least here you're safe."

"Come with us, we'll show you to the circle room." Meagan motioned everyone toward the door. It quietly opened as she and Max proceeded to leave the library. "If the crystal shows your hearts to be good, you will be given rooms."

Meagan and Max led the way. Max couldn't help but wonder. "I don't remember the crystal looking into my heart when I went into the room before."

Meagan smiled at him. "It was glowing with a bright white light, was it not?"

"Yes."

"Then your heart is good, even if you don't remember it."

Max just shrugged and continued on. Meagan and Max entered the room first and the giant crystal glowed bright white. There were now four zodiac symbols in the crystal. The new signs were Leo and Aquarius. He noticed there were now four doors instead of two. The new ones bore no names. As Cyrus and Amber entered the room, the crystal's bright white light never faltered.

Meagan smiled. "The crystal likes them."

The names Cyrus Marx and Amber Marx appeared atop the two new doors when they opened them.

Gollnick sighed from the hallway. "It's late, I suggest we all get some sleep and begin with training in the morning. That's if Max will refrain from taking any additional late night strolls."

* * *

Max and Meagan said their good nights and Gollnick departed. Cyrus and Amber were left alone in the circle room.

"Are you sure about this?" Cyrus asked. He was her big brother and he wanted her to be happy, but he had concerns about these strangers. The circle was formed to protect the world from dark sorcerers and other creatures of darkness, but that meant danger in their future. If they stayed, they would become protectors of this world. That was a big responsibility for anyone, especially two teenagers.

"I know in my heart this is where we belong." Amber appeared happy for the first time in a long while. "For once, we're needed. That's all I've ever wanted, to be needed somewhere."

Cyrus nodded as he embraced his sister for a hug. He had known what she would say. Since the dark sorcerers had been recruiting, he and Amber had been on the run. It would be nice to have a place to call home again.

He left her at her door and walked across the circle room. Looking back over his shoulder, he saw Amber smile then enter her room for the night. He quietly considered their new situation. "We may be done running, but I have a feeling we're in for a mess of trouble."

6 BREAKFAST

The next morning, Max again awoke to a knock at his door. He rolled over and saw an alarm clock on the nightstand. It was 7:00 a.m. He rolled back into bed and heard the knock again.

"It's too early! Come back later," Max moaned still face down in his pillow. For the first time, Max realized he was not a morning person.

The knock came one last time with Meagan's voice. "Breakfast is ready. You'd better hurry if you want some. I doubt it'll last long with this bunch."

Max threw off his covers and looked up at the ceiling. Sunlight lit the room, but he couldn't see any windows. Where was the light coming from? It dawned on him it had to be magical. Max literally rolled out of bed and hit the floor. "Ouch!"

He rubbed his knee then went to the bathroom to take a bath, but once there he was confused when he didn't see a tub. Instead he saw an area surrounded by a curtain and found the faucet high up on the wall... but no tub below. Max turned the water on. He noticed it fell from high above and disappeared down a drain in the floor.

After his first shower (that he could remember), he found some clothes already laid out on his bed. They were the same kind of baggy clothes Meagan had worn the night before. Max put on the grey sweatpants and sweatshirt and found them to be comfortable. As he exited his room, the crystal's bright light almost blinded him. Not a good morning so far. Hopefully the food would be better.

Max walked out of the circle room into the hallway, then realized he had no idea where to find the kitchen.

"Hello? Anyone there? Which way to breakfast?" Max felt his stomach growl.

A gentle brush against his leg made him look down in surprise. A black cat greeted him.

"Don't suppose you know where I can find the kitchen?"

The cat meowed at him and dashed down the hall to his left.

"Can't believe I'm about to follow the cat. Left again?" He kept up as best he could. Where the stairs had been on the left the night before, the cat shot around the corner to the right. Max hurried to catch up and saw the cat take another right. Once Max reached the intersection, he recognized his location. To the left was the library, where they entered the castle through the mirror yesterday. To the right, he could smell breakfast.

He hurried into the kitchen to see everyone already gathered around a large round table. They had started without him. There were five chairs with Cyrus, Amber and Gollnick already seated. Meagan was in the kitchen area. The room looked modern with granite counters and dark cherry cupboards along the back wall with a large cooking island nearby. The walls were the same grey stone, but the appliances appeared to be new—even futuristic to Max's eyes. Everyone in the room wore the same kind of grey sweatsuit as Max.

Then Max realized Meagan had prepared the food once again. *Oh no, vegetarian breakfast?* But when he approached he could smell fresh bacon, eggs, and pancakes, and on the table was a pitcher of orange juice.

"Ah, now this is a breakfast."

"I figured I should make something so you don't run away again."

Max sat down at the table then realized what she meant. "Wait a minute. You're cooking normal food?"

"I only eat vegetarian." Meagan flipped some pancakes as she explained. "But I know how to cook almost anything you can think of."

"If I'd known that, I might not have left last evening," Max joked and stuffed some food into his mouth.

Between mouthfuls, Gollnick asked, "Exactly how did you get out last evening? You wouldn't have known how to get past the spells on the main doors."

Max finished chewing then recapped his encounter with the magically animated armor. "It came after me. I jumped down to the moat, but the water rose to meet me. It lowered me to the ground on the other side."

"Why didn't you just take the stairs down to the main floor?" Gollnick appeared puzzled by Max's choice of direction.

"The stairs only went up."

Gollnick's face lit with understanding and he gave a slight smile.

"Actually the stairs can go up or down depending on which way you ask them to go. The last person to use them must have been going up."

"Now he tells me," moaned Max as he turned to the others. "Speaking of getting wet, that magic bathtub in my room is great."

Everyone regarded Max in confusion, but Gollnick was the first to speak. "Max, that's called a shower... and it's not magic."

Cyrus paused with a fork full of pancake halfway to his mouth. "I know you said he lost his memory, but exactly how long was this guy out?" He studied Max as if expecting an answer.

"Based on other things he's said since waking up, I'm guessing it's been quite a long time," replied Gollnick.

Gollnick and Cyrus may not have been best friends, but it was obvious they were at least starting to tolerate one another. Maybe a good night's rest was just what everyone had needed.

"Don't you know anyone who can help me?" Max hoped for some positive news this morning.

Gollnick sat in thought for a moment. "No one I would trust, except for Hank. He's the one who brought you to me, but I haven't heard from him since then. That was over two months ago. I'll get the word out to some of my contacts and see if anyone has heard from him. In the meantime, we all need to train." He pushed away from the table then stood up and stretched. "Finish up and we'll all meet in the training room in half an hour."

Max wasn't ready for breakfast to end, so he asked, "Hey, where did the cat go?"

"What cat?" Gollnick seemed surprised by the question. "We don't have a cat, at least not one that would be roaming around the castle."

"There was a black cat outside the circle room this morning. I followed it here. Otherwise I might not have ever found the kitchen."

Gollnick gave Meagan a glance of concern. Cyrus and Amber read the expression instantly and rushed out of the room behind the other two. Max stayed seated, chewing his bacon and looking around the empty room. "Okay, what did I miss?"

Reluctantly, Max got up. The hallways were already empty. Everyone had apparently rushed off in search of the cat.

"Hello?" Max searched around for any sign of the others.

Amber came back around the corner near the stairs and spotted him. She hesitated, but finally approached. "Where was the last place you saw this cat?" There was a good deal of concern in her voice.

"It turned the corner here and ran into the kitchen before I could catch up." Max was still a bit confused as he pointed toward the kitchen. "No idea where it went after that. What's the big deal?"

Amber took Max by the arm and led him back into the room. "Most likely this castle is protected by many powerful enchantments. For any creature to get in here without magic is unlikely. It either had help or is a sorcerer in disguise. Neither option is good news."

Max looked around the room, but saw no sign of the cat. He tried to come up with a possible solution to the feline's whereabouts. "Maybe it went under the table."

Max and Amber got down on their hands and knees to check. Just as they crawled under, Cyrus came into the room.

"What the heck is going on?" he shouted angrily.

Max was startled and banged his head on the underside of the table. *Thud!*

Amber backed out from beneath the table and returned Cyrus' angry look. Cyrus could probably tell his sister was not happy, but he seemed more amused by Max rubbing his head. Cyrus turned and walked out of the kitchen.

"Sorry about that," Amber said. "My brother can be a pain at times, literally."

"I'll be fine," said Max. "Maybe we should go find the others and see if they've turned up anything."

"Good idea."

Everyone regrouped in the hallway and Gollnick provided a warning. "No sign of an intruder. If anyone sees this cat again though, come find me immediately. Do not try to take it on by yourself. If it is a sorcerer in disguise, then he must have a good deal of power to break through our protective spells. Be careful and stay alert."

He looked at each person individually to make sure they understood the seriousness of the situation. "Okay, everyone into the training room."

Max was disappointed as he realized he'd missed out on the last of the bacon.

Mysteriously, Meagan walked past and handed him a refilled plate.

"Um... thanks," he muttered. *How did she know I'm still hungry?*

7 TRAINING

Max watched as Cyrus pushed open the big double doors to the training room. He was disappointed to see the cauldrons were already burning. Today the space felt more like a cavern with stalagmites and stalactites edging the circle of firelight. Deep shadows cast into various corners gave the chamber an eerie feel. Max knew better than to ask how—the answer was always magic.

Gollnick reached out his hand and muttered a few words. Lines of golden light appeared on the floor in four circular patterns, each with a specific design. The first had waves, the second a mountain, the third had storm clouds and the last was solid grey. Each was positioned at equal distances. All were encompassed by one larger ring. In the center was a glowing disk where Gollnick situated himself then turned to look at the other four.

"Please take your positions." Gollnick motioned Meagan, Amber, Cyrus and Max toward their respective symbols on the floor. Each recognized the sign of their elemental power and stood upon the glowing design. All except Cyrus, he had no elemental power and was left with the grey circle.

Once in place, Gollnick began his story. "Thousands of years ago, there was a group of greedy individuals who desired power. They tried to tap into the mystical powers of other realms, other dimensions and other realities. Their goal was to steal the magical energies from those worlds. They siphoned more and more power from the other worlds, until they ripped a hole in the fabric of reality."

Max observed Gollnick had the full attention of the other three teenagers. To him, this felt like old news, but he couldn't remember where he'd heard it before.

"Upon doing so, monsters, demons and the stuff of nightmares were released into our world. Three sorcerers came forward to turn back this surge of darkness. They were unable to seal the portal into our world, however they were able to create an immense door of pure magic to keep the darkness at bay. Unfortunately, many creatures had already made it through."

They each looked around to see the other's reactions. Nobody appeared comfortable with the news.

"Over the centuries other sorcerers have imprisoned many of these creatures. Their magical prisons are scattered, hidden throughout the world. The keys to these prisons were also hidden. This is why, each generation, we must form a circle of sorcerers— to protect the prisons and ensure the monsters within do no harm to this world."

"Where are these prisons?" asked Cyrus.

Gollnick appeared reluctant as he glanced at the floor to avoid eye contact, but raised his head to continue. "We don't really know. All record of the prisons was lost long ago."

"Where are the keys?" asked Amber.

Gollnick answered with even more hesitance. "We don't know that either. That information was lost as well."

Max was curious, but didn't expect much in the way of an answer. "How many prisons are there?"

Once again Gollnick was forced to reply, "We don't know."

Cyrus' concern could no longer be restrained. "How are we supposed to keep these prisons closed when we don't know where they are? Or how many there are? How do you protect something when you don't even know what it is you're protecting?"

Gollnick paused a moment. "Oh, it gets better. We don't even know what shape and substance the prisons are made from, or how to open or close them. These prisons aren't like regular jail cells. Some are caverns or mazes deep within the Earth. Some monsters were transformed into other objects. Anything that could bind a creature to a place, and not allow it to harm anyone, was used to imprison these things."

Max too felt the trepidation the others wore on their faces. "That could make things a little difficult."

Gollnick raised an eyebrow. "That's an understatement. We do know the prisons were created for some of the most powerful creatures that came through the portal. They were so powerful they couldn't be destroyed, only contained."

The others could sense Gollnick's fret by his recount of the proposed undertaking. These creatures were some of the mightiest and most dangerous from ancient mythology.

"If the prisons were opened, those creatures would be released into the world. Who knows what kind of devastation they could cause. It would make the Dark Ages look like a fun time."

Max wasn't sure how, but he knew the Dark Ages were full of death. If the release of these creatures was worse, then the world would be truly lost if they failed their appointed task. The others too appeared just as concerned.

"To protect these prisons, we practice many schools of magic. There are those who believe elemental magic is the most powerful. Others believe only in arcane spells. Some prefer zodiac magic, which is basically a form of divination. There are also enchanters, wizards, illusionists and those who specialize in alteration or shape shifting."

Max considered these other forms of magic and each felt familiar. He remembered Cyrus had indicated an affinity for illusions.

"There are other schools of magic as well, such as conjurers and necromancers. While these forms of magic are not inherently evil, summoning spirits, demons, or the dead is probably not a good idea in most cases." Gollnick made his opinion clear. "I prefer to use a combination of sorcery and elemental magic. The other forms are useful at times and should be encouraged, but for now these are the forms of magic we will concentrate on. Yesterday, Max and I discovered he is a water elemental sorcerer."

Amber smiled at Max. "That explains the water column he used to leave the castle."

Cyrus glimpsed his sister's huge smile and started scowling, but Max averted his gaze.

"My niece, Meagan, is an earth elemental sorceress," said Gollnick.

Cyrus appeared impressed, but now noted the angry gaze of his sister.

Gollnick rolled his eyes. "Why do sorcerers always start learning magic at this age? It's hard enough to control your own hormones and emotions, how are you supposed to control your magic? Can we concentrate here? I didn't think I was that boring... yet."

With everyone's attention back on him, Gollnick continued, "Cyrus, Amber, do either of you possess any elemental magic? Or do you even know for sure?"

Amber seemed reluctant. "I'm an air elemental sorceress. I also have some basic divination skills."

Max smiled at her this time ignoring the gaze of Cyrus. "That explains the tornado last evening at the Inner Harbor."

Cyrus continued to stare at Max when he announced defensively, "I may not be an elemental, but I can still cast spells."

Max got the hint and returned his attention to Gollnick.

Gollnick continued their lesson though his students' attention span was limited. "Along the walls are cauldrons. Some contain fire and others water. There is air all around us and the stone beneath our feet will do for earth. Feel free to use any elemental magic during this practice session. Later this evening, I will have tomes of arcane spells for each of you to read. Any questions?"

As everyone shook their heads, Gollnick walked out of the circle and into the shadows. "Then let the training commence. Start with defensive spells first. Let's see what you've got."

Light beams, like the ones Max's attackers had used, shot from the darkness at everyone. Whatever had discharged them stayed in the shadows of the room. The light circle and symbols on the floor faded and the only light emanated from the cauldrons of fire.

Cyrus, Amber and Meagan cast spells, but no sooner did they begin than they were hit by a light beam. The beams did no permanent damage, but hurt like crazy. The disruption forced them to begin again and again.

Max remembered what one attacker had done at Inner Harbor and tried to mimic his movement. He knelt down and placed his forearms together in front of him. A faint blue sphere appeared around him. It was shaky though, and faded in and out. It did not provide a permanent shield, but it did afford him some protection from the light beams.

Max called to the others. "Guys, try this! It's not the best solution, but it kinda works!"

Meagan and Amber followed suit. A white sphere appeared around Amber. The sphere was shaky like Max's, but did help protect her. Meagan's sphere was green and a lot more stable. It protected her from almost all of the oncoming light beams.

Cyrus continued his attempts to cast spells, but after numerous hits from the beams, reluctantly he did as Max suggested. He knelt down and placed his forearms together. Cyrus' sphere was grey and just as shaky as Max and Amber's, but he was finally taking less punishment.

The four of them heard a snap of fingers and the light beams stopped. Gollnick walked back into the circle. The four defenders released their arms and stood up where they were.

"Where did you learn that technique, Max?" inquired Gollnick.

Max was reluctant to reply. "I didn't actually learn it. I saw one of the attackers at Inner Harbor do the same thing last evening without casting a spell. It protected him from Amber's tornado. I didn't know if it would help here, but that's why I tried it."

Gollnick prodded, "Instinct?"

"Who knows? Last night I created a water column to keep me from falling into the moat. I have no idea how I did it, so it must have been instinct."

Gollnick then turned to Cyrus. "You were reluctant to follow Max's lead, why?"

Cyrus crossed his arms as his face became red with anger. "Too defensive. There was no way he could've mounted any kind of offense from that position, but I had to do something."

Gollnick addressed Amber. "You followed Max's lead immediately, why?"

Amber hesitated for a second, averting her eyes. "My attempts were too slow. Max's option was better than a futile attempt at casting a spell."

Gollnick turned to Meagan. He knew the answer, but wanted to make a point for the others. "Your sphere was more effective, why?"

"I've been practicing spells for a few months now. While I haven't seen that technique yet, I knew what needed to be done to strengthen the sphere."

"Okay, so what do we do?" asked Max quickly.

"Concentrate," replied Meagan. "Putting your arms together isn't enough. The sphere is only as strong as your concentration."

Gollnick emphasized the point. "Concentration is the key to almost any magic you use. Oh, and Cyrus, the kneeling part isn't really necessary. You can use the same sphere of protection from the standing position. The guy from last night may have just been bracing himself for a more powerful attack."

Gollnick continued with his questions, "I noticed the three of you with elemental powers didn't even attempt to use those powers for protection. Any reasons why?"

Max considered the question before he replied. "Water isn't much protection against light. It passes right through it."

"Ah, but turn water to ice and it can block more light than water alone."

"Air can't stop light," commented Amber.

Gollnick retorted, "But a dust storm can block out the sun. And unfortunately, this room could stand a good deal of cleaning."

Meagan responded, "Earth could stop the light, but encasing myself in a dome of earth would also suffocate me."

"True enough, but who's to say it has to be a complete dome? Earthen shields can block most of the beams, while as Cyrus would like, you prepare an offensive move."

Meagan didn't appear convinced. "But a multi-directional attack using fireballs could still get around a protective wall. You'd have to leave holes in order to attack your enemies."

"No defense is perfect, but it would be a lot harder to hit those holes from a distance. You have to be able to adjust quickly."

Gollnick then turned to Cyrus, "I realize you have no elemental powers, but what are your thoughts?"

Cyrus looked around the room. "I know a few illusion spells. I suppose I could have made it look like we were someplace else."

Gollnick returned his attention to Max. "This is your team, Max. What do you think?"

"Ice could diminish the effect of the light beam, but it could also be used to redirect light if formed into a smooth reflective surface."

Gollnick nodded his head in approval.

Max addressed Amber. "The dust storm Gollnick mentioned could be enlarged to blind our enemies."

Amber responded with a slight smile.

He turned to face Meagan. "The earth shields could have been erected around all of us to provide the rest of us time to react and attack."

"That works," responded Meagan.

Max finished with an idea for Cyrus. "And Cyrus' illusions could be used to make it look like there were more of us to attack."

Gollnick was impressed. "All sound ideas, Max. However, if your intention is to lead, then you need to start giving directions on the battlefield now so your team can learn to trust and follow you."

Cyrus stepped forward. "Wait a minute, who nominated the amnesiac as the leader? I was the quarterback of my high school football team. I know how to lead better than him."

Gollnick was about to respond when Max held up his hand. "Cyrus has a point. Maybe he should lead."

He faced Cyrus as asked, "How do you suggest we should've handled this exercise?"

Cyrus' face went pale as he struggled with Max's question. His mouth hung open, but no words emerged. It took a few seconds for Cyrus to respond. "I... ah... I don't know. You kinda caught me off guard there. Ah, let me think."

Max had won the point. "In a battle, your enemy won't give you time to think. You need to react quickly."

Gollnick stepped in to reaffirm Max's position. "Max may have amnesia, but his tactics are good. And he has the potential to be a very powerful sorcerer."

They could all see the reluctance in Cyrus' eyes, but he was forced to surrender to the majority who sided with Max.

Max decided to change the subject to ease Cyrus' defeat. "Are these the only weapons the dark sorcerers will use?"

"Don't worry, as the days go on, the lessons will get harder," said Gollnick with a grin. He looked at the group, "And no, the dark sorcerers have much more powerful weapons to use against you. The attackers you've met so far have been low-level flunkies. Expect much worse as you become known to our enemies."

"Awesome. Glad to hear it," Max said sarcastically and lowered his head.

Gollnick announced the next practice round. "Let's try some offensive attacks. Targets will be moving around the room. It's your job to eliminate them as quickly as possible." He turned and walked into the shadows again.

Spinning disks flew around the room at high speed. Cyrus and Amber began to cast spells. Meagan looked to Max for direction, but he was too preoccupied to respond, so she cast her own spell. Max, with no knowledge of spells, looked to the cauldrons. He tried to concentrate on the water, but nothing happened.

Cyrus finished his spell and sent an energy blast at one of the targets, but was too slow and missed. Frustrated, he began another spell.

Amber finished her spell and sent her own energy blast at one of the targets. She too was not fast enough and just singed the target without much damage. Meagan also sent an energy blast spell and clipped the edge of one, sending it spinning off into a wall.

Max continued to struggle with the water elemental magic. *This was so easy yesterday, why can't I do it now?* After a few minutes, Max ran over to one of the water cauldrons and concentrated on making ice. He reached in and pulled out a snow ball. *Not what I had in mind.* He threw the snow ball, hitting one of the targets, but did no damage.

Max continued to throw snow balls until he heard, "Ouch!"

The targets disappeared and Gollnick emerged from the shadows, rubbing snow from his hair.

"Watch where you're throwing those things." After a pause to look around he asked, "So, how did we do this time?"

He received no response, and worse, no one would meet his gaze. All eyes were on the walls or floor.

"Who wants to go first?"

Max spoke up. "I tried concentrating on the water, but all I got were snow balls. It was so easy yesterday. Why couldn't I make ice today?"

"You were over-thinking it. I know I said to concentrate, but you were forcing it. Nice try, but it's going to take some practice."

Cyrus was the next to speak. "Illusions aren't much good against flying targets."

"True. Until you have a better handle on spells, we'll need to find other forms of offensive weapons for you."

Gollnick turned to the girls. "Amber, the disks should have been easy targets for you since they were airborne."

"I barely managed to control a mini tornado yesterday. If it wouldn't have been for Max, I could've done a lot more damage." She blushed as she looked at Max. "Last time I tried anything bigger, I started a hurricane in Virginia."

Gollnick nodded. "Yes, control is something we definitely need to work on."

He then turned to his niece. "Meagan?"

"They were moving too fast for me to cast a spell quickly or try earth magic."

"Aim and patience, two more things to work on."

Gollnick then addressed them as a group. "Max, talk to your teammates. Find out their strengths and weaknesses. Cyrus, I have some spell tomes I want you to look at. Amber and Meagan, like Max, I have elemental magic tomes for you to read. The room will repeat these exercises for the next hour. Practice what I've told you so far. At the end of that time, I want all of you to meet me in the library."

He snapped his fingers and the double doors swung open and he walked out. The doors closed quietly behind him.

Cyrus looked surprised. "Why didn't he tell me he could open the doors like that?"

"Something about the doors being more imposing," replied Max.

An hour later the four of them found Gollnick in the library reading a book on memory spells. Next to him on a table were stacked four large tomes on different kinds of magic.

"So, how did things go after I left?" inquired Gollnick.

The four of them just looked at one another for a few seconds. Meagan was the first to speak. "About as well as the first time around."

"That bad, huh?"

Cyrus looked at the tomes stacked in front of Gollnick. They were huge in comparison to normal books. "So, those are the books you want us to read? And how many weeks do we have to read them?"

After noticing Gollnick's puzzled expression, Amber explained her brother's question. "Cyrus, isn't a big fan of reading."

Cyrus slowly turned his head to Amber. "Whose side are you on anyway?"

She chuckled.

Gollnick handed one book to each of them. "I think you may all find these interesting"

Cyrus replied, "I think I'm gonna be bored to death."

"Finish these as quickly as you can. You need to be up to speed before the dark sorcerers show up again. If you have questions... talk to one another and try to figure it out. I'm leaving to talk to one of my contacts for more information. No goofing off. Even when I'm not in the castle, I still have eyes in this place."

Gollnick walked to the mirror and accepted his trench coat from the knobby little arm of the coat stand. He muttered his usual gibberish and the image in the mirror began to swirl. In seconds Gollnick disappeared.

Cyrus announced with a sense of relief. "Finally, I thought that slave driver would never leave. This is ridiculous!"

Amber giggled. "Why? Because he gave you a book to read?"

Cyrus just rolled his eyes then flopped down into an overstuffed chair to read.

8 AN OLD FRIEND

It was mid-morning on the east coast and pouring rain in Philadelphia. The sky was full of dark clouds and an electrical storm hit many areas in the massive city. Lightning danced from cloud to cloud. Several buildings were ablaze from lightning strikes and it was only getting worse. Weather forecasters were calling it one of the worst storms to hit the northeast. They said it was the remnants of a hurricane, but this was no ordinary storm. Severe winds and violent rain were worse than expected. A normal hurricane would've lost strength as it passed over land this far north. It was as if Mother Nature had declared war on the city of brotherly love.

In an old abandoned house in a rundown section of town, Gollnick stepped out of a mirror. The house should have been marked for demolition if it wasn't already. Its windows were broken, the floorboards warped, and any furniture still there was broken and in no shape to be used. Dirt and debris littered the floor from a caved-in section of ceiling. The only residents were stray cats roaming in search of food.

Gollnick ducked close to the wall and crept over to a broken window. He looked out to find he was on the second floor of the old building. He could sense it in the air. This was no normal storm, magic was involved. He had come to Philadelphia at a bad time. A battle raged between sorcerers, but who? He knew he had to find his contact quickly and get out of town before he could be drawn into an unexpected battle he was unprepared to fight.

When he turned away from the window, a stray lightning bolt hit a nearby building and it caught fire. Not knowing if it was directed his way or if it was by sheer dumb luck, Gollnick made for the stairs and went down to the first level. Fire sirens from a nearby station could be heard as he ducked out the door and ran in the opposite direction.

His contact was to meet him under a neighboring bridge in ten minutes. Under normal circumstances, he would casually walk there, but with the rain pouring down, he decided to run. If he got there a little early, he'd just wait.

He ran under the bridge to the appointed meeting place, but stayed in the shadows, relieved for the shelter. The electrical storm had worsened. This was no mere battle between sorcerers, this was a war between many sorcerers. *What is going on?* he thought to himself as he pushed back his wet hair and wiped the rain from his eyes. By now, every inch of his body and clothing were soaked.

After a few minutes, he heard someone approach. Their feet splashed in the water on the wet sidewalks. He stepped behind a support column then opened his hand palm side up. Flames enveloped his hand. A single figure dressed in a trench coat had come in out of the rain and walked into the shadows of the columns on the other side of the bridge.

Gollnick could not make out who it was. Was it just some innocent person who wanted to get out of the rain? Or was it his contact? Or worse, was it another sorcerer? Friend or foe, he needed to know. With a hand of flames behind his back, he stepped out of the shadows so the other person could see him. The figure made no indication, so Gollnick coughed to alert the other person to his presence.

The figure turned and pointed at Gollnick. A wand shot out of the coat sleeve and was caught in hand. The person pointed it at Gollnick like someone wielding a sword.

"Who's there?" The stranger's voice was female.

Gollnick remained cautious. "A friend, I hope."

"Gollnick, is that you?"

Gollnick relaxed a little at the sound and realized it was indeed his contact.

"Elisa, it's good to see you again." He walked out of the shadows and over to her, extinguishing the flames in his hand. "I didn't realize you were my contact this evening."

Elisa lowered her wand and stuffed it back into her sleeve as she met him halfway under the bridge.

"It's a dangerous time to be here right now. This better be important." Her long black hair was drenched by the rain as it hung down over her trench coat.

Gollnick looked into her dark eyes and remembered a time when he was happy to see her elegant smile. She still had a slight Hispanic accent even after all these years. The smell of her perfume reminded him of old times, both good and bad.

Gollnick raised his hands toward either end of the underpass and uttered a spell, *"Vocalus non-perro atee."* A shimmering barrier appeared over either end and blocked all sound from going in or out. Out in the raging storm, the rain still poured, but the thunder was muted.

Gollnick inquired with uncertainty. "What's going on? It looks like a war."

"It is." Elisa's eyes continued to scan for unwelcome adversaries. "Malcolm is upset about something. He thinks Frederick Von Woonst knows or has something he wants. I'm not sure what he's looking for, but it must be pretty important. He wasn't even trying to cover up the attack on Frederick to make normal folk think it was a storm. Other sorcerers had to get involved to hide the magical battle and to make it look like severe weather."

After a brief pause, she continued, "Something's wrong, something's changed. This isn't the first time in the past twenty-four hours that sorcerers have battled openly in front of normal folk. The rules are changing and I don't know why."

Gollnick responded sheepishly, "I might know who he's looking for, but I have no idea why."

"Who? What do you mean, who he's looking for?" Elisa questioned.

Gollnick hesitated a moment before answering. "His name is Max. He was in a coma when Hank placed him into my custody. He just woke up yesterday and unfortunately he's lost his memory. We're guessing he's somewhere in his mid to late teens. The nurses at the hospital named him. We don't even know his real name."

Elisa looked at Gollnick with a blank stare. "So?"

"Since waking up, dark sorcerers have made two attempts to track him down. I don't know if their intention is to capture or kill him. I'm not even sure how they're finding him."

"That's why you wanted to meet? You're looking for information on a *kid?*" Elisa asked in an accusatory fashion.

"Yes," said Gollnick, "If Malcolm is willing to start a war over Max, I need to know why and fast." Gollnick couldn't help but wonder. What was it Max had or knew that was so important?

Elisa considered this before responding. "I'm not sure Malcolm's after this kid in particular. He's been recruiting heavily all up and down the east coast. There was even a rumor he captured Hank."

"Hank? Where's he being held?" asked Gollnick surprised. Hank was the only one who might be able to shed some light on Max's background.

"It was just a rumor," answered Elisa. "I don't even know if it's true. I'll see what I can find out."

"But why is he recruiting now?" Gollnick was even more confused by this new piece of information.

"You haven't heard yet, have you?" questioned Elisa compassionately.

Gollnick's expression turned to a look of concern, like he was bracing himself for even more bad news.

"What is it?" asked Gollnick.

Elisa reached out to him. "They found one."

"Found what?"

"They found one of the prisons."

Gollnick paused, realizing the consequences of her statement. "Where?"

"I don't know." Elisa sighed and lowered her head. After a few seconds, she looked into Gollnick's eyes. "Malcolm is sending Vincent to open it."

Gollnick met her eyes for a second then lowered his gaze. He turned away from Elisa to consider what she had just told him. He knew Vincent and this was not good news. Vincent was once a friend. At one time, Gollnick wanted Vincent to join his circle, but the crystal denied him access. Vincent became enraged and left. They stayed in touch for a while, but then Vincent disappeared. A few years later he re-emerged as a dark sorcerer. Gollnick never knew what happened to make Vincent join the dark sorcerers, but he knew Vincent was both a powerful sorcerer and businessman—and not someone to be underestimated.

"He still has an apartment in New York?" asked Gollnick quietly without turning around.

Elisa stepped closer and placed her hand on his shoulder. "You can't seriously consider going there?"

"I have to. It's my job to make sure those prisons stay closed. It's my responsibility."

She pulled her hand back and wrapped her arms around her own shoulders. "Yes, he still has the apartment in New York, but he also has an office in Miami. It might be safer to go there if you're trying to find information."

Gollnick pleaded, "Yes, I need information, but I also need to speak to Vincent. I need to know what happened. Why he's working for them now."

"Nick, you can't change the past. The crystal saw something in him, something it didn't like."

Gollnick turned his head to look over his shoulder at her. "That doesn't mean he was evil. It doesn't explain why he disappeared."

"Nick, if you're going after Vincent, be careful. He may not be the same person you once knew. Just remember, he's powerful. He can kill you if he wants to."

Gollnick looked into her eyes again. "I need you to see what else you can find out about Max and Hank. Let me worry about Vincent and the prison. I won't let him open it. I can't."

With raised hands pointed toward either end of the bridge, Gollnick reversed the spell. *"Dim-tar mai secul."* The shimmering barrier disappeared and they could once again hear the sorcerers' battle amidst the storm. Gollnick looked once more at Elisa then turned and pulled the collar of his trench coat high around his neck.

Elisa continued to stand there under the bridge as she watched Gollnick run out into the rain and disappear into the raging storm.

Gollnick wondered if this would be the last time he would ever see her. But he'd thought that before, yet they always made it through. This time, however, things were different. The rules had changed.

9 TRAINING FOR BATTLE

A few days later, Gollnick entered the library to find Cyrus, Amber and Meagan, but Max was nowhere in sight. The three of them looked tired and bleary eyed, but they were still reading the many tomes of magic he had given them.

"Where's Max?" Gollnick asked Meagan.

She looked up from her book and yawned. "Turns out he really likes to read. He finished the book you gave him and then read three more, in their entirety. He wanted to practice some of the spells from them, so he said he was going to the training room."

Gollnick grew concerned. Could Max really have read and understood all four books since he last saw him? Gollnick headed for the door which opened at his approach.

Cyrus looked after him and was about to follow. Without turning around Gollnick cautioned, "I wouldn't do that. As interesting as it may be, I wouldn't leave this room until you finish that book. Leaving implies you have read and understand everything it says. I will test you on it as soon as I see you outside of this room."

With a smirk, Gollnick looked over his shoulder to see Cyrus ease back into his chair and reluctantly heft the tome back into his lap.

At the snap of his fingers, the huge double doors to the training room swung open. Gollnick was assaulted by a wave of cold air. The entire room was frozen. A huge ice chandelier hung from the ceiling containing three cauldrons of fire. Where other cauldrons normally flamed, their fire appeared frozen in place.

Max stood on a raised dais in the center of the room beneath the chandelier with his back to the door. Next to him were three vessels of water. He willed the water to rise up and fashioned it into sculptures. On the left stood a three-foot scorpion. A large bird about to take flight flanked the right. From the third came a twelve-foot snake. The statues were just crude shapes, nothing detailed, but impressive nonetheless.

Gollnick wasn't sure how to respond. Only a few days ago this kid—who didn't even know his real name—could barely control the smallest amounts of water. He knew no spells and seemed lost in the world. Now he manipulated water and ice like child's play.

Gollnick approached the dais, but before he could say a word, Max called out to him. "Gollnick. I figured it was you. What do you think?"

Gollnick halted mid-step. "How did you know it was me?"

"Vibrations in the ice as you entered. So, what do you think of my elemental magic now?"

Gollnick stood there, enthralled. "You learned all of this in the past few days?"

Max smiled. "Apparently I'm a fast reader. And when it's something I enjoy, I pick things up quick. I still need to work on spells, but I really enjoy this elemental water magic."

"I see. Has anyone else been here to practice?"

Max shook his head. "Nope, not yet."

Gollnick placed a forefinger to his temple. He called out to Meagan in his mind. *Please bring everyone to the training room.*

He turned and stepped down from the dais. As he approached the doors, he pondered yet another ice sculpture in the corner, a long stick with a curved blade at the top. It reminded him of something the Grim Reaper might carry. *Interesting.* He snapped his fingers again and the doors swung open. As they parted, Amber, Cyrus, and Meagan rounded the corner and strolled down the corridor. They shivered when they entered the room and were awestruck. When the doors closed behind them it felt like a freezer.

Gollnick let them take in Max's progress for a moment then ordered, "Room reset."

The air and water inside immediately swirled around, creating a mist so thick it disrupted visibility. When the process ended, everything had returned to the appearance of a cavern.

The cauldrons were back to their normal places and filled with their correct elements.

Gollnick walked to the center of the room. "Training session. Show me what you've learned so far."

The circle appeared on the floor with the four symbols in their places. Each apprentice took their respective spots and waited for instructions.

"Offensive and defensive spells, take out the targets as quickly as possible without getting hit. Max, keep the group together," instructed Gollnick then he disappeared into the shadows.

* * *

This time, the disks were only two feet in diameter with a small black circle in the middle. They flew around the room as during previous training sessions. Within seconds, light beams shot outward from the black dots at their centers. Max took in the situation before calling out instructions.

"Meagan, stone walls for protection; Amber, stir up the wind, keep those things off balance; Cyrus, let's see if your aim has improved."

Meagan held her hands out, palms down. When she turned them palm side up, eight earthen wall segments rose out of the floor, about ten feet high, equally spaced in a circle with small gaps to see through. Amber stood at the center of the circle, moving her hands in front of her as if directing wind currents. The wind picked up, but in erratic patterns.

Max could see Amber struggling for control. He reached out to the water cauldrons and concentrated on forming ice. He ran to the gaps in the earthen walls to gauge the position of each disk. As each one passed by a cauldron, Max snapped his hand in a quick upward flick. Water jumped out of the cauldron. It ensnared the disks in a sheet of ice and froze them in place.

Cyrus also went to the gaps in the earthen walls and cast spells to shoot the targets out of the air. He managed to hit a few, though Max could see his aim was still off. After about five minutes, ten of the targets had been frozen, two smashed into the wall and three more were shattered by energy blasts.

* * *

With the capture of the final target, they heard Gollnick clap. At the snap of his fingers the disks disappeared. Gollnick walked from the shadows. "That was much better this time. We still need to work on your spell casting, but your elemental magic is doing much better, as is your leadership, Max."

"Thanks," said Max, "but this was almost a repeat of our last two sessions, even with your suggestions from last time on how to handle these things. If this were a real battle situation, I may not have known what to have everyone do."

Gollnick consider Max's comments. "I know you've all had a long day, but I'm afraid you have some more homework."

They let out a little groan, dreading the thought.

"I have some books on combat spells I need you to read and practice. Work with one another to understand these spells as quickly as possible. I may need your help in the next day or two, but only if you can defend yourselves in combat."

"What's happened?" asked Meagan.

"It seems the dark sorcerers have discovered the location of one of the prisons." Gollnick became very glum. "A former associate of mine by the name of Vincent is being dispatched to open the prison. I've been trying to track him down, but no luck so far. I'm not sure when he plans to attempt to open the prison or where it may be. I'm going to see if I can gather more information from some other contacts. If not, I may need to break into his office in Miami in order to find out what prison they're after."

"Doesn't Vincent also have an apartment in New York?" inquired Meagan.

Gollnick snapped his head toward Meagan in surprise. Wide eyed and very serious, he responded, "Let me make one thing perfectly clear, we're not going to New York City."

The determination in his eyes said this was non-negotiable. "It's the one place in the world with the largest concentration of dark sorcerers. To go there would be suicide at this point. Besides, there's apparently some sort of sorcerer civil war going on up there now and it appears to have spread as far as Philadelphia. They'll kill any sorcerer they don't know and won't bother to ask questions later. For now, we need to concentrate on Miami."

"Is it possible they're fighting over a prison in New York City?" asked Max, but Gollnick waved off the idea.

"No. There was a prison in New York City, but it was opened many years ago. While digging for the subway tunnels, some workers stumbled across the prison chamber. I don't know how it was done or by who, but that one's already been opened. What I do know is, after opening the prison a demon of some sort was released into the world. No one seems to know where he is now, but I'm sure he's still around somewhere. Waiting for who knows what."

Amber asked in a timid voice, "Is it possible he's the one who told the dark sorcerers where to find this new prison?"

"I doubt it," replied Gollnick with hopeful assurance. "If he knew where the prison was, why wait so many years to reveal its location? Why not just go there to open it right away? In all likelihood, the information was stumbled upon, just like the prison in New York City."

Max added, "It might help if we could discover how they found out about the prison's location."

Gollnick nodded in agreement. "Good point, we'll keep that in mind. In the meantime, reading and training for all four of you. Meagan, you know where the combat spell tomes are. Make sure Cyrus learns at least some effective combat spells. He's good with illusions, see if you can get him up to speed on a distraction spell. Anything to keep the dark sorcerers off balance." Then he addressed Max, Amber and Meagan. "You three have at least some elemental magic you can use. Practice."

Gollnick snapped his fingers. When the doors opened, he waited as the others exited the room. He instructed the room to reset and walked out.

Gollnick entered his chambers and snaked his way through the room to avoid the tall piles of books scattered everywhere. He sat down at his desk covered in papers, notes, maps and strange writings even he had trouble deciphering.

His hand raised to his head, Gollnick placed forefinger to temple. He called out mentally, *'Elisa, can you hear me?'*

Elisa's mental thoughts responded, *'I figured I'd be hearing from you, but not so soon.'*

'Do you have Vincent's office address in Miami?'

Within seconds, the address popped into Gollnick's mind. He pressed for more information. *'Any word on how they came by this information? I mean, ancient magical prisons don't just show up on radar. How did they find it to begin with?'*

'I can't discuss that now. I'm being followed. I'll be in touch.'

'Thanks and be careful.'

'Once again, you owe me one. How many is that now? I've lost count.'

'Too many. Be safe.'

Gollnick pulled a map from the pile of papers and spoke. "Show me downtown Miami, Florida." The image scrolled like a video screen until it came to rest on the streets of the city.

"Show me safe mirrors in the area." The map did as instructed and a few tiny blue dots appeared. Gollnick sat back in his chair.

"None close enough to get there without a fight." He leaned forward and once again looked at the map. "Okay, show me all known mirrors in the area."

Once again the map did as instructed. This time many yellow, red and black dots were added to the blue ones. Gollnick knew the yellow dots were not recommended, the red were dangerous and the black meant potential death. *Not what I was hoping to see.*

The closest dots to where he needed to go were all red or black. Interestingly enough, one of the black dots was actually inside Vincent's office, but Gollnick knew that mirror would possess traps for unknown spellcasters, just like his own mirror in the library.

If we break in, we're going to have to fight a mighty big battle and there's a good chance innocent people may get hurt. Maybe we can sneak in, but no magic or they'll detect us right away.

After a few hours of planning, Gollnick entered the library to find Max alone, seated on an overstuffed chair with his legs dangling over one of the arms.

"Where's everyone else?" asked Gollnick.

"They went to the training room to practice the spells Meagan was showing us."

"So what are you still doing here?"

"I can't stop reading."

Gollnick was surprised. "Have you practiced any of the new spells you were supposed to be working on?"

Without averting his eyes from the tome, Max held up a fist then opened it quickly with the palm of his hand directed at Gollnick as he muttered, *"Alecto orona con-vue."* A blinding light flashed from his hand.

Gollnick raised his arms a little too late. It took a full half-minute for his vision to clear from the blinding light.

"Well, that could be effective in the coming battle," commented Gollnick, still in pain. "I'm almost afraid to ask if there's anything else. How many tomes have you read so far?"

Max stopped to ponder the question.

"Seven over the past couple of days, including the combat spells. I just started this one a few minutes ago."

He pointed to a specific spell, "After the others are done in the training room, I thought I might try this fireball spell."

Gollnick grabbed the book from Max. To his surprise, it was an advanced tome on Arcane spells, more advanced than Max should have been able to comprehend. Sorcerers had to learn spells in stages, building on weaker spells in order to comprehend the more complex. Hand and body movements became more important when casting higher level spells. What Max was reading should have been well beyond his level.

Gollnick looked from book to boy. "You understand this?"

"Sure, seems simple enough. It's almost like I'm remembering the spells more than learning them."

"Your memory is starting to come back then?"

"No. It just feels like I know these spells already," replied Max. "I don't remember ever using them before, they just seem familiar."

Gollnick put the tome down. "Come with me."

The two of them left the library and headed straight for the training room. A quick snap and the doors swung open. Inside, Cyrus had just cast a fog spell and the room filled with noxious fumes.

Gollnick cried out, "Room reset."

He spotted the startled faces of Amber, Meagan, and Cyrus when the smoke cleared. Gollnick marched straight to the center of the room. "Target."

Along the far wall, a ten-foot-high disk appeared out of nothing with a bull's eye in the center. Gollnick turned to face Max. "Okay, show me what you've got."

The others stepped back as they attempted to comprehend the situation.

Max walked forward and Gollnick took a few paces back to give him space. Max stood in the center of the room and took a deep breath. He squared his shoulders with the target and placed his hands in front of him, palms facing, about six inches apart. He stepped back onto his right foot, angled his right shoulder, and a tiny glow could be observed between his hands.

"Magna fir-tor loma!" Max threw his shoulder forward and thrust with his right palm until his arm was fully extended.

A fireball about a foot in diameter shot out from his hand and slammed the outermost ring of the target, leaving a one-foot scorch mark as evidence of the hit.

Expressions of amazement were visible on everyone's face. Max—a water elemental sorcerer—had just thrown a fireball.

Gollnick was almost speechless. "Aim's a little off..."

10 BATTLE PLANS

Gollnick sent Meagan on an errand. An hour later, everyone reassembled in the kitchen. Meagan carried two heavy garment bags over her left arm and was struggling with three shopping bags in her right. Cyrus and Max each received a set of navy overalls, Gollnick a dark grey business suit, white shirt and black tie. But Amber's face flushed a deep crimson when she saw what Meagan had picked out for her—a skimpy French maid outfit.

"Seriously?" Amber said as she took the outfit and looked at Meagan who couldn't help but giggle.

"Sorry, couldn't resist." She then handed Amber a ladies business outfit with a striped top and skirt.

Amber breathed a sigh of relief. "That's more like it."

Meagan also produced a black security guard outfit with a black cap and sunglasses for herself.

Gollnick pulled out a city map to explain his plan for getting into Vincent's office. "We will split into three groups and arrive at different times so we don't draw attention to ourselves. Cyrus and Max, I've made arrangements for you to borrow a delivery truck. You will be delivering a large package. If you're stopped for any reason, tell them you've got a package for the twenty-ninth floor. If they don't buy it, knock them out if at all possible, but don't endanger yourselves any more than necessary. Just get to the twenty-ninth floor and wait for us in this office." He pointed to a different map showing the layout of the building.

"Meagan, you will arrive shortly after the boys. Some of the security guards should be on their lunch break at that time. Follow them back into the building once they're done. Wait for us in the lobby."

"Uh, what am I supposed to do? I'll kinda stick out, won't I?"

"Guard something."

"Amber, you and I will catch a cab and arrive at the same office building ten minutes later. Once we enter the lobby, Meagan will stop us, at which point she will take us past the check point to the elevators where we'll make our way to the twenty-ninth floor and meet the boys in this office."

He then addressed everyone. "Try not to use any magic unless absolutely necessary. If anything goes wrong and we need to abort, hit the nearest fire alarm and run. That will be the signal to everyone else to return home. If everything goes as planned, we'll all meet up on the twenty-ninth floor. Assuming we haven't run into any resistance, we'll take the stairs from there to the thirtieth floor."

Amber, Cyrus, Max and Meagan looked from one to another. Gollnick could tell his optimism wasn't as convincing as he'd hoped.

"At that point, we'll definitely meet resistance. Be ready for a fight."

Cyrus was the only one who appeared anxious for a fight. The irony was not lost on Gollnick that the only one who wanted a battle was the one who was least prepared for it.

"Hopefully there won't be too many guards. I'll hold them off while you four slip into the office. Find as much information as you can on this prison. Vincent isn't scheduled to arrive until 2:00 p.m. I plan for us to be out of there by 1:00 p.m."

Cyrus rolled his eyes. "In a perfect world, maybe."

"When we are ready to leave, we will escape through the mirror in the crate that Cyrus and Max will be delivering. If anything goes wrong, do not use any of the mirrors in the building. They are bound to be booby-trapped. Find your way out of the building and get to safety. To open a portal back here, use the spell 'Mirtor tolanga se-atum'. This mirror is also protected, but I've already informed it of your identities. I repeat, do not use any mirrors in the office building."

"Why don't we just carry small pocket mirrors with us?" asked Amber.

Gollnick realized she wanted a better escape plan. "Good idea, but too small. You have to be able to physically fit through the mirror in order to use the spell."

Gollnick took note of the facial expressions of his apprentices. Cyrus was eager for a fight. Max was deep in thought. Amber and Meagan registered concern.

"Any other questions?" Gollnick didn't wait for a response. "No? Good! Get some sleep and don't forget breakfast in the morning. If everyone looks as drained as you do now, we'll be a dead giveaway."

* * *

Max returned to his room both anxious and excited for the next day's events. He could sense things were not going to go as smoothly as Gollnick had explained, but judging by the faces of the others, he could tell they all knew the same thing.

He lay down and just stared at the ceiling for a while. A few minutes later, there was a knock at the door. Max got up to answer it and was surprised to find Amber. She stood with her hands clenched together behind her back. He stuttered to find the words, "Hey, ah, hi. Uh, what's up?"

"Could I come in for a minute?" asked Amber quietly.

Max just stood there dumbfounded, forgetting all his earlier anxiety, overwhelmed by a whole new kind. He couldn't help but think how beautiful Amber looked, even after a long day of practice. Her perfume sent his senses spinning. All he could do was stare.

"Is everything okay?" asked Amber.

Once again, Max stuttered. "Yeah, fine. Uh, sure, come on in." He held the door open and allowed her to enter, closing it behind her. "Have a seat," he said. Hastily he pulled out a chair for her.

She didn't sit down, but turned to look him in the eyes.

"Max, I know my brother," she began.

Max released the tension in his shoulders as he realized this visit was about Cyrus and not him.

"Is he okay?" asked Max. Though disappointed by the topic of discussion, he was still concerned about all members of their group.

"Cyrus doesn't like taking orders. I'm concerned he's going to try something on his own tomorrow. You're going to be with him.

Please keep an eye on him and don't let him do something stupid."

"I'll do my best."

"Promise me you'll keep him safe," begged Amber.

Max paused, realizing if Cyrus was that headstrong, there was little Max would be able to do to change his mind. Even still, as he looked into Amber's eyes, Max couldn't help but agree to her request. With a sigh he said, "I promise."

Amber leaned over and gave Max a hug. He felt the anxiety come back as he held her. When she released, he looked into her eyes and she smiled.

"You be safe too," she said. She opened the door, but before leaving she looked back and smiled again. As soon as the door closed, Max did a face plant into his bed.

The next morning, Max was on his way to the kitchen for breakfast. He spotted the black cat from the day before.

"Oh, so it's you again?" he bent down to pick up the cat, but it darted away down the corridor to the stairs. Max ran after it, but by the time he reached the stairs, the cat was gone.

He stood there and looked at the spiral staircase made of stone slabs around a central column. He said, "Down." But nothing happened. Then he tried, "Stairs, down." This time the stairs that had previously gone up to the next floor suddenly began to lower. One stone step at a time came down from the level above and once they were all aligned as a flat surface, they then proceeded to lower down to the main floor. The whole process took mere seconds. Max looked up, but saw no opening in the ceiling where the steps had previously led up to the next level. He looked down the stairs only to see another corridor, but then his stomach began to rumble and he remembered he was hungry and on his way to the kitchen.

Max entered to find Meagan already there. She placed a plate of food on the table in front of him. Max raised his eyebrows and shot Meagan a surprised look.

"I know you're not wild about vegetarian, but I figured we shouldn't eat a heavy meal if we're going to fight a battle in Miami today."

Max sighed. "I see I'm not the only one who had that feeling." Max reluctantly conceded the point and ate the fruit and vegetables on his plate. "So, where's everyone else?" he asked as he finished his food.

"Nick is in his room preparing for a battle if it comes to that. Amber already ate, and I haven't seen Cyrus yet today," replied Meagan.

Max reluctantly informed her of his morning visitor. "I saw that black cat again, but it disappeared before I could do anything."

Meagan stopped what she was doing. "That cat is beginning to bother me. It shouldn't have been possible for a normal cat to get in here. But if it's something else, it's keeping a low profile."

Since everyone was about to leave the castle, Max realized the cat—or whatever it was—would have free rein. *Who knows, maybe the cat is vegetarian?*

11 THINGS GO WRONG

Later that morning, Max arrived in the library to find the others already going over plans again. At first Max thought he was in the wrong place—he didn't recognize anyone. In the black security guard uniform, with her black jacket and black cap, Meagan didn't even look like herself. Her normally long curly blonde hair was pulled back in a bun, but still covered the slightly pointed tips of her ears where dark sunglasses rested.

Amber looked more like a business woman than a teenage girl. Her brown hair was also up in a bun and she was wearing glasses. Her suit and skirt made her seem older until Max heard her giggle at something Meagan said.

Gollnick was obviously uncomfortable in his dark grey business suit, tugging at his tie and pulling at the collar of his white shirt. The suit didn't appear to be snug. It just wasn't Gollnick's style.

As Max entered, Cyrus came in behind him and slapped him on the back. Like Max, he wore navy overalls.

"Let's get this show on the road," announced Cyrus anxiously.

Everybody had gone over the plan one last time before departing. Max and Cyrus were the first to go. Cyrus walked over to the mirror. *"Mirtor tolanga se-atum."* The image in the mirror swirled and Cyrus looked to Max. "You ready?" Without waiting for an answer, he reached into the mirror and was pulled into the swirling image. Max quickly followed.

Twenty minutes later, Max and Cyrus pulled up to the delivery dock behind the Miami office building. They climbed out and pulled a six-foot wooden crate from the back of the truck. Max rang the bell and waited.

A few seconds later a young kid came to the door. "Yeah, what do you want?"

Max shifted the weight from his end of the crate. "Come on, open up. We're already late in delivering this package. Where are the elevators?"

"Package? What are you talking about? No one said anything about a package."

Max shifted the weight of the crate a second time. "Look kid, this is heavy. Just point us in the right direction."

Without waiting for a response, Max and Cyrus pushed their way into the building. The teenage boy who'd answered the door was at a loss for words.

"The elevator?" Max repeated.

The kid pointed across the laundry room to an alcove.

"Hey kid," said Max, "do us a favor. Don't tell anyone we're here. As I said, we're already late. The sooner we deliver this, the sooner we can get out of here."

Max and Cyrus hefted the crate and headed for the other side of the laundry room. It was full of large, industrial-size washing machines, bigger than Max. Max was in awe as he passed by them and wondered how they worked. He started to look more closely until Cyrus whispered, "Focus, we belong here. Remember?"

Max nodded and continued with Cyrus through the laundry room. When they were halfway across, two security guards stepped out of the elevator and walked toward them.

"We've been made," said Cyrus.

Max could see Cyrus was ready to panic and attack. "No, we haven't. Just stay calm."

"They've seen us," Cyrus' voice quivered in a panicked tone.

Max tried his best to sound confident. "We belong here, remember? We're just making a delivery. They haven't noticed us." Even though he wasn't sure, he figured it was best to continue the charade. To run now would be a certain giveaway.

Max did his best to keep Cyrus calm as the two security guards came closer. They stepped off to the side to let the uniformed men pass by.

After the close call, Max looked to Cyrus who let out a quiet sigh of relief. The two of them continued on to the elevator. Even the employee elevators in this building were impressive. They were all shiny with polished copper walls. A few dents and dings, but nice for employee use.

* * *

In the next building, Meagan had just arrived at the fast food joint where the guards ate their lunch. She went inside and sat down at a table. Like many fast food restaurants, the place was noisy, busy and not the cleanest place around. She spotted three guys dressed as security guards and kept an eye on them until they got up to leave. They were dressed in the same black uniform she currently wore. With her head down, she waited until they passed. Meagan stood to follow them out and stayed five paces behind as they crossed the street to re-enter the target building. She stopped to hold open a door for some other people, and then continued inside with everyone else.

The lobby was quite large with a ceiling at least two stories high. A security desk lined the center of the back lobby wall. Elevator doors flanked the desk left and right. Some people chose to use the stairs on either side of the lobby. In the center were benches around an indoor fountain. Meagan stood near the entrance and turned to face the glass doors. All she had to do now was wait for Gollnick and Amber—and not be stopped by any of the other security guards.

* * *

Max and Cyrus were on their way up to the twenty-ninth floor in the employee elevator when it stopped on the twentieth. Two security guards entered the elevator with them. Max and Cyrus moved to the back and stood to either side of their delivery. The guards turned to face the doors. The crate took up a third of the space. There was barely room for the four passengers.

Max looked at their reflection in the shiny metal doors to the elevator. Their black caps and dark sunglasses made it impossible to see their eyes, but otherwise he thought they could've been twins. The loose fitting black jackets, black cargo pants and combat boots gave them a military appearance. The two men stood straight-faced and quiet. As he watched them, he noticed the same ring on their hands as the guys who had attacked him the other evening. He did his best to keep his composure. He had no way to know if Cyrus had spotted the rings or not, and no way to communicate it to him if he hadn't.

"Where are you two headed?" asked the one security guard with a stern face and monotone voice as he looked over his right shoulder at Cyrus.

"Delivery on the twenty-ninth floor."

Max was surprised to hear Cyrus' calm reply.

The guard glanced left at the other guard who shook his head. As the two guards nonverbally consulted, Cyrus raised his hands, palm side down. Max knew what was coming from the training room the day before. He locked eyes with Cyrus then looked to the floor as Cyrus cast his spell. *"Flo-gorto mana tam."* A thick fog poured forth from his hands and flooded the elevator.

The guards raised clenched fists with rings pointed at the two boys. The guards turned, but the vapors rose to envelope the room in seconds. Cyrus and Max immediately dove for the floor. Flashes of light told Max the guards had indeed fired the light beams from their rings.

There was a second of silence then two thuds as the security guards hit the floor next to them. Max and Cyrus exchanged puzzled glances.

"Ah, the walls are reflective. They stunned themselves!" realized Max with a sigh of relief.

Cyrus let out a little chuckle and waved his hand to release the fog spell.

Max was the first to point out, "We're going to need to hide these two until this is all over."

"We'll find a room on the twenty-ninth floor and tie them up there."

Max looked down at the one guard and noticed his ring. "Uh, oh. We've got a flashing ring, any idea what that means?"

"No, but I'm pretty sure it's not good."

* * *

In the lobby Meagan stood near the entrance and looked out the windows with her back to the security station. She spotted the reflection of a security guard approach her from behind. "Who are you?"

"'Natasha Brown," replied Meagan with a smile. "And who are you?"

The guard did not appear to be in a friendly mood. "What are you doing here?"

"I'm new. I was instructed by Vincent Maylock to wait here for two business associates of his and escort them to his office for a two o'clock meeting." They hadn't discussed what to say in the event she was discovered, so she was making it up as she went and she thought it sounded like a fairly good excuse. Now if the guard would just believe it.

The guard reached for his cell phone. As he did, Meagan quietly cast a spell. *"Memo non fizzu amond."* The guard looked around for a few seconds in a daze. He then looked back to Meagan.

"Where am I?" asked the guard.

"You were going to get me the security clearance for Mr. Maylock's two business associates who are arriving shortly. You may want to hurry." She knew it was a risk using magic in the lobby, but it was better than being caught.

"Right, security clearance," said the guard, "I'll just go get that. I'll be right back." The guard was in a trance-like daze. He obviously didn't know what he was saying or doing as he walked away.

A few minutes later, Meagan spotted him wandering the lobby looking confused. She glanced at the security station, reflected through the glass doors. One of the guards was busy on the phone, scanning security cameras and looking frantic. The other two ran to the elevators.

Meagan returned her attention to the front of the building in time to see Gollnick and Amber arrive by taxi. They stepped out of the car and Gollnick paid the driver. The two of them casually walked to the doors. Each carried a briefcase and looked very businesslike. Gollnick stopped to open the door for Amber. As they entered the lobby, Meagan approached and stopped them before they reached the security desk, as planned.

"I don't know if we have an issue or not," said Meagan anxiously. "About a minute ago, two security guards made a dash for the elevators."

Gollnick looked to Amber then back to Meagan.

"For now, we continue as if nothing has happened," said Gollnick. "We have no way of knowing if this has anything to do with the boys. If it does, they may need our help anyway."

Meagan led the two of them toward the elevators. The one remaining security guard at the station was too preoccupied to pay them any attention. The guard seemed exceedingly panicked, so they continued on to the elevators and entered the first available car going up.

* * *

On the twenty-ninth floor, Amber, Meagan, and Gollnick stepped out of the elevator to find two security guards shooting light beams down the hallway at two other figures. The elevators opened at a "T" intersection. The guards were in front of them with their backs to them on either side of the hall. They ducked around the corner after each shot.

Since the two guards were right there in direct line of sight and their attention was down the hall, Gollnick pointed an open hand at each of them and said, *"Semo nigh free."* The two security guards fell asleep.

Gollnick looked down the hall to see two heads peek around the corner. A few seconds later, Max and Cyrus came running toward Gollnick and the girls.

Gollnick looked from the guards to the boys. "What happened?"

Cyrus responded, "Two guards got into the elevator with us. We told them we were there to make a delivery, but they attacked us."

Gollnick looked around to see if anyone had noticed. Either the floor was already empty or everyone ran when the fight started. "Where are they now?"

"Down there," said Max as he pointed down the hall to their previous location. "We pulled them into an open office and were about to tie them up when these two showed up."

"Okay, let's get these two down there too and tie them all up." Gollnick hoped to expedite the situation and avoid things getting messy.

"The one guard down there has a ring that's flashing," added Max.

Gollnick looked at him in surprise. "It's an alarm. They know we're here. Change of plan, just leave these guys here. We need to move and fast. We're about to get a whole lot more company."

He pointed to the left and down the hall. "This way, to the stairs. We need to get to the thirtieth floor and into Vincent's office as quickly as we can. Boys, grab the package—that's our escape route."

The five of them ran for the stairs. When they opened the door, a very loud alarm sounded.

"Keep moving," urged Gollnick. They ran up the stairs as quickly as they could. At the top of the stairs, the door was locked. Gollnick stepped in front of everyone and pointed his hand at the door with his palm parallel to the door and announced. *"Proto torum se-ton."* An energy wave shot from his hand and the sheer force blew the door right off its hinges.

They stepped onto the thirtieth floor and ran for the entrance to Vincent's office. It was the only office on this level. The receptionist desk was empty, while a few cozy leather chairs lined the opposite wall. A picture of Vincent Maylock hung behind the desk. A huge picture window looked out over the Miami cityscape. Vincent's office had a set of large, finely crafted oak double doors. This time, not even checking to see if they were locked, Gollnick unleashed the energy wave spell. The double doors blew right off their hinges and flew into the room and crashed to the floor.

Gollnick instructed the four of them. "Get in there and find out what you can about this new prison. I'll stay here and keep everyone away for as long as I can."

12 Vincent's Office

The two girls rushed inside followed by Max and Cyrus lugging the six-foot crate between them. They propped the large package against the wall just inside the door with a sigh of relief.

The young friends stood momentarily entranced by the room. Its leather couch and chairs around a glass coffee table sat before the warm gas fireplace. The entertainment loomed above in the form of a built-in large screen TV flanked by two one-hundred gallon aquariums with all types of exotic fish. Along the left wall, Vincent's dark cherry desk with a black glass top sat on a slightly raised dais and commanded attention. Behind the desk was a mini-bar and a picture of the planet taken from space. To either side of it were wood-faced filing cabinets made to look like part of the wall. The all-glass windows of the far wall provided an impressive view of the city. From the look of the room, it was obvious that Vincent had money to burn.

Meagan and Cyrus ran for the desk, Amber opened filing cabinets and Max went to the windows. Looking down to street level, he was astounded by their sheer altitude. Once he regained his focus, his thoughts turned to dread.

"Five cars with red and blue lights just pulled up outside," announced Max.

Cyrus looked up from the desk. "Police! I figured this Vincent guy to use magical protection, not legal."

"Actually, I use both," came a voice from the far side of the room.

Max whipped his head around to locate the speaker. Gollnick even ran into the room. Max could tell he recognized the voice. They all stared at the big screen television.

"Vincent!" called Gollnick.

A larger than life picture of a man with a thin face and salt and pepper grey hair like Gollnick was on the screen. He wore a light grey business suit with a navy blue tie. He appeared to be seated in a private jet. Vincent's face lit up when Gollnick walked into view.

"Nick, my old buddy," he said in a pleasant tone as if actually pleased to see Gollnick. "How're you doing?"

Max noted Gollnick did not appear to be mutually pleased to see Vincent.

"What are you up to, Vincent?" demanded Gollnick without even saying hello.

Vincent looked shocked and hurt by the statement. "Me? Well I'm on my way to a business meeting. But, it looks like you've decided to break into my office. Is there something in particular you're looking for?"

"We know you were given the task of opening one of the ancient prisons. You can't do that, Vincent. You know what'll happen if they're opened."

"Unfortunately, I do." Vincent sat back in his chair with a serious look. "But that doesn't change the fact I was assigned this task and I must see it done."

Max watched as Vincent's gaze scanned the room. When he spotted Meagan, he once again sounded pleased. "Ah, Meagan, I haven't seen you since you were little. You've grown into a beautiful young woman. And who are your friends?"

Max suspected Vincent was stalling for time. While the conversation continued, Max searched the closest filing cabinets. The only reason for Vincent to stall was if reinforcements were on the way.

"Vincent! Stop what you're doing," pleaded Gollnick, "Tell me what you know about the prison. Help me protect it from the dark sorcerers. You were once my friend. Don't do this."

Vincent smiled. "Ah, Nick. I'm still your friend. However, I have a new employer now and let's just say he's not someone you want to disappoint. Besides, I'm working to secure my future in the new world order. Remember, the crystal turned me away and you did nothing to back me up. I had to look elsewhere for training. And I found it. Now, I'm someone you don't want to mess with."

"Vincent, it's not too late. We can still work together to protect this world."

Vincent's face saddened. "No, Nick. It's later than you think. The dark sorcerers know of more than just the prison I'm assigned to open. I don't know how many they have intel on, but I do know it's more than one. The time is drawing near when all of them will be open. Then a new world will be born from the ashes of humanity."

Max saw Gollnick look hopefully to Meagan, Cyrus and then Amber. Each shook their head in turn. They had not been able to locate any information about the prison. He then looked back to Vincent.

"Where is the prison, Vincent?" demanded Gollnick once more. Vincent appeared disappointed. He lowered his gaze then looked at his watch.

"Sorry, I've got to go. The plane is about to land. Oh, and you're about to have some company. Be nice to her, she likes to play rough." The picture disappeared from the screen.

In stunned realization that they were about to be attacked, they prepared for the worst. Gollnick held out two open hands engulfed in flames. Amber, Cyrus and Meagan moved to place the desk between them and the door. With no source of earth nearby, Meagan took a fighting stance with clenched fists. Amber and Cyrus prepared to cast spells. Max moved away from the windows toward the center of the room. He sensed the others felt as he did... the rush of adrenaline, all eyes on the shattered doors, the dry taste in his mouth from the anticipation.

Mere seconds passed by, but it felt like five minutes before a red-haired girl rushed in with five security guards. She appeared to be in her early twenties and had a nice figure accentuated by black leather pants with black boots, and a black leather shirt with black gloves. Her bright red hair was up in a ponytail and she wore dark sunglasses.

His senses still keenly attuned to the newcomers, Max considered Vincent's last on-screen act before checking his watch. He had lowered his gaze. Was his action intentional or did something draw his attention? Max retraced Vincent's previous line of sight and noticed the coffee table in the center of the room. Its base was a black cylinder, but it appeared to have hinges on the back.

The red-haired girl wasted no time in choosing a target. A quick spin and she grabbed a statuette from a nearby shelf then flung it at Gollnick. Apparently surprised by the action, he extinguished the flames from his hands to catch the fragile object. Without hesitation, she reached her right hand out to the fireplace. The fire responded to her command as it leapt from the burning coals to do her bidding. An enlarged tongue of flame shot toward Gollnick. In an instant, he crossed his arms over his head and knelt down. The fire formed a globe around him, but never actually touched him.

The security guards fired light beams from their rings. Meagan, Cyrus and Amber ducked as scorch marks marred Vincent's lavish desk. When a guard fired a light beam at Max, he dove behind the couch. The acrid smell of burnt leather upholstery filled his nostrils.

Max peered around the corner of the couch to witness the fire globe dissipate. Gollnick reached back to the fireplace and lobbed a fireball toward the red-haired girl in the same manner. Fire enveloped her and two of the guards. The guards scurried from the room screaming, but the fire didn't even faze the girl.

Two of the remaining guards ran for the desk while the third made his way to Max's hiding place.

The girl strode confidently closer to the fireplace and studied Gollnick. Max realized they must both be fire elemental sorcerers to withstand each other's attack.

A thick fog poured forth from the vicinity of the desk. Max knew it was Cyrus' illusion spell. He could hear Cyrus wrestling with one of the guards. The expanse of the cloud was cut short when a guard threw Cyrus clear of the fog and he landed on the crate. The sound of shattering glass sent a chill of panic through Max. Mirror fragments went everywhere as their precious escape route was lost.

A guard jumped over the couch and nearly landed on Max. He smiled down as he raised his hand. Max knew what came next. Acting on sheer panic, he got to one knee and rammed his right shoulder into the guard's stomach then tackled him to the floor. The sudden impact forced the air from the guard's lungs and he gasped for breath which wouldn't come. A little dazed, Max struggled free of his grasp and grabbed him by the shirt. A solid punch to the jaw and the enemy lay on the floor, unconscious. Max shook his hand in the air trying to relieve the pain from the punch.

At the fireplace, fireball after fireball was heaved back and forth between Gollnick and the girl, but it was obvious their leader was growing tired. Gollnick tripped and fell backward, landing on the chair. The girl pulled a knife from the back of her belt, did a forward flip over the couch and lunged at Gollnick. The blade plunged into his left shoulder. His right hand grabbed her arm trying to prevent the blade from sinking deeper into his flesh. His eyes squeezed shut and his teeth clenched. Through sheer stubborn will he refused to give voice to his pain.

The girl stretched out to the fireplace for yet another fireball. Without pause, Max focused on the aquariums. A sudden burst and the heavy glass shattered. Water flooded toward the girl. She looked up in utter surprise, meeting Max's eyes as a six-foot wave of water slammed into her. When the water drained away, the girl was unconscious on the floor next to the coffee table.

Max took a step toward the shroud of fog. Cyrus' disrupted illusion never made it more than five feet beyond the desk. "Everyone okay in there?"

"Yeah, okay," answered Meagan.

"Amber, you okay?"

No response.

Panic filled Cyrus' expression. He flailed his hand at the illusion and dissipated the fog to reveal Amber had been hit by one of the light beams. Cyrus and Max both ran to her side. She was alive, but unconscious. The other two guards were also unconscious on the floor.

Meagan on the other hand ran to Gollnick to tend his wound. He was bleeding badly, the knife still in his shoulder. She quickly pulled out the blade and cast a healing spell on the wound. *"Hema toe-zie fume."* The bleeding stopped. Gollnick was obviously still in pain, but stable.

Cyrus examined the mirror fragments as flames danced around the room from the fireball competition. "How are we getting out of here? The police are downstairs, maybe even on their way up now and our mirror is destroyed. Doesn't this place have a sprinkler system?"

While Cyrus asked his questions, Max ran to the coffee table and tried to open the little door in the base of the table. It wouldn't budge. He then stood up, flipped over its glass top and grabbed the entire metal cylinder base. It was heavier than he anticipated, but manageable.

"What are you doing?" asked Cyrus.

"Hopefully, I'm getting the information we need."

Gollnick stood and winced in pain with each uneasy step as he made his way over to Amber. Gently placing his hand along the side of her head, he removed the stun spell. *"Dim-tar mai secul."*

Amber woke, but held her stomach where the light beam had hit. Her face was strained from the stinging discomfort of the wound, but she was conscious.

"There's a helicopter on the roof," stated Gollnick. "Plan B was for me to fly us out of here, but that's not going to happen now. I'm in no condition to pilot the thing. We need to find another way out without running into the police."

The red-haired girl lay on the floor at Max's feet. She coughed up some water and was barely cognizant. Blood streamed from a gash on her head where glass from the aquarium had cut her. Max set down the canister and knelt to examine her. He ripped a piece of material from his uniform and used it to apply pressure to her wound.

"She's hurt," called Max. "Check the others. This place will go up in flames shortly."

"They're the enemy," protested Cyrus.

"Maybe so, but I won't let them die because of us."

Cyrus and Meagan searched for the five guards, but found only their clothing in puddles of water.

"They were water automatons," said Gollnick as he winced in pain. "They weren't real. She was the only dark sorcerer."

The red-haired girl reached up and placed her hand on Max's arm. "Twenty-fifth floor. Safe mirror. Room 2509." After her last word, she passed out in his arms.

Max looked around to assess the situation. Could her words be trusted? Their escape route was gone, the police were on the way, and they had two injured people. It didn't matter if she could be trusted. They were out of options.

"Come on, we're going. Cyrus, take the canister. Meagan, get Amber and Gollnick to their feet." Max bent to pick up the red-haired girl.

"What are you doing? We can't take her with us!" complained Cyrus.

"We covered this, Cyrus. She's helpless at the moment and I won't let her die."

They made their way out to the hall and down the stairs to the twenty-fifth floor. They dared not risk the elevators. Even so, they could hear heavy footfalls ascending quickly so Max made certain the bulky stairwell door clicked softly closed behind them. Max led the way down a hall and into room 2509. The interior was dark and the furniture covered in sheets. Max noticed tools and a can of paint. *This room must be under renovation.*

Once everyone was inside, Gollnick passed out on the floor. Meagan stayed by his side. Cyrus looked after Amber and the canister. Max knelt down and placed the red-haired girl on the floor near Gollnick. When he did, she began to wake.

She looked up into Max's eyes and squinted as she spoke with a tired voice. "Who are you?"

Meagan heard her and quickly moved to Max's side. She extended a hand over the girl's face. *"Semo nigh free."*

The girl raised a hand as the sleep spell enhanced her exhaustion. Her hand fell to her side, eyes fluttering shut.

Meagan slumped to the floor at Max's side. "That was close."

Max remembered the girl's instruction to find a mirror in this room. He stood up and scanned the area in search of something the size and shape of a mirror. In a far corner he spotted a tall thin item. When he pulled the sheet from it, he found a full size mirror. Anxious to be out of there, he moved back to the girl and picked her up as he announced to everyone, "Time to go."

Before Max could return to the mirror, Cyrus stopped him. "Hold on! Gollnick gave us specific instructions not to use any mirrors in this building."

"I know, but our two planned escape routes are lost to us. The police people and possibly more dark sorcerers are on the way. We're running out of time."

"What makes you think that mirror isn't trapped?" questioned Cyrus with a hint of anger.

Max was reluctant to admit his reason. "She told me it was safe." He nodded at the red-haired girl who lay limp in his arms.

"What?"

"Do you have any other options?" When Cyrus didn't respond, Max took his silence as a no and moved to the mirror. *"Mirtor tolanga se-atum."*

Once the mirror portal was open, he looked back at his three friends and their unconscious mentor. "Are you coming?"

Meagan took the canister from Cyrus and helped Amber to her feet. Cyrus reluctantly picked up Gollnick's flaccid body and carried him to the mirror. Max was the first to step through with the girl in his arms. When nothing disastrous happened, Meagan led Amber through. Cyrus and Gollnick were the last to pass. The swirling stopped and the mirror was normal once again.

13 A CRYSTAL SURPRISE

Once everyone arrived safely back at Ravenicon Castle, they all breathed a sigh of relief. Max looked around at each member of the group and realized how lucky they were. Their information about Vincent was obviously incorrect. Security had been far greater than anticipated.

Meagan placed the canister on a nearby table and examined the wounded. "We need to get these three to the infirmary."

Meagan led Amber from the room, Cyrus guided a semi-conscious Gollnick, and Max continued to carry the red-headed fireball of a girl. Outside the library they headed for the stairs.

Meagan called, "Stairs, infirmary."

The stairs lowered to another level. Descending, Max realized they led to a different level than when he'd told the stairs, "Down," earlier that morning. This time the steps led directly into a room that looked like a medical center. Once at the bottom he put the girl on a bed, and looked back at the stairs, but they were gone. All that remained was the door to the room. *This is one strange castle. I'd hate to have to draw a map of this place. It keeps changing.*

Once Amber and Gollnick were in their beds, Meagan approached the red-haired girl. With her hands extended over the girl, she uttered a spell. *"Norta movum etu."* Nothing appeared to happen.

Max gave her an inquisitorial glance.

"It's an immobility spell. She won't be able to get out of bed until I say so." Meagan then moved to attend to Amber and Gollnick.

Max joined Cyrus at Amber's bedside. She was still tired but smiled as he approached. A moment later she was fast asleep.

"I guess we made a pretty good team today," said Cyrus.

"Well, we all made it out in one piece." Max looked at Gollnick then returned his attention to Cyrus. "Mostly."

They joined Meagan at Gollnick's bedside. Max was concerned about their mentor's condition. "How's he doing?"

"He'll be alright," replied Meagan. "He just needs some rest. They all need some rest. I left the canister back in the library. Why don't you two see what we have. I'll keep an eye on these three."

Max wondered if that was her way of asking them to leave. Regardless, he was still too wound up from the excitement of the day's events to relax. "Good idea. Keep us posted if there are any changes."

"Oh, and take it to the training room to open, just in case," added Meagan.

Cyrus appeared to think about her suggestion for a few seconds. "Just in case of what?"

"Just in case," said Max. He knew it belonged to Vincent and wouldn't put it past the dark sorcerer to booby trap it.

Cyrus followed Max toward the door with a perplexed look. Before they could open the door, Meagan called out, "Stairs, second floor corridor."

In an instant, a staircase lowered from the ceiling. Looking up, Max realized they went up to exactly where Meagan had named. He and Cyrus ascended and returned to the library.

The black cat sat on the table sniffing at the cylinder.

"See, there's that cat!" exclaimed Max. "I'm not imagining things." He was glad someone else was finally able to see this mysterious creature.

Cyrus took one step toward the animal, but with cat-like speed, it ran past them and out into the hallway. Cyrus pursued with Max close behind. By the time they made it to the hallway though, the sneaky feline was gone. Cyrus looked around obviously frustrated. "Whatever you do, don't turn me into a mouse."

Max fetched the canister from the library table. On the way to the training room, Max noticed that Cyrus stayed a good distance behind. He figured Meagan's comment must have spooked him about the contents.

They entered the training area and Max set it down in the middle of the room. The two boys stood on either side, neither making an attempt to open it.

Cyrus looked at Max inquisitorially. "So, how do we open it?"

"Good question."

Cyrus sighed. "Oh, this is going to be fun."

They sat down on the floor to examine the hinge on the side of the cylinder and found the other side of the door, but no latch or lock. There appeared to be no way to open it.

With an encouraging look, Cyrus sprang to his feet. "I'll be right back. I think I saw a tool set of some kind in the kitchen." Cyrus sprinted from the room.

Max wasn't sure if he'd actually seen a tool set or if he was so spooked by the canister, he didn't want to be in the same room with it. While Max continued to examine the object, the cat strolled in, but soon disappeared into the shadows. Max jumped to his feet and attempted to locate the mysterious feline, but yet again it was gone or well hidden.

When Cyrus returned, he found Max looking behind cauldrons. "You lose something?"

"That cat came running in here after you left." Max didn't withdraw his attention from his search. "It's hiding behind one of these cauldrons."

"Oh, let it go. It's not like we're going to catch it anyway, it's too fast. Here, I found a spell book on opening locks. I also found this crowbar." Handing the book to Max, Cyrus attempted to pry the door open with the huge piece of metal.

Max was in the process of skimming the spell book when Cyrus looked up, having made no progress with the crowbar. Max paid no heed to the astonishment on Cyrus' face as he continued his rapid perusal of the magic tome.

"Cyrus, step back," instructed Max. Once Cyrus was about ten feet away from the cylinder, Max called out a spell. *"Lo-toc altu rocom."* A few seconds passed before it began to shake. Suddenly, the cat ran from the shadows and jumped on top of the unstable object. As it jumped off, the container tipped over and slid to the other side of the room. The cat sprinted for the corridor and was gone. As Vincent's secret safe continued to shake, Max and Cyrus exchanged terrified looks then followed the cat's lead and ran for the corridor. The doors began to close upon their exit. In its last inches, a sliver of bright light between the doors followed by a low boom and vibrations throughout the hall indicated the object had indeed been booby-trapped.

After a few minutes of silence, they regained enough confidence to open the doors slightly. Max entered the room with Cyrus a few steps behind. Max noticed the walls were darkened by scorch marks and a circular blackened pattern around the epicenter. The cylinder was indeed blown open and its contents singed around the edges with a small fire burning one corner of a folder. Max patted the fire out and pulled some files from the remains. He looked them over and handed some to Cyrus. "Can you make heads or tails out of this?"

"Looks like gibberish to me. We'll probably need Gollnick."

Max paused in his examination of the paperwork and cocked his head to one side as he pondered the recent events of the past few minutes. He laid the files down on his lap and with a quick glance in search of the mysterious feline, he considered the intelligence of the animal. "Is it me, or did that cat just save us from an explosion?"

"Kinda looked that way, didn't it?"

The two of them picked up the files and headed back to the infirmary. As they turned a corner, they spotted the cat near the kitchen entrance. Their rescuer sat calmly licking a paw and using it to clean the fur on its head. Max called out, "Thanks."

The cat hesitated with paw in mid-stroke. It looked right at Max and meowed as if to say, "You're welcome," then disappeared into the kitchen. As they passed the room though, the cat was gone once again.

Cyrus commented, "There's something strange about that cat."

Max considered his friend's observation. "Really? It was smart enough to get out of there before the explosion. And we followed it. If the cat's strange, what does that make us?"

"Never mind."

Max knew they had found the infirmary level when he smelled the pungent stench of disinfectant cleaners. He wondered if Gollnick and Meagan were arguing over the sleeping arrangements or something more severe like the odor.

"I'm fine. I need to get back to work," stated Gollnick as he attempted to get out of bed.

Max knew Gollnick well enough to realize he didn't like being remanded to bed while there were things that needed to be done.

"No, you need to rest," ordered Meagan and she blocked his attempts at leaving. This was one of the few times Max had seen Meagan refuse to back down to Gollnick's authority.

"How about we bring the work to you?" Max tried to offer a compromise.

Meagan shot him a quick look, but he couldn't tell if she was happy about the offer or not. Either way, Gollnick resigned from any further endeavors to leave.

"Fine, at least it'll keep him in bed." She turned her back and walked away to tend to the red-haired girl.

To Max's surprise, he did not see Cyrus' sister. "Meagan, where's Amber?"

"She went back to her room to lie down. She wasn't hurt badly and didn't like the infirmary beds. She just needs some rest. Unlike that one who still needs observation."

Max and Cyrus approached Gollnick and handed him a stack of folders an inch thick. The folders may have been singed, but the contents saw little damage. Max felt this Vincent must be very methodical as the documents were well organized. Gollnick looked surprised by the information they discovered. "It will take some time to decipher these. How did you open it? I would have expected it to be trapped."

"It was," chuckled Cyrus. "Max found a spell, but the mystery cat decided to play 'kick the can' and then ran when it started shaking. We decided he might know something we didn't, so we followed. It exploded a few seconds later."

"Strange," said Gollnick with a little hint of suspicion in his voice. "I would have expected Vincent to have it explode immediately, with no warning. Actually, this whole thing seems strange. He knew we were there, but only sent a small force to deal with us."

"A small force?" interrupted Cyrus.

Gollnick disregarded Cyrus' remark. "He provided a hint to where the information was kept. The red-haired girl provided an escape route after our plans were disrupted. The booby-trapped canister gave a warning. And on top of that, Vincent knows where my castle is. There hasn't been any attack on us yet to get the information back. Either he feels the information is useless or..." he leaned back against the headboard as he sighed and his brow creased, "...he wanted us to find it. But why?"

Amber entered the room and ran to Gollnick's bedside a little breathless. She appeared tired, but alarmed. She was still winded when she explained the reason for her excitement. "Gollnick, the crystal in the new circle room, it created a new door, but there's no name on it yet. The zodiac sign in the crystal is Aries."

They all stood in a circle around Gollnick's bed and looked to one another. Their expressions revealed the replay of memories they each had over the past day. Max realized they were trying to recall everyone they'd recently met who could be considered an ally.

Gollnick sat up in his bed. "The door will appear first when one of you meets someone who is destined to join your circle. There's no name on the door until the person actually opens it for the first time. The question is, who is the new member of your circle?"

"The only new person we've met is..." replied Amber, but she didn't complete the sentence. Everybody in the room turned to look at the red-haired girl at the other end of the infirmary.

"Aw... you can't be serious?" whined Cyrus. "Not her. I knew it was a bad idea bringing her here."

Gollnick corrected him, "Actually it was a good idea. The door appeared once you met her. Had we not brought her here, we would've had a very difficult time finding her again."

"But she's the enemy!" reminded Cyrus.

Amber interrupted, "I also checked the old circle room, just in case." The possibility of more news heightened Gollnick's attention as he leaned forward to focus on Amber's next words. "You have a new door there as well."

"*What?* My team is gone, except for Hank and Elisa." He fell silent for a moment. The confusion in his eyes revealed this was more than unexpected. He appeared troubled as he processed the information. "It's not possible. The only person I've met recently had already been approached to join, but the crystal rejected him."

"Maybe he just wasn't ready back then." Max had a suspicion, but looked to Gollnick for confirmation. "Maybe he wasn't meant to join you until now. So, who is it?"

After some hesitation, Gollnick replied, "Vincent."

"WHAT?!" cried everyone, except Max.

14 PLAYING WITH FIRE

The next morning, Max entered the infirmary to see how everyone was doing. He wore his comfortable grey sweatsuit and white sneakers. He wasn't surprised to find Meagan had never left from the night before. She was fast asleep on a spare bed, still dressed in her security guard uniform. Gollnick was also sleeping.

While Max checked on Meagan and Gollnick, a voice with a slight Irish accent surprised him. "They've been fast asleep all night and so far this mornin'."

Max turned to look at the red-haired girl, but she was still in her bed with her eyes closed. No longer wearing her black leather outfit from the day before, it lay folded on a chair next to her bed. The bed sheet covered most of her, except for a black tank top. Uncertain if it was she who had spoken, he approached her and looked closely at her eyes to see if she was awake.

"Boo!" she shouted. Her eyes popped open and Max jumped and primed himself for attack, but the girl remained motionless on the bed, except for her laughter.

"Are ye really that easy to surprise?" questioned the redhead.

Max realized Meagan's spell must be keeping her restrained to the bed. "After you attacked us yesterday, I wasn't sure what to expect from you."

Her expression darkened as her brow furrowed and the smile faded from her face. "Ye attacked us!" said the girl accusingly. "Ye were the ones who broke into Master Vincent's office. Ye were the ones goin' through his personal files. We were merely defendin' the place."

Max opened his mouth to speak, but hesitated as he realized she was right. He sat down on the chair next to her bed, closed his mouth and began to consider her point of view.

"I guess it could've looked like that," said Max almost surprised by the fact, "but Vincent is about to do something very dangerous, very bad for the world, and we had to find a way to stop him."

"Had ye considered maybe talkin' to him?"

Once again, Max had to sit there in thought as he pondered her question. "No, I guess not."

"At least two security guards are badly burned or dead and I have no idea what happened to the other three. And all ye can say is 'I guess not.'"

From the far end of the room came another voice. "I wouldn't worry too much about the security guards."

Max and the redhead looked toward the sound. Both Gollnick and Meagan were now awake.

Gollnick sat up in his bed rubbing his wounded shoulder. "We already know the guards were water automatons created by Vincent. They weren't really alive. That's why they disappeared when you rescued the young lady here."

"Ye," the redhead pointedly returned her gaze to Max, "saved me?"

"The place was on fire," stated Max as if trying to defend his actions. "I saw you use fire elemental magic, but I wasn't sure it would protect you while you were unconscious. Besides, you were already injured from the exploding aquariums."

"Thanks." After a brief pause, she asked, "So, what do I need to do to get some food around here?"

"Meagan, would you please get our guest some breakfast?" asked Gollnick. "Meanwhile Max and I need to have a little chat with the young lady. Oh, and please ask the others to join us."

Meagan got up out of the bed, keeping an eye on the girl as she left the room, through the door this time.

"So, do you have a name or do we keep calling you 'young lady'?" asked Gollnick.

"Me name is Taryn O'Donnel. Ye are Gollnick Strom and yer niece there," looking toward the door, "is Meagan Strom. And ye," now looking at Max, "I don't know ye. I heard the others call ye Max, but Master Vincent never mentioned ye before. I'm guessin' ye're a water elemental sorcerer based on the way ye took me out yesterday. I promise, that won't happen again."

"What do you know about the ancient prison Vincent is attempting to open?" asked Gollnick.

"Ah, so now we get to it." She looked back to Gollnick.

The door opened and in walked Cyrus and Amber. They both were wearing grey sweatsuits and white sneakers.

Taryn looked at them with an accusing eye. "And now the rest of the assailants join the party."

Cyrus looked at her with contempt.

Amber sat on the bed next to her. "How are you feeling?"

"I'm immobilized on a hospital bed, in a castle somewhere, after bein' captured by thieves and I'm starvin'," said Taryn rattling off her complaints. "How would ye feel?"

"Oh," said Amber, still looking at the girl, not knowing how to respond.

As they talked, Meagan returned with a small tray of food. It held fruit and raw vegetables with a glass of orange juice. Taryn looked at the tray and asked, "What? Are ye guys vegetarian?"

Everyone but Meagan answered, "She is."

Meagan glanced around the room with a look of surprise.

"Okay. I'll see what else I can find for our guest." She turned and walked out of the room.

Max proceeded to introduce the redhead. "Guys, this is Taryn O'Donnel. Taryn, this is Amber and Cyrus Marx." They all looked at one another without saying a word.

"So, Taryn," said Gollnick trying to continue the earlier conversation. "We were discussing the ancient prison."

Taryn did her best to turn her head far enough to address Gollnick while still immobilized in her bed.

"No, ye were discussin' the ancient prison," she said, "I was starvin'."

Gollnick sighed then asked again, "What do you know about the prison?"

"I know ye don't know where it is. Otherwise, ye wouldn't be askin' me about it," said the girl obviously not wanting to divulge too much information.

"Look, we're not going to get anything from her," interrupted Cyrus. "What was in the cylinder?"

"What cylinder?" inquired Taryn.

"The base of the coffee table in Vincent's office was a little metal cylinder. It was also a safe, of sorts, and it contained information about the ancient prisons. At least we hope it did," said Max as he regarded Gollnick.

Gollnick sat up straight in his bed now and pulled out the papers from Vincent's office. "According to the information I've been able to decipher, they have information on at least five prisons so far. The first was the one in New York and was opened many years ago while digging a subway tunnel. We already knew about that one. There's one in Africa, but its exact position is still uncertain and they don't know what the prison actually is yet. There's also one off the coast of Japan, but it appears to be underwater somewhere. Also, no information on the prison itself. There is a fourth prison in England. They believe it has something to do with Stonehenge, but they're still researching that one. Now, the prison Vincent is attempting to open is in the Middle East."

Cyrus raised his hand to draw attention. "The Middle East is kind of a big place. Can you narrow that down a bit?"

After a brief glance at Cyrus, Gollnick continued. "The place is in southern Iraq in what used to be the Babylonian empire."

Cyrus rolled his eyes. "Babylon? Seriously? Why do I feel like I'm about to get a history lesson?"

"Near the city of Babylon are the remains of the Etemenanki Ziggurat. It is one of the pyramids some believe could have possibly been known as the Tower of Babel. No one knows its location for certain. A ziggurat is a type of step-pyramid, or at least it used to be; it's mostly ruins now. At the top was said to be a temple to Marduk, a god of Babylonian mythology. Actually, he was another sorcerer and a powerful one at that."

Taryn reminded everyone of her presence. "If ye're plannin' on goin' to Babylon, I would suggest ye be afraid. The prison in Babylon holds many dangers."

Gollnick did not disagree. "As we've previously discussed, each prison contains a creature from the other realm. When the prison in New York was opened, a demon was released. There's no telling what's in Babylon."

"Ye don't know what's in each prison? Even I know what's in the Babylon prison," said Taryn in response to Gollnick's uncertainty.

"Well..." Cyrus whined, "are you gonna tell us, or do we have to Caber-Toss you off one of the towers?"

Taryn rolled her eyes apparently annoyed by Cyrus' comment. "Are ye daft? The Caber-Toss is Scottish."

"Oh," replied Cyrus.

"It's a dragon."

Everyone looked at her, but said nothing.

"What? It's a dragon that's imprisoned in Babylon," said Taryn defensively.

Max was standing in the middle of a desert. His arms were raised up to the sky and energy poured forth from his hands. He looked up and realized he was creating a huge shield of energy. Turning his head, he noticed many other sorcerers around him. They were all dressed similarly, loose-fitting long sleeve shirts and long pants with a belt. Some carried scimitars, others held a staff or spear. They all fired off spells that penetrated outward through Max's shield and hit their enemy.

Max returned his gaze to the front and realized the enemy they faced was an enormous dragon, hundreds of feet long with a wing span as equally impressive. The dragon sat atop a massive ziggurat and could easily swallow Max and his friends whole. Its teeth were nearly the same size as Max. Upon seeing the dragon, Max instantly knew the creature's name—it was Tiamat of ancient Babylonian mythology.

The dragon was breathing fire at the sorcerers and it was only Max's shield that protected them. The other sorcerers threw fireballs, lightning bolts and energy blasts at the dragon, but it was a stalemate. The sorcerers could not do enough damage to the dragon, but the dragon couldn't penetrate Max's shield.

Suddenly Max was back in the here and now. Everyone was staring at Taryn.

Max was the first to ask the question. "How do you know it's a dragon? And why are you telling us this?"

"I didn't believe Master Vincent when he told me, but somehow he knew ye would capture me," said Taryn. "There were some pieces of information he gave me because he wanted ye to know. Primarily, the dragon."

Max's eyebrow popped up and his mouth dropped as his confusion hit a peak. "Okay, I'm losing track here. Are we the good guys or the bad guys? After all, we did break into Vincent's office."

Cyrus turned a reproachful eye to Taryn. "Yeah, and it looks like Vincent was expecting us to do just that. So, Taryn, what other information do you have for us? And how do we know we can trust a word you're saying?"

Meagan returned to the room with a new tray of food. This time, the plate was full of scrambled eggs, bacon, sausage, and toast.

Taryn looked at the appetizing food with a smile. "Ah, that's more like it. So, who's goin' to feed me since I can't move? Or do ye want to let me up so I can eat?"

"We don't even know if we can trust what you're telling us," Cyrus said. "There's no way we're letting you up."

Taryn did her best to look at Gollnick. "I assume ye know the truth spell?"

Gollnick pursed his lips for a moment. Max could see Gollnick contemplate her question.

"Very well." Gingerly he climbed out of bed and slowly walked over to Taryn. With his hands over her head, he spoke the words, *"Tarmu las-na migh."* A glow settled from his hands onto Taryn.

Gollnick stepped back a few paces and leaned on a nearby bed. "Taryn, who do you serve?"

Taryn stared straight ahead and responded in a very monotone voice even with her Irish accent. "Vincent Maylock has been me teacher for two years now, but I have been instructed to aid the new circle in the comin' battles."

"Why is Vincent helping the dark sorcerers?" asked Gollnick.

"Malcolm has placed a bindin' spell on Master Vincent. He must do as instructed."

Cyrus interrupted with an angry tone, "Then why is he helping us?"

Taryn replied without hesitation. "When Malcolm is not around, the spell weakens. He has been preparin' me to help ye and to have me ask ye for help to free him from Malcolm's power."

Gollnick resumed the questioning. "Why did you try to kill us yesterday?"

"Ye're slower than I thought. I didn't expect to even get close to ye with the knife."

Gollnick pursed his lips. "Not exactly what I meant. Why did you attack all of us yesterday?"

"Like Master Vincent, Malcolm knew ye were comin'. He was also watchin' the office battle through one of the security guards. I had to make it look real to protect Master Vincent."

Max decided to move to a different line of questioning. "What is in the prison in Babylon?"

"A dragon," responded Taryn still in her monotone voice.

Gollnick continued with Max's line of thought. "Does he have the key?"

"I don't know anythin' about a key."

"How does Vincent plan to open the prison?"

"All prisons are trapped," responded Taryn. "He doesn't know what will happen when they try to open it. He plans to send in a series of water automatons to test the prison chamber first before enterin'. He has taken a jet to Egypt and will stay there tonight to create more water automatons before travellin' to Iraq. Another sorcerer named Frederick Von Woonst will meet him in Babylon. When they are ready, they will test the prison for weaknesses."

"Frederick Von Woonst and Malcolm are enemies. They were dueling in Philadelphia a couple nights ago," said Gollnick. "Why would they work together?"

"Malcolm won," said Taryn simply, "and now Frederick works for him."

"When do they plan on entering the prison?" asked Gollnick.

"If all goes as planned, they will enter it the day after tomorrow," answered Taryn.

Gollnick looked around the room to see if anyone else had questions. When no one spoke, he stood and approached the bed. Waving his hand over Taryn, the glow faded and she returned to her normal self.

"So, does this mean I can get out of bed now?" asked Taryn. "I'm still starvin'."

Gollnick looked to Meagan and nodded. Meagan approached Taryn and waved her hand, releasing her from the confines of the bed.

Taryn sat up and stretched her arms and legs, then held out her hand for the food tray. Meagan passed it to her. The redhead began to eat ravenously. After a few bites, she looked up.

"Is everyone goin' to sit there and watch me eat?" asked Taryn somewhat annoyed by the attention.

Max, Cyrus and Amber got up and left the room. Meagan instructed Gollnick, "You, back to bed. You still need to rest. You were up all night deciphering those papers."

Out in the corridor, Cyrus turned to Max and Amber, "So, what do you think? Do we trust her?"

"The crystal seems to trust her," replied Amber, "and Gollnick seemed satisfied with her answers."

Max agreed. "She could prove useful in the coming battle. She is a fire elemental sorceress after all."

Cyrus didn't look happy with their answers. "Okay, but keep an eye on her just in case. I still don't trust her. She's up to something."

Max attempted to ease Cyrus' concerns. "I think she was right about the dragon."

"How do you know?" asked Amber.

"When she said it was a dragon, I had another memory flash." Max was happy to be remembering anything. "I was with a group of other sorcerers and we were fighting this enormous dragon. The dragon's name was Tiamat."

"What happened?" asked Cyrus.

"I don't know. I was creating an energy shield to protect us all while they attacked, but it was a stalemate. Then I woke up."

Cyrus didn't appear convinced. "Even if she is right about the dragon, I still think we should keep an eye on her."

Later that morning, Max and Cyrus were in the kitchen looking through some comic books that were on the table. Still dressed in their grey sweatsuits, they were waiting for Meagan to finish making lunch.

Amber walked in and saw once again, Meagan was doing the cooking and no one was helping her. "Can't you guys at least help? Meagan's not your servant here."

"It's okay, Amber," smiled Meagan. "I enjoy cooking. Besides, like the Training Room, the cleanup is handled with magic. The kitchen will clear the empty plates, clean them and put them away when everyone is done. Actually the entire castle is self-sufficient when it comes to cleaning. It's one of the reasons I like doing the cooking."

Amber sounded angry as she looked at the two guys sitting there reading comics. "They could still at least offer to help."

Max and Cyrus looked at each other then to Meagan. "Meagan, can we help?"

Meagan smiled. "No. Thank you."

Disappointed, Amber sat down at the table with the guys. She saw one of the comics they were reading and picked it up. On the cover was a picture of a beautiful and interestingly shaped sorceress wearing an outfit so skimpy it could only have been drawn on paper, not actually worn.

"I wouldn't be caught dead in a get-up like that," said Amber. "Do people really think that's what a sorceress wears?"

No sooner did she finish her statement than footsteps were heard coming into the room. Everyone turned to see Taryn enter the kitchen. She was wearing skin tight black leather pants and black shoes with four-inch heels. Her bright red hair hung down past her shoulders. She also had on a black string-bikini top that barely covered her and showed off her well-defined abs.

"How's it goin'?" asked Taryn with a mild Irish lilt.

Amber turned and flopped the comic book on the table. "Forget I said anything." When she looked up, she realized the guys never heard a word she'd said. They both had their mouths open, gaping at Taryn. Amber rolled her eyes and hung her head. Max was closest to her, so she elbowed him in the ribs to stop him from staring. He rubbed his side then returned his attention to the comic book.

Taryn strutted over to the table and sat down between the guys. "So, who's the leader of the group? Or don't we have a leader yet?"

Cyrus spoke quickly. "That would be me."

"Right." She spoke with an air of disbelief then turned her attention to Max. "So, Max, ye're a water sorcerer. Are there any other elementals in the group?"

Amber answered in his place as if protecting him from Taryn. "I'm an air sorceress and Meagan is an earth sorceress. With you joining the group, we now have all four of the elementals covered."

Taryn glared at Amber. "I see, and what about the other schools of magic?"

Returning the glare, Amber replied, "Cyrus has some talent with illusions and I have limited divination powers."

Max and Cyrus looked at each other. Obviously they were in the middle of another battle, but this time Amber was fighting back with more enthusiasm.

Meagan broke the tension. "Lunch is ready!" The guys quickly got up from the table and raced to get their food—also to get out of the line of fire. After removing themselves from the table, Cyrus and Max glanced back to see what would happen next.

Amber and Taryn were still locked in a staring battle until Gollnick entered the room with his arm in a sling.

"Smells good. What's for lunch?" Reluctantly, Amber got up from the table and joined the others in the food line. Taryn hesitated, but followed.

After lunch was over, Amber sat next to the group's mentor. "Gollnick, you and Meagan share this telepathic link. Isn't this something we should learn to use within our group?"

Gollnick raised an eyebrow. "It's not that simple. There is a spell to create a telepathic link with someone, but it only lasts for about an hour. To create a permanent link, you must share a special bond. Elisa and I, well let's just say our bond isn't what it used to be. As for me and Meagan, she's my niece; we'll always have a special bond. I suppose we could try the spell with you and Cyrus. Being brother and sister, you should have a strong connection."

"I was thinking more like me and Max," Amber blushed. She turned to Max and asked, "What do you think?"

Surprised but not wishing to upset Amber, Max agreed.

Gollnick cleared his throat. "I would recommend against this. Such a link can be attempted only once. If it doesn't work, it never will. Perhaps we should try in a few months... if you're still interested."

Gollnick stood and proposed a plan for the afternoon. "Taryn, you seem to be experienced in magical combat. Perhaps you'd care to lead a practice session in the training room this afternoon?"

"Excellent," replied Taryn. "It'll give me a chance to see what we have to work with. And reveal any strengths and weaknesses."

"Okay." After a brief pause he continued, "According to Meagan, I still need to rest. I also need to contact Elisa to see if she's found any new information, or if she was able to track down Hank. He's the one who brought us Max, but with no explanation as to where he came from."

Taryn grinned. "Don't ye worry. I'll have 'em workin' as a team in no time."

Gollnick held up a hand as he tilted his head left and squinted with one eye. "Just make sure they're still alive when you're done." Gollnick left the room followed by Cyrus and Taryn.

Amber caught Max's arm as he was leaving. Meagan was still putting things in the sink for the room to clean later.

Amber held tight to Max's arm. "Meagan, you know the telepathic link spell, don't you?"

Meagan snapped her head around, eyebrows clearly raised. "You heard what Nick said. Give it a few months."

Amber pleaded, "Please help us try. I'm still working on my divination skills, but I have this feeling if we don't do it now, we won't have the chance in a few months."

Meagan looked to Max who shrugged his shoulders.

"Amber, we're talking about a permanent telepathic link. Once created, it can't be broken. You really should think about this." She looked at Max and continued her cautionary advice. "As should you, Max!"

Amber continued to plead. "We have to try."

Meagan sighed, looking back and forth at Amber and Max. "If Nick finds out about this, we'll all be in trouble." It was obvious to Max that Amber would not back down from her request. Meagan appeared to sense it as well when she conceded, "Okay. Sit down at the table."

Meagan sat between them. "Join hands and repeat after me. *'Inlecto vo inlecto sem-zom co-nectium'.*"

Amber spoke first, *"Inlecto vo inlecto sem-zom co-nectium."*

Max followed, *"Inlecto vo inlecto sem-zom co-nectium."*

"That's it?" asked Amber.

"Yep," acknowledged Meagan.

Amber stood and ran from the room as she called, "Max, stay here. I'll go back to my room and see if you can hear my thoughts."

Max asked curiously, "Will this really work?"

Meagan shrugged, "It's hard to say. As Nick pointed out, you need to have a special bond with someone for this to work. But once tried, if it doesn't work, it will never work with that person."

After about fifteen minutes, Amber walked back into the room crying. "I guess it didn't work. I couldn't contact you."

Max and Meagan tried to console her. She wrapped her arms around Max's neck and held on. Meagan stood there a few seconds then decided it best to leave.

Max looked into Amber's eyes. "We've only known each other a few days. I have no memory of who I am or what I was. You might be better off not being able to touch my mind."

In a way Max was relieved it hadn't worked. He had no memory of his past. Was he a dark sorcerer? A monster of unthinkable horrors? Or worse?

"I've lost too many people in my life," replied Amber. "I don't want to lose you, too."

15 FINDING FRIENDS

Early that evening, Gollnick crept out of the infirmary and headed for the library. He no longer had his arm in the sling, but it was still very sore. As he rounded the corner near the kitchen he heard, "And just where do you think you're going?"

Gritting his teeth, he knew he'd been caught. As he turned around, he responded. "Meagan, look, I have work to do before we face Vincent, Frederick and Malcolm over in the Middle East. And I can't do it sitting in bed resting."

Meagan stood at the entrance to the kitchen with her arms crossed. "Your room is the other direction. So where are you going?"

Gollnick responded sheepishly. "That doesn't matter."

Meagan grew visibly concerned. "You're not going to New York?"

"No, no. Elisa is in Philly," Gollnick said, trying to alleviate her fears. "As for Hank, I'm hoping Elisa has a lead on him too."

"Fine," said Meagan with a very stern voice, "but you will keep in touch. This group will fall apart if you get yourself killed. And I won't be too happy about it either. You're the only family I have left."

Gollnick walked over to Meagan and gave her a hug. "You're my only family too, you know. I'll be fine."

He released her and headed for the library once again. As he entered, he found Max seated on an overstuffed chair reading yet another book.

"Max, exactly how many tomes have you read so far?"

"Lost count. You're going to find Elisa and Hank, aren't you?" responded Max without looking up.

Gollnick replied quickly and passed Max on his way to the mirror. "Elisa has been trying to gather information for me. And I need to find Hank to learn more about you."

Still seated on his chair, Max closed the book and looked up at Gollnick. "I'm coming with you."

Gollnick's head snapped around. "No! You need to stay here and train with Taryn and the others."

"You're going to need help, and you know it. They may not have attacked us here, but they are looking for us now. In addition, you haven't heard from Hank in a long time, which means he may be in trouble. Experience or not, you're going to need backup."

Gollnick thought for a while, staring at Max and that gigantic book. Though Max seemed inexperienced, he picked things up so fast he must've known magic before. His accelerated study of water elemental magic could prove helpful and Gollnick had to admit he didn't know what kind of trouble he would be walking into.

"Fine." Gollnick raised his hand to his forehead and touching his temple, he contacted his niece. *'Meagan, Max will be accompanying me on my excursion. Please inform the others.'*

Meagan's voice responded, *'I had a feeling he might be able to talk you into letting him come along.'*

Gollnick raised an eyebrow only Max could see, but he knew Meagan could sense the slight surprise. *'You two had this planned, didn't you?'*

Meagan didn't respond, but he could almost feel her chuckling. No sooner did Gollnick return his attention to Max, than he found the young man already dressed in his brown trench coat ready to leave.

"Understand one thing before we go," stated Gollnick with authority. "You will follow my instructions to the letter. Agreed?"

Max just smiled. "We're wasting time."

Gollnick continued to stare at Max for a second then sighed and turned to the mirror. He touched it and muttered, *"Mirtor tolanga se-atum Elisa."*

As the image in the mirror began to swirl, Max asked, "I thought you needed to think about the location when using that spell? Not just the name of a person."

"When you don't know where they are, you can use the person's name. It will take you to the mirror closest to that person. The only catch is you have no idea where you'll end up and no idea if it's safe or not."

"Didn't you contact Elisa to let her know you were coming?" asked Max with more than a hint of concern.

"She hasn't been responding to my telepathic connection."

"That doesn't sound good."

"Still want to tag along?" asked Gollnick.

"Let's get going."

* * *

As they emerged from an unfamiliar mirror, they found themselves in a tiny bathroom. Its walls were made of plasterboard with the screws still showing and edges that had never been covered. The toilet and sink were stained from years of use and stank of sewer. The framework appeared in poor condition as the wall shook when they opened the door.

As they exited the small room, Max looked around to get his bearings. They were in a large cluttered warehouse. Smashed crates were piled along one wall. Racks and racks of other crates filled most of the warehouse. Small single-bulb lights hung from the ceiling dangling from their power cords. The place smelled like sea water and rotten fish.

Max whispered to Gollnick. "This Elisa of yours hangs out in some real upscale places."

Gollnick just scowled and raised a finger to his lips. He motioned for Max to stay close behind him. They quietly crept through the warehouse sticking mostly to the shadows. Max knew they had arrived there because Elisa was nearby, but he had no idea where she might be.

As they were sneaking around, Max found a hole in the warehouse wall and looked out. It was difficult to see much of anything because of crates outside the warehouse as well. He could tell they were on a pier, but no idea where that dock was located. Then he caught the glimpse of a skyline and an unmistakable figure. He had to take a second look, then realized they were in a lot more trouble than expected.

Max caught Gollnick by the arm and pulled him back to the wall. Gollnick looked surprised by Max's concern. Max pointed to the hole in the wall, and Gollnick did as Max indicated. Max watched as Gollnick scanned side to side until he spotted what had concerned Max. Gollnick whispered, "The Statue of Liberty. We're in New York. Aw man, are we in trouble!"

In a harsh whisper he said, "Back to the mirror, return to the castle and stay there. I'll find Elisa and return as soon as I can."

Max just looked at him with an expressionless face and shook his head.

Gollnick sighed.

There was no way Max would be talked into leaving. They then continued their stealthy exploration.

While the two made their way through the warehouse, its stench became stronger until they realized they no longer smelled rotten fish, but something much worse. They peered around a corner and spotted the source of the odor. A large creature stood in the shadows leaning up against some crates. It stood around eight feet tall and was very muscular, wearing a pair of ragged brown pants. The monster was green with long brown hair hanging down its back and an angry expression above its huge protruding jaw. A wooden club with metal bands stood nearly six feet in length and was propped against the giant as it kept its left hand on it at all times.

Gollnick whispered to Max, "Ogre."

They peered around the massive figure. In the middle of an open space was a wooden table with a simple wooden chair on either side. Above the table was a single light hanging down from the ceiling casting a glow on the table, but its illumination only extended a few feet past the table. Beyond was shadow and darkness. In the one chair sat a security guard in a black uniform. In the other chair with her hands bound behind her back was Elisa. Standing behind her was a second security guard. Max could tell there was yet another presence, lurking just beyond the ring of light. It seemed quite large, but it wasn't an ogre. He could barely make out what looked like wings. It remained in the shadow too much to get a good look at it.

The security guard across from Elisa slammed his hand on the table. "What does the circle know about our plan to open the prison?"

Elisa was barely conscious. Her head slumped forward as she whispered, "I don't know."

Max and Gollnick pulled back from the scene to discuss in whispers what they saw. "What tomes were you reading earlier?" asked Gollnick.

"Water elemental magic," replied Max.

"Too bad we don't have any water."

Max looked at Gollnick with a surprised expression on his face. "We're in a warehouse, near the waterfront, on a pier. There's water all around."

Realization dawned on Gollnick's face. "Can you swim?" he asked.

Max opened his mouth to answer, but then hesitated. "I don't know."

"It's still light out," said Gollnick, "and the creature in the shadows is staying out of the light... so I'm guessing it doesn't like the sun either. I'll take the ogre; you go after the security guards. When we figure out what the other creature is, we'll have to improvise. Worst case, sink the pier. Even if you can't swim, as a water elemental, you should at least be able to breathe underwater. Find Elisa and get her back to the castle. If I don't meet you at the mirror, I'll find my own way back."

"I'm not leaving without you," said Max. "There's no way I'm going to tell Meagan I lost you. She'll kill me."

Gollnick quietly chuckled then motioned for Max to circle around to the other side of the pile of crates. As he did, the ogre was now between them. Gollnick threw a fireball and hit the ogre's giant club. Ogres never were the most intelligent creatures. It picked up the club and began waving it around as if it expected the fire to go out.

The security guard behind Elisa ran over to the beast to calm it down. As he made his way to the ogre, Max motioned with a clenched fist and made an upper cut swing with his right arm. A giant icicle shot up through the floor and speared the security guard who exploded in a shower of water.

A loud screeching sound came from the far side of the circle of light where the mysterious creature continued to stalk, but still would not enter the illuminated space.

The ogre continued to swing his burning club, igniting the crates around him. He then started pounding the club on some of the boxes, smashing them to splinters and spreading the fire even more.

Gollnick maneuvered around the frantic ogre and into the light. The second security guard got up from his chair holding his right arm straight out toward Gollnick and aimed his ring. Gollnick let loose a fireball at the guard's feet, being careful not to hit Elisa. The guard ignored the fireball and shot Gollnick in the right shoulder with a light beam. Gollnick spun to his right and crashed onto the floor.

The security guard looked down to see his clothes were on fire. He turned toward Elisa. Max stepped out from the shadows and called to the guard. The man stopped to look at him. With his hand pointed and his palm perpendicular to the guard, Max announced, *"Proto torum se-ton."* The guard was hit with a shock wave from Max's hand, propelling him backward into a pile of crates. As the boxes shattered under the impact, the guard burst into water.

Max ran to help Elisa, but before he was able to untie her, the ogre screamed at him. Max spun to see the giant beast completely surrounded in flame still beating the club on anything nearby. The ogre could not get to him, so instead it flung the burning club at Max. Instinctively, Max raised and slammed his forearms together in front of himself. Instantly, a faint blue sphere enveloped him. The club deflected and crashed into the overhead light as it continued on to the crates behind him.

The ceiling light was now gone, but flames still lit the room around the ogre. In a panic, the creature crashed through some burning crates and headed down the warehouse in the direction Max and Gollnick had originated, away from the fire.

Max proceeded to untie Elisa who was still groggy. She looked up, but Max could tell she didn't recognize him.

"Who are you?"

"Good question. For now, call me Max."

"Max? Gollnick? Is Gollnick with you?"

Gollnick started pushing himself up on one elbow, enough to reply, "I'm here, barely."

Max heard heavy breathing from behind. He whirled to see a monstrous figure behind him, no longer hidden in the shadows. The fire's light was not enough to keep it at bay.

The creature was over twelve feet tall. Its long spindly arms ended in hands of razor sharp claws. Attached to each arm were thin leathery wings reaching from its wrists down to its body. The hind legs looked like that of a goat, but with talons in place of hooves. It had a long thin tail ending in spikes. The firelight cast an ominous glow upon the creature's blood-red leathery hide. It appeared to have the head of a bald human with two-inch fangs. The creature lumbered forward toward Max and Elisa, screeching with those fangs bared.

Gollnick called to Max, "It's a demon, probably one of Malcolm's servants. It won't like the cold."

The creature turned its attention on Gollnick. It leapt over Max and Elisa and pounced on the old sorcerer, driving its razor sharp claws into his left leg. Gollnick cried out in pain as it moved in on him.

Max raised his hands to either side of him with palms face up. As he turned those hands face down, the temperature of the room dropped radically. Within ten seconds, it had gone from ninety degrees, due to the burning fire, to below zero. Everyone could see their breath in the air.

The creature cried out in pain then turned an angry glare at Max. Releasing its grip on Gollnick's leg, it pounced toward the boy. Once again, Max raised his forearms together in front of him. The faint blue sphere appeared, but the creature landed on top of it. It tried biting at the sphere, but was unable to break through. After a couple minutes, the strain of trying to maintain the sphere with the heavy creature on top was beginning to weaken Max. He realized without some help soon, he would no longer be able to hold the protective sphere. And when it failed, he would be demon dinner.

Max looked around and spotted Gollnick who was passed out on the floor behind the creature. Max redirected his focus back to the demon in an attempt to find a way out of the situation. As his strength to maintain the sphere was about to fail, one of the claws pierced the protective shell dangerously close to Max's face. As the bubble collapsed, a lightning bolt shot at the demon from behind. It fell and landed on its back. Before it could right itself, Max clenched a fist, made an upper-cut motion with his right arm and a huge icicle shot up from beneath the pier, punching a hole in the floor and skewering the creature in the chest. The demon let out a painful cry then disintegrated into a cloud of red smoke.

Max turned to find Elisa lying on the floor with her hand pointed up at where the creature had been. He hadn't even heard her cast the spell, but she had saved him.

Drained of strength, Max crawled over to Gollnick followed by Elisa. Gollnick was bleeding badly from his left leg. Elisa held her hand over the wounded limb and said. *"Hema toe-zie fume."* The bleeding immediately stopped.

Gollnick regained consciousness, but was still very groggy. "Did we win?"

"We're alive. I suppose that counts," replied Elisa, "Please tell me you have a plan for getting us out of here."

"There's a mirror in a restroom at the other end of the warehouse," answered Max. "That's how we got here, but that's also the direction the ogre was headed."

Elisa looked to Max then sighed. "None of us are in any shape to face an angry ogre, least of all Nick. We need to find another way out."

As if on queue, the warehouse made a loud breaking noise. Max and Elisa looked at the fire and giant icicles then realized the pier on which the warehouse was built was giving way.

"We don't have time. We have to go through the ogre," said Max. "This pier isn't going to last much longer."

Max and Elisa stood up and gently raised Gollnick between them. They made their way around the flames and through the warehouse, back the way they had come.

They moved through the stacks of crates and could hear the creaking and groaning of the warehouse weakening under the burning flames. In the distance, they heard fire sirens approaching.

The three turned a corner and Max spotted the restroom. Pacing there before it was the angry ogre. Instantly it spotted them and let out a blood-curdling scream as it charged toward them. Max shifted Gollnick's weight to Elisa.

"Get him out of here," instructed Max. "I'll keep this guy busy while you do."

"No," groaned Gollnick. Elisa gave him no other choice as she pulled him away and headed for the restroom.

Max grabbed a slat of wood from a pile of broken crates. At the end of the slat were three nails protruding from the wood. When the ogre came within range, he swung the slat like a baseball bat. Unfortunately, Max was apparently no good at baseball. He swung the board, missed the ogre and slammed it into a nearby crate. The nails hit the crate with enough force to embed themselves. He was unable to quickly free the slat, so he left it hanging there.

The ogre took a swing at him and smashed the crate that held Max's baseball bat. It then turned to follow Max. He led the monstrous creature down one aisle after another snaking through the crates trying to buy Elisa the time she needed to get Gollnick out safely.

As he made his way through the crates, the creature took a wrong turn. Max paused momentarily to see where it went. When he couldn't spot the ogre, he headed back to the restroom only to be cut off by the beast. It took another swing and caught him in the left arm. It hit with enough force to send Max flying over two crates and smashing into a third.

When he regained his senses enough to look up, the ogre was standing over him with a large metal oil drum in its hands, suspended above his head. Max quickly raised his right hand pointing at the ogre with his palm parallel to the creature and cast a spell. *"Proto torum se-ton."* A massive wave of force hit the ogre square in the chest. The ogre stumbled backward and released the barrel. The creature crashed into a pile of crates as the drum came tumbling down on its head.

The ogre was not unconscious, but it was dazed by the impact. Max ran as fast as he could for the restroom. As he neared, another metal oil drum flew through the air and crashed into the poorly built restroom, shattering the fixtures. Max turned to see the ogre lumbering toward him again. He took a quick look at the restroom and realized there was no way the mirror could have survived the impact.

Once again, the trembling and groaning of the warehouse caught Max's attention. He looked behind the ogre to see parts of the building already starting to collapse into the water below. He realized his chances were better in the water than trying to stand toe to toe with an ogre so he rushed past, heading for the collapsing section. The giant beast, as dumb as it was, still knew better than to follow. It stood there watching in confusion at Max's actions.

While Max was running, he spotted a section of broken boards in the wall. He smashed through the damaged section and out onto the pier, landing next to ten large metal drums. He looked back to see the ogre had not followed. It continued to watch Max until the warehouse around it began to give way and collapse into the harbor below. When Max turned again, he noticed the metal drums he'd landed next to were marked 'Gasoline' and they were on fire. His memory may have been faulty, but he knew enough to realize gasoline and fire didn't mix. Without pause for thought, Max took a deep breath and dove over the edge as the whole dock exploded, propelling him far out into the water.

Max was standing outside a Greek temple on a mountaintop overlooking the countryside. Somehow he knew this place, Mount Othrys, and it felt like home. The temple was pristine and the surrounding area well maintained. The scent of flowers hung in the air as well as the burnt stench of electricity. He was tired and weak, but knew he had to continue fighting... but who was he fighting?

As he cast a spell to prepare another fireball in his left hand, he blocked an electrical strike with the large scythe he carried in his right. Looking around, he saw three attackers. One threw lightning bolts, another carried a trident and a third kept to the shadows.

The attacker throwing lightning bolts was off to his right. He was tall and wore white robes with gold bracers and tan leather boots. He had a short brown beard and a determined expression on his face. Max realized this was Zeus from Greek mythology.

The attacker carrying the trident was off to his left. Muscular and tanned, he moved as though the trident was a natural extension of his arm. He wore short pants, no shoes, and appeared wet from head to toe. It could only be Poseidon.

The third attacker was somewhere behind him in the shadows. Max could not get a good look at him, but sensed he was wearing dark clothing of some sort. Most likely Hades.

After blocking the last lightning strike, he felt a searing pain in his back from what appeared to be black fire. Next the attacker with the trident pointed his weapon and an energy wave shot from its three points. Max raised his left hand allowing the fireball to dissipate and creating an energy shield to block the trident attack. No sooner did he block than another lightning strike hit in his right side. The pain was overwhelming. Already weakened, his strength was fading. He raised the scythe to block the lightning again, but too slowly. The searing rear attack plunged him to one knee.

Dropping his scythe he wrapped his arms around himself and an energy shield enveloped. He cast a spell, "Crono mon tra-ton." As he did, he flung his arms wide and the energy shield expanded at blinding speed, knocking his attackers to the ground. The energy it took to cast the spell weakened him even further. He placed his left hand to the ground to steady himself. As he looked up, a final bolt of electricity hit him square in the chest. The intense pain blinded him and everything went bright white as he lost consciousness.

16 Taryn's Training

After Gollnick and Max had departed to look for Elisa, Meagan entered the training room to find Cyrus, Amber and Taryn waiting for her. The room had once again changed its shape. It appeared to be a giant circle with walls arcing up to a domed ceiling. At the dome's peak was a large glowing orb, which illuminated the entire room. The floor was compacted sand. No other objects were present. Everyone, including Taryn, was now wearing a grey sweatsuit.

Taryn stood in the center of the room with her hands on her hips as she heralded Meagan's entrance. "Ah, one more to the team. And where's Max?"

Meagan replied politely, "He's gone with Nick to find Elisa."

"Brilliant, so we're one person short," said Taryn, disappointed Gollnick had not informed her of the change in plans. "It would've been better had he stayed to train with us. But since that's not possible now... I'll have to concentrate on ye three. I'll have a talk with Gollnick later."

She paced the center of the room. The others spread out around her not knowing what she had planned. Taryn glanced around the room to measure her trainees and their positions.

"I want all of ye to attack me. Don't hold back. Yer enemies won't hold back either. I guarantee ye won't hurt me." Taryn knew she sounded arrogant about her abilities, but she was confident in her assessment of the team of greenhorns. Without Gollnick and Max, she felt the other three posed no threat.

"Don't be so sure," replied Cyrus confidently. "Max beat you in Miami with a fish tank. I think we can do just as good." Cyrus cast a spell, *"Flo-gorto..."*

As he was speaking, Taryn flung a small fireball at him to disrupt his speech.

Amber raised her arms over her head and the wind in the room began swirling around like a tornado. Too late did she realize Taryn, standing in the center of the room, was less affected than everyone else, since the eye of the storm was its calmest place.

Taryn glanced her way, but ignored Amber for the moment. She shifted her attention to Meagan.

Meagan held two clenched fists at her sides. As she raised them, the ground beneath Taryn began to rise in a column of rock. Taryn was briefly caught off guard, but did a flip off the rising rock to land on the ground only a few feet from Meagan. Taryn held out her left hand and a burst of flames shot toward Meagan.

Meagan raised her forearms in front of her and placed them together to form a green sphere of protection. This surprised Taryn, who redirected her attention back to Cyrus.

"Flo-gorto mana tam," she heard him say.

The tornado-force wind from Amber began filling with a thick fog. Visibility worsened so Taryn was only able to see a foot or two in front of her.

Nobody could see anyone else. Gradually, the temperature in the room rose noticeably, and continued to rise. Taryn added fire to the wind to raise the temperature. Being a fire elemental sorceress, she knew she would be immune but it should have a strong impact on the others.

She figured Cyrus had come to the same conclusion when she heard him cast a cold spell. *"Loma ici mon-tue."*

The temperature in the room returned to normal, but the humidity from the clashing heat and cold increased.

Clouds formed at the top of the dome. Taryn's voice echoed from the center of the room. *"Electro stra tol-nay."* Lightning flew in all directions. She used the clouds and humidity to create a small electrical storm.

As the winds died down and the fog lifted, Taryn glanced around to find Amber and Cyrus both unconscious. As she looked for Meagan, she spotted a semi-formed shield of rock. When the storm passed completely, Meagan stepped out from behind her rock shield of protection.

As Meagan walked the perimeter of the room, Taryn mimicked her movement so they circled one another. Their gaze focused, neither blinked.

"I'm impressed," offered Taryn. "Ye knew enough to protect yerself when the lightnin' started, but ye made a mistake by leavin' the protection of yer shield."

"Not exactly," said Meagan. She clenched her left fist and in doing so, the earth around Taryn rose up to envelope her feet in stone, effectively paralyzing her.

Taryn looked down in shock. How could she have been taken off guard so easily? She looked up just in time to see Meagan finish her spell. *"Semo nigh free."*

Taryn became drowsy. She attempted one last fireball, but it was more like a puff of smoke. Sleep overwhelmed her.

A few minutes later, Taryn woke to find Cyrus, Amber and Meagan sitting in a semi-circle around her. "It seems I was defeated after all," she admitted. "I underestimated Meagan's earth magic."

Taryn directed her attention to Amber and Cyrus. "Yer attacks were diversionary at best. Have ye not been workin' on offensive spells?" Taryn could see Cyrus grind his teeth and knew he was not happy. She hadn't tried to be mean. Just constructive criticism.

Amber was the first to respond, "I hadn't considered everyone's position in the room. My wind power did us more harm than you. Had I been in the center of the room, it might've been more effective."

While Taryn agreed with the assessment, she could also see Amber was being too hard on herself. "Next time, try directin' the wind up or down in the center of the room, or maybe a burst of concentrated air similar to an energy wave punch. Ye needed to find a way to knock me off balance."

She then looked to Cyrus whose brow was furrowed and his stare didn't waver. She could tell his displeasure with her had only grown.

"Fine. My illusions are pathetic and my energy blasts are weak," shouted Cyrus. "I don't have elemental powers like the rest of you. I have to learn spells and I don't know any good ones yet to use in a battle. What do you want me to do? Start a fist fight? The dark sorcerers will just laugh at me. Or maybe that'll distract them long enough for you to fry them. Will that make you happy?"

Taryn couldn't tell if it was his lack of powers or his feelings toward her that made Cyrus angrier. "Illusions can be a powerful tool when used at the right time. Don't discount your abilities. And ye're correct in sayin' elemental magic is useful—but even that kind of magic can be disrupted. Find a way to knock your target off balance or do somethin' to make it difficult to concentrate. We need to find ye some useful offensive spells or perhaps a magical item. When Gollnick returns we'll talk to him about gettin' you a staff or somethin' you can carry. Like the elemental magics, some items can be used without arcane spells."

Taryn could see the tension in Cyrus' face ease a little as he thought about her words. She knew it would take far more to make him trust her, but time was not on their side.

They prepared for another round of practice. Meagan seemed distracted, staring at the floor. Taryn noticed and approached. "Are you okay?"

"Something's happened." Meagan turned pale and looked at Taryn with wide eyes. She ran from the room, calling out, "The library. Nick's been hurt!" Everyone dropped what they were doing and followed.

In the library, Meagan found Elisa kneeling next to Gollnick. He had collapsed on the floor beside the mirror. There was no sign of an open portal... or Max.

Amber followed, slightly out of breath. "What happened? Where's Max?"

"We were all too weak to fight. An ogre was blocking our way," answered Elisa as she looked up in tears. "Max lured it away from the mirror so Nick and I could make our escape." She looked Meagan, the only familiar face, in the eyes. "He was supposed to be right behind us," drawing in a stuttered breath, "but he never made it through."

"What mirror did you use?" asked Taryn quickly. She ran to the library mirror, waiting for direction.

"We were in a warehouse, on a pier in New York City," replied Elisa.

Taryn stopped as everyone looked at each other. New York City was the worst place for a sorcerer to be, even in the best of times.

"New York?" questioned Meagan breathlessly. "Nick told us never to go there."

"It wasn't by choice," replied Elisa. "Frederick Von Woonst captured me in Philadelphia and took me to New York to await Malcolm's return."

Amber ran to the mirror and touched it. *"Mirtor tolanga se-atum Max."* She waited for a second, but nothing happened. Impatiently, she tried again. *"Mirtor tolanga se-atum Max."* Still nothing happened. She looked to Elisa, but Elisa just hung her head.

"The warehouse was on fire and in the process of collapsing at the time we made our escape. It must have been destroyed."

"There has to be another mirror in the same area we can go to," Amber pleaded, looking to Taryn for an answer. "Max could be hurt. We have to help him,"

"No!" said Gollnick groggily, still lying on the floor. "We were on a pier. With any luck Max made it to the water. If he did, he's safe for the time being. If not, then he's already dead."

Amber inhaled sharply, but did not release the breath. She ran from the room calling, "The crystal! If he's alive, his name will still be on the door in the circle room." Taryn followed.

A moment later, the girls sighed deeply when they saw Max's name still on his door. Amber collapsed to her knees crying. "He's still alive."

"Amber?" said Cyrus as he entered the room a moment later.

"He's still alive," said Amber.

"I'm glad to hear that," replied Cyrus in a calm voice. "But um... the weather above the castle is going crazy. Almost hurricane-force winds. Do you think you could maybe calm down a bit?"

"Me?" questioned Amber. "I did that? I didn't mean to."

"I know. It's okay, just breathe and relax."

Amber closed her eyes and did as Cyrus instructed. She sat calmly, trying to control her breath.

Taryn considered the possibilities. "Interesting. A lack of emotional control produces some powerful results. If we could just find a way to focus that power."

Taryn noted Amber's intense stare and furrowed brow and realized now was not the time to test the idea.

Taryn, Cyrus and Amber returned to the infirmary to check on Gollnick's condition. Meagan and Elisa were tending his wounds. They had used magic to stop the additional bleeding and had performed healing magic as best they could.

"He's stable, but he took a beating," said Meagan. "He won't be able to walk well for some time. I'm afraid he won't be joining us in Babylon when the time comes, neither will Elisa. She's in no condition to fight anyone right now. They both need to rest. We can only hope Max made it through okay."

"So what are we going to do?" asked Amber with trembling hands. "We can't just leave Max in New York by himself."

17 AN UNEXPECTED ALLY

It was late in the evening when Max woke up groggy and with a serious headache. He found himself in a brightly lit room surrounded by vertical black metal bars. After rubbing his head for a few seconds, he looked around and realized he was not alone. "How did I end up in the dungeon?" The comment was intended as a joke until he realized he really was in a dungeon.

The other two occupants, who previously paid him no attention, each raised an eyebrow. A man around Gollnick's age rested a hand on the knee of his tan pants and leaned against the wall. His matching tan vest covered a white shirt with rolled up sleeves, all of which appeared in need of a good cleaning. Including the man himself. He rubbed his short dark curly hair and studied Max with a tired expression. Max guessed him to be of Egyptian origin, based on skin tone and the small Egyptian Ankh on a chain around his neck. The other was a young kid around Max's age. The boy's jeans were torn in multiple places and his t-shirt was covered with images like graffiti. He was thin, but when he grabbed Max by the collar, it was obvious he was also very muscular.

"Yo, nut job, ya got any money on ya?" asked the kid with a strong New York accent. This was not the greeting Max had hoped for so he tried to back away, but the kid would not let go of Max's shirt collar.

"Please leave me alone," said Max. "I'm tired and need to get some rest." It was true he was tired and in need of rest, but he also didn't want to hurt the kid.

"I said, do ya got any money?" demanded the kid as he punched Max in the stomach. Max doubled over in pain, unprepared for a punch that knocked the wind out of him.

The older man stood and walked over to the kid. The man held out his hand. *"Semo nigh free."* The kid slumped over and fell asleep.

Max looked up in appreciation. "Who are you?"

"My name is Hank. I'm the one who brought you to Gollnick. How did you get here?"

Max's face brightened when he heard the name. "Long story. Thought we were going to Philadelphia to rescue Elisa, but ended up in New York." He swallowed hard wishing he had something to drink. Fighting to keep his eyes open, he said, "We saved her, I think, but Gollnick was injured. Hope they made it back. I got stuck while covering their escape."

"Does anyone know you're here?"

"If Gollnick and Elisa made it back to the castle okay, then yes," replied Max barely able to keep his eyes open. "If not, then no. By the way, where is here?"

Hank smiled. "We're in a dungeon in Malcolm's fortress in New York City. Hopefully, he doesn't know who you are yet. He has many spies in local law enforcement. They found you in the water near the burning warehouse and Malcolm had you brought here."

"Do you know who I am?" asked Max, searching Hank's features with anticipation.

"I just told you I was the one who brought you to Gollnick," replied Hank as he tilted his head to one side in question.

"No, I mean do you know my name? Or where I'm from? Anything?" pleaded Max still trying to maintain consciousness.

"You don't know who you are?"

"I've had no memory of anything before I woke up a few days ago in the hospital. The nurses called me Max and we've gone with that name ever since, but I have no idea what my real name is."

As desperate as Max was for knowledge, fatigue was winning the battle. He propped himself up on one arm, trying to keep his eyes open.

"Your name," Hank began, "is one of the most ancient and feared in all the ages. Not only for your deeds, but also for your powers."

Max's eyes widened as he pushed the idea of sleep from his thoughts.

"Your name..." Hank reiterated, "is Chronos, Ruler of the Titans and Master of Time."

18 Friends to the Rescue?

It was a bright sunny day in New York City not far from Central Park. The normal big city traffic provided a noisy backdrop to another busy morning. Car horns sounded as cabs moved through traffic. People crowded the sidewalks trying to make their way around the city. The smell of car exhaust was strong in the air.

Some movers were carrying a large mirror into the front door of an office building when the reflection turned to a swirling image. Cyrus, Amber and Taryn stepped out of it and surprised the movers—who dropped the mirror, shattering it into a thousand pieces. The trio ducked around a corner and started running. Twisting through alley after alley they stopped to look back and make sure no one was following them.

Cyrus was wearing blue jeans, a black t-shirt, white sneakers and his brown trench coat. Amber was dressed similarly in a white t-shirt. Taryn, however, looked more the part of a New York City model in her black leather pants, black boots, black bikini top and black trench coat. She wore mirrored sunglasses and her bright red hair was pulled back in a ponytail.

Barely winded from the short jaunt, Cyrus questioned Taryn. "How did you know there would be a safe mirror in front of that office building this morning?"

Taryn peered around the corner looking for trouble. "Easy. I ordered it last evenin' when we decided to make this crazy trip. It was supposed to already be in the buildin' by now! So much for expedited shippin'. "

"What?"

"'Come on, we're in New York City. Almost every mirror in the city is controlled or monitored by dark sorcerers."

"Right," replied Cyrus. "And how do we get out?"

"Improvise."

"Not quite the well thought-out plan I was hoping for."

"Okay, so how do we find Max?" asked Amber with alarm. "This is New York, there's going to be tons of dark sorcerers. What are we going..." Cyrus clapped his hand over her mouth to silence her.

"We'll think of something," he said, perspiration streaming down the side of his face. "For now, calm down. We don't want another hurricane on our hands."

Amber brushed his hand away and shot her brother an angry look.

Taryn turned from the corner, grabbing them by the arms as she started to run. "We need to move! And fast! We've got company."

The trio was half a block away when Cyrus looked back to see three black-clad security guards heading their way. Taryn, being in better physical shape, began to outdistance the other two. The security guards raised their hands and aimed their rings at the trio. Light rays shot past them as they continued down the street.

"What happened to not letting people know about magic?" asked Amber as best she could while running.

"Apparently these guys never got the memo," replied Cyrus, slightly ahead of his sister. "Follow Taryn. Hopefully she knows where she's going and isn't leading us into a trap."

After a few blocks with the guards on their tail, Taryn led them into the southeast corner of Central Park. She stopped and waited for the others to catch up, scanning the area for trouble. Once Cyrus and Amber arrived, she suggested, "Split up. Hopefully we can lose them in the park. We'll meet up at the swimmin' pool."

Cyrus headed northwest, entering the park near West Drive and ducked in among the trees and around the pond. One security guard followed each of them.

Cyrus hid behind a tree and waited for the security guard to run past. After a minute or so, he was still waiting. He peered around the tree but did not see the guard anywhere. *Either I lost him or he's stalking me. Neither option is good news.*

Cyrus stepped out in the open. A light beam hit the tree next to him leaving a small scorch mark. Cyrus raised his arm to shield himself from the attack. He turned to see the guard was about fifty yards in front of him on West Drive. His way was now blocked from his intended destination. He took off running with the intention of finding another way through the park.

He made his way around the softball fields without incident, but as he turned to make sure he wasn't being followed, he spotted the guard, again gaining on his position. There were a couple of people playing softball so he ran over and grabbed a baseball bat then ducked in among the trees for cover. One of the players spotted him and tried to stop him, but a light beam hit a nearby tree and changed the boy's mind.

The guard was scanning the area when Cyrus stepped out from behind a tree and slammed the bat into his back. Apparently unhurt, he raised his hand to fire at Cyrus again. Cyrus grabbed the guard's ring-bearing hand and the two of them wrestled. Cyrus managed to pull the ring from the guard's finger. As soon as it cleared the digit, the guard exploded like a giant water balloon. A drenched Cyrus looked down in surprise.

"Well, that gives new meaning to 'Pull my finger!' " He looked at the ring in his hand then dropped it into his pocket. "I'll have Gollnick look at that later. For now, I need to find the others."

He took off to the northeast following West Drive around the reservoir, when he spotted another security guard in the distance. He decided to get off the main road and take the smaller paths through the park. He headed down past the Loch and out onto a road that circled around to the pool.

Cyrus looked around thinking that he couldn't be the first to arrive after all of the detours he'd taken. *What could have happened to them?* He looked skyward for any signs of a storm, but it was a clear day in the Big Apple.

If something happened to Amber, I'll never forgive myself. We should've stayed together. We should've stood our ground and faced those guys. And when they called for reinforcement, we could've fought off a hundred more of them... and died. Okay, not a good plan either. What is taking them so long? Maybe I should go look for them. He sighed as he considered the size of Central Park. *I'd never find them in a place this big.*

After waiting five more minutes, he spotted Taryn in the distance. Her pace was more of a jog than a run.

"Where's Amber? Have you seen her?"

Taryn looked back the way she came with wide eyes. "No, I haven't. She took the most direct route. She should've been here first."

"That does it! I'm going to look for her."

Taryn grabbed him by the arm. "Wait!"

Through some trees Taryn saw someone. It didn't take long for both of them to realize it was Amber. They ran to meet her at the tree line.

Cyrus was the first to greet his sister with a hug. "What happened? What took so long?"

Amber was tired and out of breath. "Look, you two are in better shape than me. I'm not an athlete. That was a long run that turned into a longer walk. And that black-suited guard didn't help matters any."

"The one following me is gone," stated Cyrus. "All that's left of him is this ring." He pulled it out and showed it to the other two. "When I pulled this from his finger, he exploded."

Taryn looked at the small prize. "Gollnick may want to see that. Maybe he can find an easier way to defeat these guys."

"My thoughts exactly," said Cyrus. "What about the other two?"

"I fried the one followin' me around Cleopatra's Needle," replied Taryn.

"Mine took an aerial view out of the park," answered Amber.

Taryn was apprehensive about Amber's answer. "But, did ye destroy him?"

With raised eyebrows, Amber defended her actions. "I can't see how he could have survived a fall from that high up."

A twitch of his eye indicated Cyrus' reluctance to side with Taryn. "I've seen these guys take a hit. Impact alone may not take them out."

No sooner did he say it than a light beam hit him in the left arm. The impact of the strike spun him around and down to one knee. The girls turned to see the guard approach their position at a brisk pace with his ring pointed right at them.

"I really wish Max were here right now," said Amber. "He could use the water in the swimming pool to get rid of this guy."

Taryn created a fireball, but before she could throw it, Amber pointed out, "People will see."

"People have already seen... we just need to get out of here!" shouted Taryn. She let loose the fireball and the guard exploded into a mist of water.

A few of those who had witnessed the incident ran away screaming and calling for the police. Most kept walking, as if nothing out of the ordinary had happened. But then... this was New York City. 'Strange' is somewhat normal in these parts.

"Are you okay?" asked Amber. She attempted to help her brother to his feet and examined the burn mark on his coat's left arm.

"Stings something fierce and I can't move my arm," replied Cyrus through clenched teeth, strain evident in his voice.

"We need to get ye back to the castle," stated Taryn.

Amber turned to look at her. "We can't just leave. Max is still here somewhere. I thought I saw a castle in the middle of the reservoir, but it isn't there anymore."

Taryn was familiar with dark sorcerer tactics. "A cloaking spell! Like the one Gollnick uses on the castle in Baltimore. The place will be protected by Malcolm's security guards and who knows what else. We need to regroup at Ravenicon Castle and figure out what to do."

Amber bit her lip, looking south. She couldn't argue knowing Cyrus needed attention. Then her face lit up. "What about our telepathic link?"

"Ye tried that even after Gollnick told ye not to?" queried Taryn. She watched as Amber looked toward the reservoir and mimicked Gollnick's movements, holding her finger to her temple.

After a minute of silence, Amber relayed her attempt. "The connection isn't strong enough, but I got the impression he's safe for the moment."

"Well at least we know where he is now," replied Taryn.

They could hear police sirens in the distance. Suddenly, an explosion followed by a geyser of water being shot into the air could be seen from the direction of the reservoir. As they stood observing the mist, two more security guards appeared from the swimming pool. One fired a light beam at Amber, but Cyrus stepped in front and took a second hit to his injured arm.

People were hustling and bustling in all directions around them. Taryn knew if they didn't get out of there soon, they would be facing off against sorcerers as well as guards. "Amber, it's too late to conceal our presence, we need a blast of wind to clear the way."

Amber held up her hands and the winds started building. As she lowered them in the direction of the guards, the wind blast hit the ground between them. One guard was knocked into the trees near the pool, the other went flying over the tree tops, and Amber, Taryn, and Cyrus were knocked from their feet. Scrambling up, they spotted three police officers coming from the direction of the pool.

"Watch your aim," cautioned Cyrus. "Back to the Met, we'll find a mirror there to get back to the castle." They ran south toward the Metropolitan Museum of Art, but didn't get far when they saw two police officers in the distance coming from that direction.

"This way," called Taryn. She took a left and ran out of Central Park. They went to the first small shop they could find. After bursting in the front door, they made a bee line for the restroom. The shop keeper screamed at them for disrupting his customers as they passed through. The three of them made their way to the small restroom and disappeared inside.

A few minutes later, four police officers followed them into the shop and to the restroom, but found it to be empty.

19 Escape From New York

A little before noon, Max woke to find Hank seated on a nearby bench. They were still in the dungeon, but the other kid was no longer there. The cell had black metal bars on one side and dull grey stone walls on the other three which matched the floor. There were many other cells in the hallway. A small magical orb floated in the corridor, lighting the entire area. Max could just make out a wooden door at the end of the hallway.

Hank sat on the bench with his legs crossed, apparently meditating, so Max did his best to remain quite. He sat up and stretched. A few minutes later, he leaned over toward Hank to see if he was asleep.

"Feeling better?" asked Hank with his eyes still closed.

Max jerked back in surprise. "Yes." Sleep had helped but the bench wasn't very forgiving on his back. He stretched again to work out the stiffness. "So where are we?"

"I told you last night. We're in Malcolm's dungeon, in New York," said Hank, both eyes now open and looking at Max with a raised eyebrow.

"Yeah, I got that much already. I mean where in New York is this dungeon?"

"No idea. Malcolm controls a large area of the city, but there are boundary disputes all the time. Gollnick explained the situation already, didn't he?"

"Yeah, yeah," said Max trying to get past the obvious. "Malcolm and the dark sorcerers are the bad guys, we're the good guys. They want to open some ancient prisons and destroy the world. Our job is to keep that from happening. New York is a bad place and we should never come here... yada yada."

"Then why did you?" asked Hank.

"As I said last night, Gollnick wanted to save Elisa," responded Max. "She was being held in a warehouse somewhere nearby. We thought she was in Philadelphia, but when we traveled through the mirror, we ended up here instead."

"But you did rescue Elisa, right?" asked Hank trying to confirm his hope.

"Kind of. Gollnick was hurt and she was helping him to the mirror. I can only assume they made it out. I was covering their escape, but the mirror was destroyed before I could get away."

"Unfortunate," said Hank.

"Hey, look on the bright side. I found you!" said Max with mock excitement.

Hank looked around the dank cell. "Yes, I can see that worked out really well."

"Gollnick also wanted to find you and was hoping Elisa might know where you were," offered Max.

"Well, nice of him to give it a try. Unfortunately, he missed the mark on that one. Now we're both lost to the circle."

"Last night you said I was a powerful sorcerer," said Max. "Do you know anything else about me? Where I'm from? Friends or family I can contact? I still can't remember anything about myself. Just brief memory flashes that don't make sense."

Now that he'd finally found someone who might be able to fill in some of the blanks—since actually most things were blank—he wanted to know everything Hank could tell him.

"An old rogue sorcerer in Cairo, dumped you in my lap and asked me to bring you to the circle. He said you would be very powerful." Hank waved his hand in the air at the mention of power.

He hesitated before continuing. "According to legend, the three sorcerers who sealed the portal to the nightmare realm became immortal. From what I was told, you are the immortal Chronos. Unfortunately, we were ambushed and I barely escaped with you. I haven't been able to find him since."

Max was skeptical. "You believe this guy?"

"I don't know. I trust my sources who put me in contact with him, but I only met him that night."

"According to the doctors, I'm seventeen years old. How can I be immortal?" asked Max with frustration in his voice.

"According to mythology, Chronos was the master of time. Only your power could've done it, if in fact you really are the Titan King."

"But why can't I remember anything?"

"How would I know? You're supposed to be the powerful one."

"Do you know why the dark sorcerers are after me?"

"I'm afraid that's my fault," confessed Hank with a sigh. "Using some dark magic I've never seen, Malcolm forced me to tell him who I had taken to Gollnick. We both thought you would wake up and be a powerful ally for whoever got to you first. I didn't realize you would have no memory though. Malcolm wants you to work for him or no one so he sent out instructions to capture or kill you."

"Well. That explains the past few days, but I still need to know more. How can I find this rogue sorcerer? What's his name?"

"He went by the name Nido, but I don't know where to find him. He found me. However, there's a group of sisters I know who may be able to shed a little more light on your identity, if we ever get out of here. For now, I would recommend staying with the name Max. If Malcolm finds out who you truly are, we could be in real trouble. Right now, we need to find a way to stop him from opening the prison in Hades."

"You mean Babylon," corrected Max.

"No, Hades," said Hank with a confused look. "I don't know anything about a prison in Babylon, but I do know Malcolm is on his way to Greece to find an entrance to Hades. He plans to release Cerberus."

"Who?"

"Cerberus, the three-headed guard dog of the Greek underworld. He allows the dead to enter and keeps the living out. He also prevents the dead from leaving. The sorcerer Hades was one of the gods of Greek mythology. He imprisoned Cerberus in the underworld and forced him to guard the entrance, but never be able to leave, at least not without permission. Hercules once took Cerberus from the underworld, with Hades permission, but later returned him to the underworld as instructed."

"Well, Vincent and his water automatons along with Frederick Von Woonst are planning on opening the prison in Babylon tomorrow. We'll have to stop them too," said Max.

Hank lowered his feet and turned to face Max with wide eyes. "Vincent Maylock is helping Malcolm?"

"He's under some kind of binding spell. He doesn't have a choice."

"That's not good news," replied Hank. "Do they have the key?"

"Gollnick asked Taryn the same question, but she didn't know anything about a key," replied Max while he tired of going over the information in his mind.

"Who's Taryn?" asked Hank.

"Long story," said Max getting a little frustrated. "Do you know where these keys are?"

"I know the key to keeping Cerberus in the underworld is supposedly kept somewhere in Hades. And if they don't know where it is yet, we need to make sure they don't find it. However, before we do anything, we need to find a way out of here."

Max stood up and walked to the cell door.

"It should be easy to break out of here," said Max confidently. Hank tried to stop him just as Max touched the bars to the cell.

"No!" called Hank, reaching out a hand to grab Max by the shoulder, but it was too late. The magic protecting the cell bars gave Max a serious jolt and sent him flying backward as if punched in the stomach. He landed flat on his back in front of Hank.

"Ow," croaked Max.

"You... didn't think the bars would be protected?" questioned Hank as he stood next to Max's head with hands on his hips. He looked down at the boy lying flat on the floor. "Oh, and there are no mirrors in here. So unless you know of another way out, we'll be staying put for a while."

Max slowly propped himself up with his arms behind him, but remained on the floor as he looked around.

"There has to be another way out. We can't just sit here," said Max determined to escape.

Max once again stood, this time without touching the cell bars. He glanced around the dungeon. Eventually, he found what he was searching for—a restroom in the far corner of the dungeon.

Hank stood up too and walked over beside Max, looking down the corridor toward the measly excuse for a restroom. "Even if we get out of here, I doubt there's a mirror in there we could use to escape."

"I'm not interested in the restroom for the mirror, but the toilet," smiled Max.

Hank shot him a strange look. "You're going to escape through the toilet?"

Max grimaced. "Not exactly."

Without touching the bars of the cell, Max reached out his open hand toward the restroom. A few seconds later, its door burst open, a tentacle of water shooting toward the bars of the cell. As the liquid contacted the bars, magical bolts of energy were discharged into the water, but had no effect on it. When Max clenched his hand into a fist, the water between the bars solidified into ice. As more and more ice built up between the bars, the strain of the expanding ice forced the bars further and further apart. Once the bars were far enough apart, Max released his fist and the ice shattered, allowing an opening in the bars. Max and Hank stepped through.

Hearing the commotion, two ugly looking goblins lumbered into the dungeon. They looked like little old men with green bodies and long pointed ears. Bare-chested with torn pants, they each carried a sword in a scabbard slung over a shoulder.

Max swung his arm toward the green guards and the remnants of the water tentacle shot between the goblins. As Max dropped his arm, the water fell to the floor in huge puddles. Max extended a flat hand and the water froze into a sheet of ice. The goblins lost their balance and slid everywhere, falling flat on their backs. Once they were on the floor, Max clenched his fist. The ice reached up, like crystal manacles from the frosted white floor, and grabbed the goblins by the wrists and ankles, holding them in place.

Hank rushed to the creatures. With his hands over their heads, he muttered, *"Semo nigh free."* The goblins fell fast asleep.

Max looked into the restroom to find it as Hank had predicted, no mirror. Hank ran to the dungeon door to see if anyone else was coming. Through the window in the door, he spotted three more goblins in the next room.

"Now what do we do?" asked Hank.

"I haven't thought that far ahead yet," responded Max.

"Oh, great!"

"Got any bright ideas? I'd love hear 'em," said Max.

Hank tried the dungeon door to find it too was locked. *"Lotoc altu…"* A sudden shock zapped Hank with a magical jolt from the door knob. He flew backward and landed flat on his back.

Max just looked down at him as he stood over Hank. "It stands to reason, if the cell was magically protected, the whole room would be protected in the same way."

"Yeah, well, now we know for sure," said Hank in a strained voice as he stood up and dusted himself off.

Max quickly looked around. Their surroundings hadn't improved much. Everything was still dull grey stone or black metal bars with only one way out. The idea of fighting their way through Malcolm's fortress was not his first choice. There had to be another way out. He scanned every inch of the room for another option when he spotted a crack in the outside wall. He placed his hand over the crack and paused for a moment. "There's a large body of water on the other side of this wall. I can feel it."

A huge grin spread across his face. "Do you know how to swim?"

"No, why?" responded Hank.

Max stepped back a few feet and cast a spell. He held his hands out in front of him, palms facing forward and said. *"Proto torum se-ton."* Upon finishing the spell, an energy wave of distorted light shot from his hand toward the crack in the wall. The energy ricocheted off the stone. A wave of energy struck Max in the chest and threw him against the opposite wall.

"Everything seems well protected," commented Hank.

Max held his head for a few seconds and tried to focus his vision while the ringing in his ears subsided, then stood and dusted himself off. With a straight face, squinted eyes and pursed lips, he regarded his nemesis. An extended hand toward the crack was followed by concentration. He could feel the water on the other side of the wall. With a clenched fist he swung his arm around in a right hook. The walls of the castle shook. They could feel something had impacted the castle just below them.

"What was that?" inquired Hank.

"Bad aim."

Max concentrated again and this time when he swung his clenched fist in the right hook, a huge block of ice crashed through the wall followed by thousands of gallons of water.

Max pointed at the hole and the huge block of ice dissolved. He grabbed Hank by the arm and yelled, "Deep breath!"

He rushed into the oncoming flood of icy water with Hank in tow. Using his water magic to fight the violent deluge, he quickly pulled them clear of the current and out into open water. Light glimmered on the distant surface above, but Hank's fervent struggle slowed their gradual ascent. Once on the surface, Hank gulped in huge breaths of air while clinging to his rescuer. Max swam for shore pulling Hank along as he splashed around trying to find something solid to grab on to.

As they were making their way to shore, Max spotted a large dark shape swimming beneath them underwater. "Any idea what Malcolm kept in the lower dungeons?"

"Bad stuff," was all Hank could say as he continued to gulp down water, trying to stay afloat.

Moments later, another creature shot up in a huge spray of mist from the water near the castle wall. With wings spread, it launched itself into the sky and circled Max and Hank.

The large dark shape under the water's surface closed in on Max and Hank from below while the winged creature above dove straight at them. Max raised a hand toward the sky to cast a spell when a huge mouth twenty feet across and full of teeth breached the water's surface. With paws larger than a human hand, the winged creature snatched them out of the water as the immense jaws closed around them. A powerful flap of its wings and the sky creature pulled them free of the huge mouth and returned to the heavens above.

Max looked down, recognizing the reservoir in Central Park. As they flew away, he looked back for the castle but it was gone.

"It's magically hidden," said Hank. "It would kind of stick out in the middle of Central Park, don't you think?" He looked down at the water. "Malcolm is not going to like you if his fortress sinks."

It was a bright sunny afternoon as the warm wind rushed by Max and Hank, hundreds of feet in the air above Central Park. The cityscape fell far below as they ascended to the few clouds in the sky. Levitation was not a spell Max had studied so gravity became a serious concern for the water sorcerer. Furry arms and paws held him in place against the body of a large lion, but this lion had an eagle's head and wings.

"Since when do lions have wings and a bird's head?" asked Max as he directed his question to Hank.

"I'm a gryphon and my name is Sorrin," said the creature as it looked down at him.

Max looked up to the eagle head with wide eyes. "Thanks for the rescue."

"My pleasure," replied Sorrin. "After all, it was your iceberg slamming into the lower dungeons that freed me and the Megalodon. It was the least I could do. Is there some place you would like me to drop you?"

Hank's eyes shot up to the gryphon's face in horror.

"Forgive me. Is there some place I may safely take you?" amended Sorrin.

"Someplace out of sight and out of the city," replied Max.

"Preferably on dry land," added Hank.

After flying a few minutes north along the Hudson River, they spotted a small wooded area to conceal their landing. Sorrin took a sharp turn and plummeted into a steep dive. The trees approached Max at an alarming rate. He grasped Sorrin's arm with all his might and extended his legs like landing gear. A few flaps of Sorrin's massive wings and he placed them gently on the ground. A few more flaps to shift his position then he landed beside them.

The feathers from his eagle head stretched down to his chest, but his body and paws were that of a large lion. Sorrin's wings were tucked at his side, but during flight had been a good ten feet long on either side. His upright eagle head brought him eye level with Max.

"Thanks for the ride, Sorrin," said Max. "Were there others in the lower dungeons with you?"

"Not that I was aware of," replied Sorrin. "The Megalodon was there, but he's not very talkative. His pea-sized brain had only one thing on his mind—and that was to eat me. I owe you my life. If there is ever anything I can do, please do not hesitate to call."

"Call?"

"Call my name and I shall be there." Sorrin bowed his head then launched himself into the air once again. As he flew higher and higher, he appeared to be no more than a large bird.

"Sounds like traffic in that direction," said Hank pointing east. "Hopefully, we're not too far from a town. We need to get to the key before Malcolm."

After a short walk, they came upon a house. It looked more like a cabin to Max with the exposed wood logs. After further inspection of the site, they noticed the two-car garage, swimming pool and tennis court around back. As they approached the front door, they heard a dog barking from one of the windows, but saw no other movement. Max and Hank walked up to the front door and knocked. The endless yapping from the little dog was their only response. After two more unanswered knocks, Hank stepped ahead of Max. He pointed his little finger at the door lock. *"Lo-toc altu rocom."* The door unlocked and swung open.

A little black furball, no more than six inches high, came running out still barking at them. Hank and Max merely looked at one another.

"Yappy little fellow," commented Max.

As they entered the house, the little dog followed right along behind them, still barking madly. Immediately they made their way to the bathroom to look for a fairly large mirror.

Just as Hank was about to touch the vanity mirror above the sink, Max asked, "Shouldn't we contact the circle first? To let them know where we are and where we're headed?"

Hank glanced at Max, hand still poised mid-air in front of him. He pondered the question for a brief second. "We can't waste time, but you're right. We should let them know where we're headed. *Mirtor a mirtor tong-la.*" The mirror turned all fuzzy, then a clear picture emerged in the center. The castle library. Sitting there on the table in front of the mirror was the mysterious cat cleaning itself.

"Hey, cat," called Max.

Hank looked sideways at Max with a single raised eyebrow. "You're calling to a cat through a mirror?" but to his surprise the cat turned around and looked right at him through the mirror.

"Cat. Go find Gollnick or someone. Go."

The cat turned slightly and raised a paw, but then looked back at the mirror as if to say, "Must I?" But then it jumped down from the table and ran out of the room.

"Talk to cats often? And since when do they obey commands?" asked Hank.

"This one's a little unusual. It's very intelligent... I hope."

A minute later, the cat ran back into the room with Meagan following close behind. As she entered the room, she started looking around for the cat until Max called out to her from the mirror.

"Meagan, over here," said Max.

Startled, Meagan quickly spun around, trying to locate where the voice was coming from.

"Max?" questioned Meagan recognizing his voice. When she spotted them in the mirror her eyes widened. "Hank?"

After a few seconds to sink in, she continued, "Are you two alright? Where are you?"

"Not sure exactly," replied Max. "Somewhere outside New York City. We don't have much time. You have to get to Babylon and stop Frederick and Vincent from entering the prison. In the meantime, Hank and I are going to Greece where Malcolm is trying to open another prison in Hades. We'll stay in touch as much as possible, but we have to move."

Meagan looked over her shoulder to the door, then returned her gaze to the mirror. She pursed her lips and extended her hand to the mirror. *"Mirtor tolanga se-atum Max."* Once the visage of Max and Hank shifted to a swirling image, she then stepped through the mirror and into the bathroom with Max and Hank.

"I'm coming with you," she said.

"Yeh, I ah... I see that," commented Max.

"I can communicate with Nick telepathically," said Meagan. "I'll keep Nick and Elisa apprised of our situation. Everyone else went to New York City to rescue you."

"I'm really liking this telepathy thing," said Max.

"It doesn't work for everyone. Remember what happened with you and Amber?" Meagan pointed out the problem with his first attempt. "You have to already have a special connection with the person you're trying to link with."

"I take it that means Gollnick and Elisa are more than just friends?" asked Max, realizing it was really none of his business.

"Yeh, they were married once," said Meagan as if it were no big deal. "So, where are we headed?"

Hank stepped in between Max and Meagan and touched the mirror. *"Mirtor tolanga se-atum."* Max and Meagan both continued to stare at him with raised eyebrows.

"Mount Helicon. In Greece," Hank reminded Max. "Remember those sisters I told you about?"

20 Mount Helicon

Hank, Max and Meagan stepped into a circular room about thirty feet in diameter. The walls, floor and ceiling were polished marble, smooth and seamless. A glowing orb hovered a few feet above the mirror where they had just emerged. The full-length mirror was also floating, about a foot off the ground. They each searched the room, but it became obvious there were no secret doors, no entrances or exits. In fact there were no doors or windows at all.

"Where to now, Hank?" asked Max. His voice echoed, repeating his confusion.

Hank took a seat along one wall, facing the mirror. "Now, we wait," he replied.

Max couldn't believe waiting was their only option. The dark sorcerers planned to open two of the ancient prisons within the next twenty-four hours. He felt they needed to do something, anything, other than wait. Time was short and options were few. After thinking things through for a few moments, he realized waiting was their only option. They had no idea where Tiamat was located in Babylon or how to get to Hades. If the Muses couldn't help them, they were sunk, and so was the world.

"What are we waiting for?" inquired Meagan, slumping against the wall next to Hank. "Looks like a dead end."

"Our arrival will have been noticed," replied Hank. "Someone will likely be along shortly to collect us."

"Correct me if I'm wrong," commented Meagan, "but according to Greek mythology, Mount Helicon was the home of the nine muses."

"Correct," replied Hank. "They inspired mortals in the different arts and literature."

Max had a feeling he knew the Muses, somehow. "They were just sorceresses, though, kind of like us, right?"

"The Muses of Greek myth died long ago," said Hank. "Their descendants, however, are still on the job."

"And why exactly are we here?" asked Meagan.

Max agreed, they needed information not inspiration. Then it hit him. "To see Clio—or at least her descendant. She was the muse of historical literature. If anyone is going to have accurate knowledge of the history of this world, it would be Clio."

"That's correct," said Hank as he glanced sideways at Max with a smile, "I take it your memory is coming back?"

"Just bits and pieces. Being somewhere or seeing something seems to trigger it. I don't remember seeing this room before, but I sense we are on Mount Helicon."

"And so you are," said a voice from behind them. "Welcome, everyone. I am..."

Max turned upon hearing the voice and completed her sentence. "...Terpsichore." There behind them stood a beautiful young girl in her late teens. Her long brunette hair flowed as she moved. She wore a white blouse and skirt that showed off her figure.

"Alas, merely the descendant of Terpsichore, the muse of dance. My real name is Emma," replied the young girl, "but you may call me Terpsichore while here on Mount Helicon... if you like." The young girl smiled flirtingly at Max and bowed. "Veena had a feeling you might come to see her at some point. She was in the old section of the historical library all day."

"And Veena is?" inquired Max as he did not recognize the name as one of the ancient Muses.

"Oh, sorry. Veena is a descendant of Clio, the muse of historical literature. As members of the new Circle, she figured you'd be looking for information on the magical prisons around the world, with the dark sorcerers on the move as they are. If you'll follow me, I'll take you to her."

"How did..." started Meagan, but Emma had already anticipated the question.

"There isn't much that gets past us. Especially Veena. She seems to think we are at the beginning of a new chapter in the history of this world. Come."

As Emma turned and walked toward the smooth wall, a section of it faded to reveal a hallway. Its path was seamless marble with columns on either side every ten feet. They walked about a hundred feet until the hall opened into a garden. The sun was bright, birds chirped, and the air had scents of every herb and flower imaginable. A slight breeze made the whole garden seem to come alive. In front of them, at the top of a small hill, Max saw a series of columns built in a circle with a domed roof. The temple stood twenty feet in diameter with a marble floor. Seated in its center at a finely crafted wooden table was a girl reading. A pile of scrolls were heaped on the table next to her.

The trio approached, led by Emma. Barely looking up from her parchment, the girl at the table said, "Took you long enough to get here. Or are you not worried about dark sorcerers, mythical creatures and the end of the world?"

With her brunette hair up in a librarian's bun, she appeared to be in her early twenties. Despite the reading glasses, she was still exceedingly attractive—but then all muses were said to be beautiful. She wore white robes and shuffled through the scrolls on the table in front of her.

Max approached. "Veena? Hi, I'm..."

"Max, Meagan and Hank," said the girl as she stood to address them. "Sorry for being so abrupt, but Malcolm is already combing the southern points of Greece in search of the tunnel Hercules used to enter the underworld."

"Does he know where to find the key?" asked Hank anxiously.

Veena turned sharply to look at Hank. "You have to understand, the keys to each prison are not like keys to a lock. They are items, spells and puzzles. According to some of Hades' last writings, the key to keeping Cerberus in the underworld was Hades' Helm of Darkness. So long as the helm remains in the underworld, Cerberus can never leave."

"Do you know where in the underworld it might be?" asked Max.

"No," answered Veena, "but as the underworld was the final resting place for many spirits, I would think Hades would have kept it someplace safe, most likely his fortress. I have never been to the underworld, so I can offer little advice in finding it.

However, it must be found and protected... but it can never leave the underworld."

"It seems the underworld needs a new Hades," offered Hank. "Know anyone looking for a job?"

Max didn't say anything, but the idea of remaining in the Underworld for the rest of his life with only Cerberus and the spirits of the dead to keep him company was not a pleasant one. However, the helm must be protected no matter what.

"Where's the entrance?" asked Max, breaking the awkward silence. "We need to beat Malcolm to the fortress."

Veena pulled out a crude map. "The entrance to Hades is in one of the sea caves beneath a series of cliffs in southern Greece. They are the Diros Caves and are a couple miles south of Areopolis."

"What about our friends?" interrupted Meagan. "They're going to Babylon to stop Frederick and Vincent from opening another prison. Taryn said a dragon was entombed there."

Veena laid down the map and searched through the pile of scrolls on the table until she discovered the correct one. She unrolled it and began to read. The others looked over her shoulder, but were unable to decipher its cuneiform text.

"Do Frederick and Vincent have the key?" asked Veena without looking up from the scroll.

"What is its key?" asked Meagan.

"The Tablets of Destiny. They are clay tablets written in the same cuneiform as this scroll. They contain many pieces of information including a spell to release Tiamat."

Veena looked up from the scroll, but saw no confirmation or acknowledgement. "Tiamat was imprisoned somewhere in Babylon beneath a temple. She has been described as both a dragon and a sea serpent, but I have no manner to confirm which is correct. Either way, the Tablets of Destiny were taken from Tiamat by Marduk, a powerful sorcerer of the time. With them, he was said to have ruled over the Babylonian gods. Before he died, he passed them on to one of his descendants. Over the centuries, they migrated west. Their last known sighting was in Petra, which is in present-day Jordan. You may want to tell your friends to start their search there. Petra was a center of commerce along many trade routes and was later controlled by the Roman Empire. Now they are just ancient ruins. If your friends can beat Frederick and Vincent to the key, they won't have to worry about Tiamat."

Max placed a hand on Meagan's shoulder. "Let Gollnick and the others know where we're headed and tell them where to find the tablets."

Meagan closed her eyes and placed a finger to her temple. After a few minutes of mental communication, she told Max, "I've informed Nick. He'll let the others know as soon as they get back from New York."

Max could tell from her voice she was concerned they had not yet returned. If they spent too much time in New York searching for Max, they could be in a lot of trouble. Max considered returning to New York to find their friends.

Max realized Meagan could tell what he was thinking. She wore a serious face and crossed her arms then shook her head no. Max reluctantly agreed and nodded without saying a word. They would be safe and return home soon, he hoped.

"Are there any mirrors in the Underworld we could use to get there?" asked Max after regaining his focus on the task at hand.

"If Malcolm is searching for the entrance to the Underworld, I would think it is safe to assume he's already tried that... and failed," said Veena as she raised an eyebrow. "And even if there was one, it would most likely be trapped. Hades was never fond of visitors. Well, unexpected ones, at any rate."

"Good point," replied Max.

Hank strained his neck a few times as he looked around. Max wasn't sure if he was enjoying the scenery or if he was anxious to get going. "What's the fastest way to the Diros Caves?" inquired Hank.

Veena appeared to think for a second. "As Malcolm is already in the area, the closest mirrors are probably already being watched. I would suggest flying. Pegasus was grazing the fields just outside the garden earlier today. He might still be there."

"Like Pegasus from Greek mythology?" inquired Meagan with wide eyes. "Wouldn't he be dead by now? He'd have to be thousands of years old."

"He is thousands of years old," replied Veena in a calm tone. "Pegasus is, like the creatures in the prisons, immortal. They can't be destroyed while in our world. Fortunately, not all of the creatures from the other realm are dangerous or evil. Some, such as Pegasus, are very gentle, but do be careful. If he doesn't know you he may put up a fight. Emma will lead you to him. I need to continue my research. I'll send word if I find any new information."

"One last question," said Max, pulling Veena aside to ask her something in private. "Hank told me a sorcerer named Nido brought me to him with instructions to deliver me to the new circle. This Nido said my real name is Chronos. But I don't know if we can trust him. Do you know where I can find him? Or who I am? Or why I can't remember my past? Anything?"

"I understand you've lost your memory," replied Veena in a sympathetic tone, "but other than what Hank has already told you, I have no record of you before Hank brought you to the new circle. I've heard of this Nido. He is an ally, but he can also be a little strange at times. As for Chronos and the other two immortals, that's just a legend after all. I'm afraid I can't tell you any more than you already know."

Max hung his head in disappointment as once again any information about his past was still unknown.

Emma had already started to lead Hank and Meagan away, but turned to get Max's attention. "Come with me, I'll lead you to Pegasus."

They followed a winding path through the gardens and around some ponds into a clearing. Emma's steps looked almost as if she were dancing along the path rather than walking, but then Max remembered her ancestor was the muse of dance. It would only be natural.

The grassy fields stretched out forever. Max thought to himself, *This is a beautiful place. It doesn't even feel like a mountaintop... but then magic can make things seem very different than reality.*

There, grazing at the edge of the field, stood a magnificent white-winged stallion, Pegasus. His head popped up as did his ears at the group's approach. Emma stepped forward and said a few calming words to him. He seemed to relax a little.

"Will he be able to carry all three of us?" asked Max while looking at the majestic creature.

"Not likely," replied Emma, "he is strong, but you're in a hurry and over such a distance it may be too much of a burden."

"Any chance you might have some saddlebags or maybe even a backpack?" asked Hank.

Max looked at Meagan with a furrowed brow, attempting to figure out Hank's meaning. Meagan returned the expression.

Emma paused a few seconds to think before answering. "We have collected many lost items from wayward travelers over the years. Let me see if I can find something." Emma then danced off down the path.

"I can cast a shrinking spell to reduce the two of you down to about six inches tall. I'll put you in the pack and carry you with me until we reach Diros."

Max and Meagan looked at each other wide eyed with concern.

"You're sure there's no other way?" asked Max. "I'm not wild about being six inches tall."

"It's only temporary," replied Hank. "The spell will wear off in a few hours. Or I can remove it if we get there sooner. You'll be perfectly safe."

Emma returned carrying a navy backpack that had seen better days, but it was still intact. She placed it gently in Hank's hand and bid them farewell, dancing away into the garden.

Hank turned to Max and Meagan who stood next to one another. "Hold hands," he instructed, and then cast his spell. *"Mino zor-ti redu."*

At first nothing happened, but gradually the world around Max started getting bigger and bigger until he and Meagan had to strain their necks to look up at Hank, towering above them.

One at a time Hank carefully placed Max and Meagan into the backpack and fastened the clasp so they wouldn't fall out.

For people who were six inches tall, the backpack was fairly roomy. After a few minutes of jostling around, they felt the winged stallion lift off. Max peered out the top of the pack to see the view as they ascended into the heavens.

"We're mini-sized, on a winged horse, headed to some sea caves. Never thought the day would end like this."

21 WE NEED A NEW PLAN

Taryn and Amber descended the stairs into the infirmary while supporting a wounded Cyrus between them. Cyrus held his left arm as he slumped down on one of the beds, his back to Gollnick and Elisa. He recoiled at the spike of pain when he rolled from his left side onto his back.

Elisa tottered over to him with bloodshot eyes, drooping eyelids and a face drained of all color. Her eyes traveled from Amber who stood at the head of his bed to Taryn at the foot. It took a few seconds before she asked, "Where's Max?"

"We weren't able to save him," replied Amber almost in tears. "He's still in New York."

Elisa's gaze fell. "That's not good."

"If Taryn is right about Vincent, then time is running out," said Cyrus still wincing. "We have reason to believe Max is safe for the moment. Right now, we need to make plans with or without him. Where's Meagan?"

"She's with Max," responded Gollnick.

Amber and Taryn turned wide eyed to look at him. Cyrus rolled over and almost spilled out of his bed. Everyone but Elisa looked at him as he rested in bed with his eyes shut. He opened them to find everyone's gaze upon him. "She just told me telepathically right before you arrived. Meagan, Max and Hank have gone to Greece to stop Malcolm from opening a second prison."

Amber's mouth hung open for a few seconds as she stared at the floor. When she returned her gaze to Gollnick, she asked, "How did Meagan find Max and Hank? I thought she was here with you."

"She was," answered Gollnick, "but when they contacted us through the library mirror, she left without telling us."

"We don't have time to waste worrying about them," Cyrus pointed out the obvious as he swung his legs down from the bed and sat on the edge facing Gollnick. "If Malcolm is going after a different prison, we would've had to split up anyway. Any chance we can lock Frederick and Malcolm in one of those prisons?"

"Unfortunately, no." Gollnick sat up a little straighter. "They're magical prisons. Each holds only one occupant. The laws of physics don't always apply." Gollnick paused and considered the question. "Moreover, what's already in the prison, is much worse than either Frederick or Malcolm. I've heard rumors. One creature was frozen as a stone statue for all eternity. Another was sentenced to a prison outside of the physical world... a prison in which height, width and depth have no meaning. They aren't jail cells, Cyrus. These prisons are meant to hold creatures of such power they can never be destroyed, merely contained."

"Thanks for that cheerful thought," Cyrus slouched.

Gollnick then began to fill the others in on what Meagan, Max and Hank had found at Mount Helicon and about the Tablets of Destiny possibly being somewhere in Petra, Jordan.

Cyrus tried getting out of bed, but Taryn and Amber stopped him.

"I'm fine," he complained. "Just patch up my arm good enough for me to fight. We can't waste any more time."

Taryn placed a firm hand on his left shoulder. "I'll work on a plan to find the Tablets. Ye just rest. It's going to take all three of us to pull this off."

Cyrus was reluctant to take orders from Taryn, but he had to admit a nap sounded good. He wanted to resist, but turned away with a scowl on his face instead.

After a few healing spells and an hour's rest, Cyrus was anxious to get going. He, Amber, Taryn and Elisa went to the library. Cyrus dashed over to a pile of maps he had seen on an earlier inspection. He dug through hundreds of maps until finding the one for which he was searching. "Okay, Petra is in present-day Jordan, and Babylon is in present-day Iraq. Not exactly the most calm parts of the world these days. There's always a skirmish, battle or war going on in the area. I doubt there'll be any useful mirrors in either place. We'll have to find one close by and walk to the ruins. There's a small town a mile north of Petra."

Taryn looked at the map. "We have no idea who we'll run into. We'll need to be battle-ready as soon as we step out of the mirror. Once we arrive, we'll take this road south to the Lion Temple. The Great Palace should be nearby. My guess is an artifact that powerful would have been taken to the leaders of Petra at that time. It's a place to start. Amber, if things get too out of control, whip up a sand storm. That should cover our presence."

"Sandstorm? Sure. Controlled sandstorm? That's another story," commented Amber. "Won't we have trouble understanding what people are saying? I'm not sure what language they speak, but I am sure I don't know it."

"We should probably avoid contact with the locals if possible," said Cyrus. "Frederick may have dark sorcerers among them waiting for us."

"I know a language spell we can use just in case," offered Taryn, "and oddly enough, the spell was created in ancient Babylon. It's called the 'Spell of Babble.' It will allow us to hear and speak the local language no matter where we are in the world."

Cyrus looked up from the map. "If we can get to the Tablets of Destiny before Frederick and Vincent, we won't need to worry about Babylon."

"And if we fail... or if... if they already have the tablets?" questioned Amber hesitantly.

"Then we're in for a battle," replied Cyrus. "Vincent's water automatons won't be very effective in the desert. It'll be too hot and dry. Taryn, what do you know about Frederick? Will he have anyone with him?"

"I don't know. Master Vincent didn't like him very much. If he does bring anyone," Taryn paused, "or anything along, it might be some lower level demons, ogres, or other creature he finds along the way."

"Wonderful," said Cyrus. "At least they'll stick out like a sore thumb. Unfortunately, we will too."

"I know a disguise spell," suggested Elisa. "It'll at least make your clothing stand out a little less."

"You're not coming with us?" inquired Amber with wide eyes and high-pitched voice.

"No, my dear, I'm too tired and weak. Gollnick can barely walk. We'd only slow you down. I'm afraid it's up to the three of you to stop Frederick... and if possible, free Vincent. Remember, Vincent is there against his will. If you can free him, he and his guards may be able to help you."

"Okay. Amber, I need you to go shopping," suggested Cyrus. "We're going to need some kites."

"Got it," replied Amber without hesitation.

Taryn regarded Cyrus with a furrowed brow. "Kites? We're not going to have time for fun. This is a race."

"Relax, I know what I'm doing," said Cyrus calmly. "Besides, I'm still not convinced we can trust you. While Amber is getting the kites, I want you to check in the library and on the internet, to see what you can find out about Petra and Marduk. My guess is this descendant probably hid the tablets somewhere so others wouldn't easily find them."

Taryn raised a single brow. She opened her mouth to speak, but paused and closed it again. Shaking her head, she turned and strode to the door. "And who said I trust ye?"

Cyrus then turned to Elisa. "Elisa, I know you're tired, but I need your help. My magic isn't up to par with the others yet. Are there any magical items here I can use to boost my powers?"

"Follow me," she said and led him out of the room. "Gollnick has a chamber of magical artifacts. Some are too dangerous, but I know a couple that may help."

When they reached the stairs, Elisa commanded, "Stairs, weapons vault." The stairs hesitated then lowered into a dark room.

They descended into the chamber. Torchlight gave the room an eerie feel as shadows danced across the red brick walls and cobblestoned floors. There were numerous crates, weapons racks and tables of all sorts. Elisa walked over to one table and picked up a ring etched with Celtic scrollwork and runes. After a brief examination, she handed it to Cyrus.

"What's this?" asked Cyrus studying it.

"It's a ring of magical protection. It should protect you from the light beams used by the water automatons."

As Cyrus studied the copper band, he remembered the ring he had taken off one of the security guards in Central Park. He pulled the object from his pocket and placed it on the table with some other trinkets.

Elisa made her way to the other side of the room with Cyrus close behind. When she stumbled, Cyrus caught her by the arm and helped her to her feet again.

"Are you alright?" asked Cyrus. "I should take you back to the infirmary."

She shook her head and started digging through a chest. She pulled out a bracer made of rawhide leather with ancient runes finely etched into the surface. She handed it to Cyrus who affixed it to his right forearm and placed the ring on his left index finger.

"This bracer can throw fireballs," said Elisa. "It's half of a pair, but the other one was lost long ago. Together they gave the wearer the power and control of a fire elemental sorcerer. Alone, it can still throw fireballs, just not very powerful ones. But I figure any offensive weapon at this point is better than none."

"Thanks for all your help. You should get some rest. We'll let you and Gollnick know before we leave," said Cyrus.

After a light supper, they all regrouped in the library. Gollnick could barely stand and Elisa still appeared ready to pass out. Elisa stepped forward and cast a spell, *"Viso mon-alt dolong."*

As they looked at one another, they could see their clothing had changed. They were each wearing light tan, long-sleeved shirts, long pants and sandals.

"It's a concealment spell," said Elisa. "If you need to travel to a different area of the world, cast the spell again and think of where you are going. It will make your clothing look a little more normal for that area of the world."

"Do you have everything you need?" asked Gollnick.

"Yes, mom and dad," answered Cyrus as he rolled his eyes. "We each have a backpack with water, food and a few other items should we need them. We could do with some more information about the Tablets of Destiny, but otherwise we're as ready as we're going to be."

Gollnick and Elisa both wished them luck then the trio turned to the mirror. *"Mirtor tolanga se-atum,"* Cyrus chanted.

The image in the mirror swirled. Cyrus looked back at the other two then reached his arm into the mirror and was pulled in. Taryn and Amber followed right behind.

22 PASSING THE TIME

The inside of the backpack was dim with only a hint of light from the opening at the top. Max and Meagan sat in the bottom of the pack pressed shoulder to shoulder with their backs to Hank who carried the pack. Their knees were scrunched up tight with minimal room to move. They had done their best to clean the pack out, but it still had the stench of rotted food.

"Do you think Hank can hear us in here?" inquired Max as he craned his neck.

"I doubt it," replied Meagan. "The wind rushing by would probably block out our voices, but if we need to get his attention, we could poke him through the fabric."

"That's okay," said Max. "Actually I just wanted to talk to you without Hank overhearing."

Meagan smiled as she attempted to adjust her position to face Max. "What about?"

"Amber."

Meagan's enthusiasm evaporated with her smile as she regained her original position. "Oh, what about Amber?" She turned her head away, giving Max a cold shoulder.

Max furrowed his brow. He was afraid he had offended her, but decided to press on.

"This isn't exactly easy to talk about, but... Well, she's kind of attractive and she seems really nice," said Max as he blushed a little.

"If you say so," commented Meagan somberly.

"Well, my memory obviously isn't up to date in a lot of areas," stated Max. "I was just wondering, what are the customary courtship practices these days?"

Meagan's head snapped around as her mouth dropped.

"Customary courtship practices?" repeated Meagan. "You mean you want to ask her for a date?"

"What does today's date have to do with courting?" asked Max.

Meagan stared at Max for a moment.

Max felt uncomfortable in the awkward silence. The lighting in the pack was poor, but he could see the confusion in Meagan's eyes as she tried to process the question.

"You really have been out of it for quite a while," she said. "A date is... well... a date. It's when two people spend time together, to get to know each other better."

"Oh, and that's called a date?" asked Max curiously.

"Yeah. Max, when was the last time you were on a date?"

Max had to think for a moment. There were several memories he was able to access, but none of them involved dating. "I'm not sure, there's still a lot I can't remember. I get images sometimes, but they're mostly of combat and magic. There is one of a woman's face that I do remember, but I don't know who she was."

"Was? She's dead now?" questioned Meagan.

"I would guess so," answered Max. "Most of my memories are from long ago. I mean like ancient times. I can't explain it. There are times when I think my memories are from multiple people I don't even know. My guess is she was from ancient Greece."

"Was she your girlfriend or wife?"

"I'm not sure, but I don't think so. Either way, that's in the distant past. How do I go about asking Amber for a date?"

Meagan didn't answer right away. He could see her study his face as if looking for something or trying to decide how to answer. She took in a deep breath then let out a sigh.

"Sometime when the two of you are alone, just ask her." suggested Meagan.

"Do I need to get her father's permission?"

"You are out of place and time," responded Meagan. "Maybe if you wanted to marry her, you might, but not for a date. Although, I wouldn't ask her when Cyrus is around. He seems very protective of her and I'm not sure how he would respond."

"But if it's against his wishes," started Max with a bit of concern, "wouldn't it be best to get his permission first? He is, after all, her older brother."

"In this day and age, it's her choice, not his."

"And what do people do on a date?"

"Uh... the standard date nowadays is dinner and a movie," replied Meagan, "but you can do other things too. There's theatre, opera, ballet, museums, dancing, maybe a romantic walk on the beach. Or things like miniature golf, bowling or shopping. Girls really like shopping."

Max tried to imagine doing each of those things with Amber, but realized that he didn't even know what some of those things meant. A walk on the beach seemed pointless to him. The sand would get everywhere and be uncomfortable. He wasn't sure, but he didn't think he knew how to dance. At least nothing like Terpsichore. The idea of miniature golf confused him. Perhaps people shrank down to six inches and used a three-inch golf club to play.

He regained his focus to realize that Meagan too had drifted off in thought as well. Her eyes had sunk to the left as she tilted her head. Max tried to get her attention. "Meagan?"

"What?" she asked in surprise.

"You were daydreaming," commented Max. "Are all of these things in Baltimore near the castle?"

"Some are, yes."

"Where should I take her first?" continued Max.

"'What do you like to do?"

"I don't know. As I said, most of what I remember is about magic and combat. Everything else seems like a jumbled mess of images."

"You'll just have to pick something and give it a try," suggested Meagan. "Maybe ask her what she likes to do. If you don't know if you'll like it, you'll just have to try everything until you decide what you do like."

"Thanks, Meagan. It's easy to talk to you."

Meagan's eyes brightened with a dazzling smile. A sudden shift in the wind direction jostled horse, rider and backpack. They each pitched forward knocking heads. Through the mild pain, they began to laugh.

"You're a good friend," he said as he helped her back to her seat. "Even if you are a vegetarian."

She smiled back. "Hey, it's healthier than the stuff you normally eat. You should give it a try sometime."

"What made you decide to be vegetarian?" asked Max.

"When I was little, before I came to Ravenicon Castle to study magic with Nick, my parents and I had been staying with a small group of druids out in California. They taught us about nature and the benefits of healthy eating. That plus my mother was already a vegetarian."

"Are your parents still in California?"

Meagan lowered her head as the light in her eyes dimmed. "No, they died in an attack. The dark sorcerers thought the druids possessed information on one of the prisons. Only three of us survived. The two druids brought me to Uncle Nick. I've been at the castle ever since."

"I'm sorry to hear about your parents," said Max as he bit his lip and looked away. The last thing he wanted to do was cause her to think about a painful memory.

"It was a few years ago, but I still miss them," Meagan said with a distant look in her eyes.

Max reached over and gave her a hug. Meagan's eyes grew wide as she looked sideways at him.

"What was that for?" she asked in surprise.

"You looked like you could use a hug and definitely needed some cheering up," replied Max.

Meagan smiled softly. "Thanks."

Another sudden shift in direction and speed jolted the occupants of the pack back to the here and now. The course correction indicated they were headed down. They arrived at the southern point of Greece near Areopolis. The Diros Caves, where Hercules found a way to the underworld, were a couple miles south. Hank removed Max and Meagan from the backpack and returned them to normal size.

"I hope the ride wasn't too rough," said Hank as he looked them over.

"The company made it enjoyable," said Meagan as she looked at Max.

"It wasn't bad, but I'm still confused about dating," replied Max.

Hank's eyes widened as he looked from Max to Meagan.

"I'm thinking about asking Amber for a date." Max sensed Hank's concern. The last thing he wanted was for word to get back to Amber or Gollnick that he was dating Meagan.

Max looked off into the starry sky. *I wonder if Malcolm is any closer to finding Hades than I am to understanding dating.*

23 PETRA

Just before dawn, Amber, Cyrus and Taryn made the mile-long journey south from the small Jordanian village to the northern outskirts of Petra, an abandoned city carved into the stone. The remains of temples, an aqueduct system, rooms carved into the hillside, a palace and even a roman amphitheater adorned its red desert cliffs. The temperature was cool, but rising quickly. It would soon be another scorching day in the sun.

Amber examined a map they had downloaded from the internet. "It looks like the standard tour starts at the southern end of Petra and follows a path northwest from there, but we're already on the northern end."

Taryn scanned the horizon. "If the Tablets of Destiny were so important, they were probably kept in the Great Temple. That's where we'll start our search."

Amber looked at the map for their destination. "According to this, once we reach the Lion Temple, The Great Temple of Petra should be just a little further southeast."

The Great Temple covered a large area, but was mostly in ruins now. When they arrived, they found themselves alone. If there had been any tours that day, they had not made it that far north yet. This would make their search much easier.

Amber looked around in despair as she shaded the sun from her eyes. "These ruins are thousands of years old. Chances aren't very good that the tablets are still here. Even if they were, they may have been smashed to dust hundreds of years ago or even taken by the Romans during their occupation of the area."

Taryn retorted, "If Marduk's descendants hid the tablets here at Petra, they would have made it difficult for anyone to find. It may even require the use of magic to locate 'em."

"I assure you the tablets are here at Petra, my children," came a voice from behind them.

They turned to find a tall, thin man in his late forties. He had a greying goatee and spoke with a German accent. He wiped the sweat from his brow and placed a tan hat on his bald head. Dressed in a safari-style outfit, his clothes didn't quite fit in with the local garb. With his right leg up on a rock in front, he leaned over and rested his right arm on his knee.

Cyrus stepped forward. "Who are you?"

"Ah, allow me to introduce myself," said the man as he straightened up and puffed out his chest to look more imposing. "I am Frederick von Woonst." As the man spoke, his accent got thicker. "I am in the service of master Malcolm. I assume you are the children of the new circle based in Baltimore, yes?"

"Maybe," replied Cyrus.

"Ah, I see that I am right," continued Frederick. "As we are obviously here for the same purpose I will kindly ask you to leave and allow me to complete my task of finding the Tablets of Destiny."

Cyrus shook his head. "I don't think so."

"I figured as much," said Frederick then pursed his lips. "I had hoped for a more peaceful resolution to this situation, but I would have been disappointed had you complied. I fear this leaves us at an impasse. I cannot allow you to find the tablets before me and I am sure you will not permit me to find them before you."

"Yes," said Cyrus, "but there's one thing you seemed to have overlooked. You are one, where we are three."

Frederick smiled. "Ah, my young friend, you should know in the practice of magic, things are not always as they seem."

With a snap of his fingers, they heard the approach of massive footfalls and the flap of leathery wings. A few seconds later, two huge ogres entered the palace area behind them and a manticore landed atop a boulder beside Frederick as its flapping wings kicked up a cloud of dust.

The ogres were each ten feet tall and very muscular. They wore no shirts, but had dark leather pants. Tribal tattoos covered the green skin of their upper arms and each carried a huge stone hammer with six-foot tree trunks for shafts. Their hair was shoulder length and drenched with sweat from the desert heat.

Their jutting jaws and dark scowls gave both monsters an ominous appearance.

The manticore looked like a male lion with its furry mane. But it also had huge dark bat-like wings and a tail with sharp spikes. It gave an angry roar and snarled like a lion.

"I'll allow the six of you to get acquainted while I continue my search." Frederick then turned to the manticore. "Don't kill them too quickly. Have some fun before you finish them off." He nodded to the members of the circle and walked away to the north around some large ruins.

"Amber, one of those dust storms we talked about would be really good right about now," called Cyrus. "See if you can slow down the two oafs over there. Taryn, see what you can do to help her out. Fry those guys if you have to. I'll deal with the beastie over here."

Amber raised her hands and within seconds had stirred up a sand storm. It engulfed the ogres who hopelessly swatted at the sand blowing in their faces. She stood like a statue with her eyes focused on the ogres. Taryn threw a fireball at the one, but missed as the blowing winds threw off her aim.

"I can't hit anythin' with the wind blowin'," Taryn called to Amber, "Can ye keep the storm on only one ogre at a time while I deal with the other one?"

"I'll see what I can do," replied Amber.

Holding her arms straight out, she concentrated solely on the ogre on the right. The second ogre was freed from the blowing winds. Its first move was to attack, but Taryn stepped in front of Amber.

The massive creature raised his hammer above his head and with little effort slammed it down as Taryn dove to the side at the last second. She quickly shot a fireball, hitting the ogre's left knee and searing its flesh. The creature let out a howl and swung its hammer up toward Taryn. Once again she dove out of the way.

Amber looked over her shoulder and saw Cyrus had engaged the manticore. The lion part alone would have been enough of a challenge, but the fact the thing could fly and had a spiked tail didn't help matters. "Where do they get creatures like this anyway?"

Using the bracer, Cyrus hurled a fireball. The creature leapt into the air to avoid it, then turned and dove at its attacker. A tuft of desert grass burst into flames. Cyrus did a quick tuck and rolled to his right as the creature landed where he previously stood. He snapped his head around to see the manticore's spiked tail pound into the sand next to his face. He rolled backward and recovered into a crouching stance to prepare for another pounce.

The creature trapped in Amber's sand storm screamed and swung its arms feverishly, attempting to free itself. It threw its huge hammer in Amber's direction, but just like Taryn's fireball, the blowing winds knocked it off course.

The ogre then picked up a nearby boulder and lobbed it at Amber. This time it only missed by ten feet. Amber could feel the stress build inside her, but continued to concentrate on her task. "Guys, I'm not going to be able to hold this thing much longer. His aim is getting better."

"Strengthen the storm," called Cyrus. "Keep him off balance. Whatever you have to do to keep him tied down until one of us can help."

Taryn continued to dodge blows and throw small fireballs at the opposing ogre. The creature randomly swung the hammer and its free arm in a desperate attempt to hit the fiery annoyance. Finally, it threw its massive hammer at Taryn who dodged once more. As she recovered, it grabbed her from behind with its massive arms. The creature squeezed her. Taryn's expression of pain soon turned to anger. Seconds later, Taryn burst into flames.

The ogre tried to hold on, but was forced to release her or be burned to a cinder.

Taryn dropped to her knees and looked at her hands. "How did that happen?"

Fearing for Taryn's safety, Amber called, "Cyrus, Taryn is on fire! She's burning up!"

Cyrus turned to look and drew in a sharp breath. From the corner of his eye he saw movement. The manticore's spiked tail caught him in the left side just below the rib cage and sent him flying. Cyrus crashed hard into a stone wall and collapsed to the ground.

Amber saw Cyrus was down. She was now alone with two ogres and a manticore. Her stress level had peaked. The dust storm intensified. The winds blew harder and faster, turning into a tornado and only continuing to increase. The ogre at the heart of the storm was lifted off the ground and thrown hundreds of feet into the air. There was no sign of where or if it ever landed. The other ogre and manticore tried to take cover behind the ruins.

Taryn called to Amber, but it sounded more like a bad phone connection as the noise from the rushing wind drowned out all sound. Amber looked around to find Taryn still aflame, but the fire streaked away from her like the tail of a comet.

"Amber, turn it down a notch. I can't get these flames under control."

Tears filled Amber's eyes. "I can't, I can't control it. It's too big."

"Shut it off then," yelled Taryn.

"I don't know how," said Amber, tears streaking her face.

Another voice called from behind her. "Amber, calm down," said Cyrus. "Close your eyes and focus on your breathing. Slow steady breaths."

Amber did as her brother instructed. She lowered her arms to her sides, closed her eyes and took slow steady breaths. In a minute, the tornado had died down to a dust storm again and continued to slow. Eventually the wind subsided to a gentle breeze.

A growl from the manticore quickly forced her eyes open once more. She looked around to find it cautiously stalking her.

A dazed ogre stood up from behind some of the ruins. Taryn's blaze had receded to just the flames engulfing her hands. Amber watched as Taryn grabbed the nearby ogre hammer and set its shaft ablaze. She followed with a spell, *"Mi-tro hercu amon."* Taryn lifted the huge fiery hammer and hurled it at the remaining ogre.

The monster caught only a brief glimpse of stone before it slammed him square in the chest. Ogre and hammer slammed against a wall of the ruins, bringing the disintegrating stone wall down upon the creature. Taryn collapsed to the ground looking pale faced and bleary eyed, drained of all strength. She crouched on her knees as she watched the flames around her hands die away. When Amber called to Taryn, she looked around in a daze.

The manticore kept its eyes on Amber as it stalked her from a distance. Cyrus, though conscious, was still lying face down on the ground.

The manticore continued to circle at a distance. Perhaps it wasn't sure if she could harm it or not. It bared its fangs and gave a low grumble showing its impatience. Small puffs of dust were kicked up with each step as it paced. When it finally took a single step toward Amber, she raised a hand in its direction, but did nothing else. The creature froze in mid-step like it expected Amber to do something.

Amber called out, "I can't risk another tornado. If I lose control again, I may not be able to stop it. What do I do?" But she received no response.

Using the same spell Taryn had cast to lift the hammer, *"Mitro hercu amon,"* Amber felt a reservoir of strength welling within her. She grabbed the nearest slab of stone—weighing over a ton— and hurled it at the manticore.

The creature easily dodged as the stone crashed into another nearby wall. The manticore continued to pace at a distance, stalking its prey.

Amber grabbed a second chunk of stone. This time her muscles trembled under the weight. Sweat beaded down the side of her face as she clenched her teeth and struggled to lift the boulder. The spell's effects were clearly short-lived, just as they had been for Taryn. She threw the stone and it landed half the distance between her and the manticore.

The creature took a cautious step forward and another, with no retaliation. It took a few more steps then launched itself through the air toward her. A few feet before it landed on a terribly weakened Amber, came a low whooshing sound. A fireball slammed into it sending it crashing to the ground and permeated the air with the scent of burnt flesh. She turned to see Cyrus, leaning against a large stone. He held his side with his left hand, the bracer strapped to his right forearm. He was weak, but alive.

The creature was burnt and angry as it regained its footing. It stood and turned toward Cyrus. It let out a loud roar, but before it could attack, another fireball hit it from the opposite direction. Amber turned again to see Taryn, still weakened and slumped against a boulder, had just thrown the other fireball.

Caught between two fire-crazed spellcasters, the creature lunged for Amber, the weakest of the three. Without a moment's pause, she cast the strength spell again. *"Mi-tro hercu amon."* Just as the manticore landed inches from her, Amber punched the creature on the side of the jaw, snapping its head right. It just stared at Taryn for a few seconds before collapsing to the ground.

Amber looked down at the motionless body for a second. As she raised her head, her gaze returned to Cyrus. Her eyelids drooped and she wavered side to side before collapsing next to the unconscious manticore.

The trio was nearly wiped out in a single confrontation with the minions of the German sorcerer who had already begun his search for the Tablets of Destiny.

The region was peaceful and spotted with vegetation. The nearby cliffs overlooked the blue waters of the Mediterranean. The smell of the sea and the sound of water lapping at the rocks seemed peaceful from the top of the cliffs. It was early morning and the sun was rising higher in the sky.

Max, Meagan and Hank had heard about the tours that took visitors on a set pattern through the caves, but rejected the idea. It was unlikely "Entrance to Hades" would be on the tour. There were other ways into the Diros Caves not on the maps. After an hour of searching, they found a local who was willing to rent them a rowboat.

As they floated round a corner and headed into the bay, Meagan asked, "Okay, so how do we figure out which cave entrance leads to the underworld? There must be hundreds of tunnels branching off in there."

Max noticed Hank's attention was far from the coastline. Turning to follow Hank's line of sight he asked, "Something out there?"

Hank paused a moment before replying, "I thought I saw a shark fin."

Meagan suggested, "Maybe it was just your imagination."

Max then got a drained look on his face. "Malcolm is looking for the Underworld, too. You don't think he would've brought the megalodon along?"

"Actually, I think that's exactly what he did. At least that's what I would've done if I were in his overpriced shoes."

Meagan's attention remained on the coastline. "I don't know what this megalodon is, but I don't really want to hang around long enough to find out. Can we just focus on the sea caves and find the right one? Maybe once we're inside, we'll be..." Meagan went silent and didn't finish her sentence. "Guys, I think it found us."

A few seconds later, Max felt fingertips press into the crown of his head, physically rotating it toward the caves. Hank's gaze followed. The shark fin appeared to be ten feet above the water's surface.

"How big is this thing?" asked Meagan.

"Not sure," replied Max. "We never had a chance to measure it. Probably the size of a whale, give or take."

Hank pointed toward the walkway to the tour entrance. "Malcolm."

Then Max noticed a single man of African origin stroll along the path. He stopped and spoke plain English.

"Ahoy. I brought you a little present," called Malcolm. "As much as it doesn't like me, it seems to like you even less. Oh, and be careful, it hasn't eaten in a few days. It normally likes whales, but I'm sure you'll do fine."

Malcolm laughed to himself as he continued to follow the path to the tour entrance and disappeared within.

Meagan turned to Hank. "Do you think he knows where he's going?"

"I'm not sure, but I figure he wants to get as far away from the megalodon as possible," replied Hank.

"He's going into the wrong cave entrance," interrupted Max.

Max was standing on the shore near a small village. It was late at night, but he could see someone holding a torch and climbing into a small rowboat. It was dark and there was a fog rolling in. As he stood there watching, he somehow knew it was Hercules. Max climbed into the boat with the Olympian hero. He sat at the front and took the torch as Hercules began to row. They skirted along the coast until arriving at the sea caves. They ducked in and out of a few before disappearing into the dark recesses.

The ceiling of the cave was very high at first, but lowered quickly as they floated along. Max asked, "Are you sure you know where you're going?"

Hercules chuckled, "Don't worry, old man. I know exactly where we're headed." Max looked down at his reflection in the water to see his grey hair and wrinkled face. He indeed was an old man.

About half an hour later they came upon a shore of red dirt. The cave ceiling was merely eight feet above them now. Hercules exited the boat and pulled out another unlit torch, lighting it from the one Max held.

"This is where you turn around, old man. Thanks for your help, but I go alone from here."

Hercules then pushed the boat away from the red shore. Max watched as the hero of myth went down a tunnel. A few seconds later, his torchlight faded from sight.

Max wasn't sure how he knew all of this. It was almost like he was there when it all happened, but how? How could he have been there? Was this another life he was remembering? But how could he recall it so clearly. Could he really be the immortal Chronos?

Max was jolted back to reality when Meagan grabbed him by the arm. "Max, row! That thing is coming back for another attack."

Max grabbed the closest oar and Hank rowed with the other. No matter how fast they paddled, Max knew there was no way they were going to outrun the megalodon this time.

Max pointed his hand toward the creature and concentrated. The water between them and the megalodon froze. The creature collided with the frozen mass, lifting it out of the water almost ten feet before both it and the chunk of ice crashed down with a splash. The megalodon could be seen under the water as it swerved around the frozen obstruction.

"I wish Sorrin was here," said Max. "He saved our butts last time against this monster."

As if on cue, the cry of a great eagle came from above. Max swung his head around to look skyward just as Sorrin dove toward the boat. It swooped low overhead then banked toward the megalodon.

The great maw of the enormous creature elevated out of the water toward the gryphon. Sorrin banked hard again and swooped around behind the giant sharklike sea creature. The megalodon splashed back down into the depths. A sharp turn underwater and the megalodon had given up on the tiny rowboat, now more interested in its old nemesis the gryphon. Its tail slammed into the side of the boat, rocking it violently, as if to say one final farewell. It then followed the gryphon back out to sea.

After a hasty recovery from almost tipping, Max and Hank continued to row toward the sea caves. Max could see in the distance the megalodon continued to lurch itself out of the water toward the swooping and swerving gryphon high above.

Hank placed his hand on Max's shoulder. "I'm sure Sorrin will be fine. He's definitely smarter than the big brute. He won't let that thing get him."

Max nodded and continued rowing.

As they neared the sea caves, Max pointed to their right. "There, that one. That's the one Hercules used to go to the underworld."

"Hercules? As in the son of Zeus? You're sure?" stammered Hank. "You'd better be right, Chronos, because we can't afford to be wrong here. Malcolm's already got a head start on us. We have to beat him to Hades' fortress."

"I'm not sure how, but I know this is the right cave," replied Max confidently.

"At this point, that works for me," continued Hank. "We have no idea where Malcolm went, so we might as well follow your instinct."

"Chronos?" questioned Meagan in a whisper.

Max winced, "I'll explain later."

Hank created some light, *"Alecto orona na-see."* A small orb hovered above them casting just enough light to see. Meagan sat at the front of the boat to guide them away from hidden rocks beneath the water. Max and Hank continued to row for almost half an hour with Max guiding their way like it was second nature.

They entered a small chamber full of densely packed stalagmites and stalactites. "This is it," said Max. "This is where

Hercules left the boat and headed down a tunnel toward the Underworld."

Hank sighed, "I'm sorry Max, but this is a dead end. I don't see a tunnel anywhere."

"It's been a few thousand years. Maybe the water levels have risen, but I'm sure it's here." Max stood and leaned against a stalagmite for support so the boat didn't tip. He peered behind other rock formations until he found his objective. "It's here, behind the rocks."

"How do you know all of this?" asked Meagan as she looked Max in the eyes.

"I'm not sure. It's almost like I'm remembering it, like I've been here before," replied Max.

"When we get back to the castle, we really need to work more on restoring your memory," said Meagan. "There must be other things we can try. You have something locked away inside your head. I'm not sure what, but we definitely need to find out what it is."

"Agreed, but for now it'll have to wait," said Hank.

The trio disembarked and crawled through a narrow opening. Behind the rocky façade was a tunnel. As the passage went on, the incline took them up twenty feet before leveling off. The chamber looked like a burial site with skulls littered around a floor of red dirt. On the other side of the chamber was another tunnel leading down. The descent was long and grueling. At one point, Meagan commented about reaching a depth of over five hundred feet.

An hour later, Max noticed the temperature had risen as he wiped sweat from his brow. He wasn't sure how far down they had gone or how far they had walked when the tunnel opened up into a large cavern. The ceiling here had risen up to almost thirty feet. The cavern seemed long, stretching out to the left and right for what seemed like forever.

As they started to cross, Meagan grabbed Max by the arm. "Stop!" she cried, her voice echoing through the cavern. "There's a deep crevice here. It looks like it goes on forever in both directions, just like the cavern."

Hank looked over the edge into the deep dark fissure. "No idea how deep it is, but it's a good hundred feet across. Any ideas?"

Max looked around and found an old gondola-looking craft off to their left. The wooden boat was intact, but wasn't much to look at. It was brown and made of a dark wood. A long single paddle lay on the ground nearby. He estimated the craft could hold five to six people at a time.

"Okay, this may be a wild guess," commented Max, "but I'm thinking this was Charon the boatman's... and this," Max pointed to the dark fissure, "must have been the river Styx. Unfortunately, it looks like it's either dried up or was diverted somewhere further upstream."

Meagan walked to the edge of the crevice and held her hand out over the deep opening. She closed her eyes and stood there for a minute. When she opened her eyes again, she looked to their left and said, "Yes. An earthquake. A long time ago, but the water is still nearby. The blockage is about two hundred feet upstream. Max, if we work together, we might be able to redirect the river and bring it back here."

Max was surprised by her suggestion, but figured it might be their only way to the other side. He joined Meagan near the edge of the crevice. He took her left hand in his right and they stood there together for several minutes. With their eyes closed, they each extended their free hand toward the water source. Max could hear earth shift and water flow. With a final loud crack, water began rushing into the cavern.

Hank watched wide eyed as the water once again flowed into the river Styx.

It had taken about ten minutes for the river to really regain its flow. The crevice was almost filled to the level where they stood.

Hank turned to look at the two teenagers. "I've seen some impressive things in my days, but bringing back the river Styx from the dead. That's a new twist."

Together the three of them maneuvered the gondola to the edge of the river and gently lowered it into the water, which was flowing rapidly at this point. Max knew the single paddle was not going to be enough.

"Get in," instructed Max. "I'll make sure we stay afloat and make it across the river safely."

Everyone piled into the boat which now appeared seaworthy even without Max's assistance. Once they pushed off from the shore, Max held his hand over the water and tried to guide the small craft to the other side.

Max struggled to keep the boat moving in the right direction, but it wasn't easy or fast.

They were only a quarter way across the hundred-foot girth. "The river is fighting me," said Max with a strain in his voice. "It's been magically protected. The spell is old and weak, but it's still fighting me. Hold onto something. This could be a bumpy ride! Hank, use the paddle to help steer us to the other side."

Meagan diverted a rock or two away from them so they didn't crash. After a half hour of struggle, they finally reached the other side.

As they climbed out of the boat, Max collapsed on the shore completely drained of strength. "I need a few minutes to catch my breath."

Seated by the riverbank, Max looked around. He estimated this part of the cavern was a mile or so downstream from where they'd started.

"Okay, we're on the Hades side of the river Styx. Any idea what Charon did with the silver coins he collected from the dead?" asked Hank.

"Sorry," replied Max, "I apparently never made it this far into the underworld."

Meagan scouted around while Max and Hank talked. "Hey guys, over here. It's the red dirt again. I'm guessing it'll lead us to the underworld."

Max and Hank quickly joined her and followed the red dirt. It travelled about fifty feet away from the river to a giant circular opening in the side of the cavern.

The entrance looked like it once may have been finely carved into the rock wall, but the details had long since faded. The effects of time had grown stalagmites and stalactites with an array of colors all around the edges of the circular opening with only small sections of the circle still visible. The red dirt path led right through the giant circular aperture. There was a sound coming from the other side, a heavy breathing.

As Max, Meagan and Hank approached the opening, a foul scent and loud thudding gave them cause for concern. They stopped twenty feet short of the giant breach just as a massive creature bounded up to the other side—it was Cerberus.

25 THE TABLETS OF DESTINY

Amber awoke to find her brother and Taryn standing over her with concerned looks which shifted to joy upon seeing her wake. They had just defeated two ogres and a manticore, but at great risk. They still needed to find the Tablets of Destiny and stop Frederick Von Woonst.

The sun was nearing midmorning and the temperature was rising.

Cyrus pulled her up to a sitting position and gave her a big hug. "Are you crazy?" he asked rhetorically. "You could have died. Never use that spell more than once."

"I didn't have many options at the time," said Amber. "What happened?"

"Taryn used a healing spell on you, otherwise you would've been dead," answered Cyrus.

"If I didn't, the manticore would've killed me anyway," responded Amber defensively.

"True enough," said Taryn, "but it was still a bad idea."

"Where is Frederick Von Woonst?" asked Amber trying to change the subject.

"Not exactly sure," answered Cyrus as he started looking around for the mysterious German. "Last I saw him, he was headed off to the northwest."

Amber stood up, still a little groggy, and noticed the bandages on Cyrus' left side. She looked him in the eyes with a sudden sting of concern. The spikes of a manticore were poisoned.

Cyrus read her eyes and smiled. "Taryn cast a spell to slow the poison. I'll be fine until we can get back to the castle and remove the poison properly. I've got at least a day or two before I die."

"That's not funny," said Amber protectively. "We need to get you back to the castle now."

"We need to stop Frederick before he finds the Tablets," corrected Cyrus.

"He'll be fine," interrupted Taryn, "We just need to keep an eye on 'im. If he passes out or gets a really high fever, then we'll need to find more immediate help. Until then, I think it best we find a way to stop Frederick."

Amber pulled out the map. "We're here at the palace. If Frederick headed off to the northwest, there are all sorts of temples, tombs and the Ad-Deir Monastery in that direction."

"If the tablets were that important and they're not here, the next logical place is in the monastery," suggested Cyrus. "We'll head in that direction. Keep your eyes open in case that wasn't his destination."

The trio headed off to the northwest at a fast walk. None of them had the strength to run at this point. They climbed over rubble and peeked into as many tombs and temples as possible on their way to the monastery, trying to catch a glimpse of Frederick in case he'd veered from the expected course.

As they approached the monastery, Taryn stooped to examine some footprints. "Someone came by this way recently," she said. "Whoever it was, they were alone."

They quickened their pace and arrived at the entrance to the monastery. Cyrus motioned for the other two to hang back a bit while he peered around the corner. Inside he saw Frederick Von Woonst casting a spell. Cyrus couldn't make out what spell he was using so he decided to wait and see what happened.

When Frederick finished and looked around, he seemed confused. Whatever he was trying to do, it didn't seem to be working. Without warning, Frederick cast a different spell and threw a fireball at the monastery's back wall in apparent frustration.

"Where are the blasted tablets?" He'd seemed so calm and collected at the palace, but now his emotions were getting the better of him.

Cyrus motioned for the other two to follow him back and away. Once they were at a safe distance to talk without being heard, he relayed what he had seen.

"Obviously Frederick doesn't know where they are either," said Cyrus. "If the tablets are here, then where are they? This is a big place. We could spend months looking for them."

Amber started scanning the map once again.

"We assumed they were religious artifacts and would be brought here to the monastery," commented Taryn, "but what if Marduk never told anyone what they were? Maybe they were just treated as valuables. They could've been taken to the Khazneh—also called the Treasury of Petra—though no treasure was ever found there. South of the palace is the Roman amphitheater and southeast of there is the treasury. It's quite a distance."

"Then the three of you had better start walking," said a voice from behind them. "As for me, I brought a camel. Too bad I only have the one." Frederick sat atop his desert mount. His steely glare was matched by his evil smile. No sooner did he speak than camel and rider were headed south.

"There's no way we're goin' to beat him to the treasury at this rate," commented Taryn.

"Don't be so sure." Cyrus smiled and looked to Amber. "You feel up to a little parasailing?"

Taryn looked confused. "We're in the middle of a desert. How do ye plan on sailin' anywhere?"

Amber returned her brother's smile as she opened her pack and took out three little bundles, then chanted to remove a previous spell. *"Dim-tar mai secul."*

The miniaturization spell was broken. The three bundles returned to their original size, but the trio's clothes returned to their normal appearance as well. The removal spell had undone more than just the size of their bundles. Cyrus and Amber started opening the packages, leaving one for Taryn. Taryn examined hers to find what looked like a small surfboard, a parachute and a pair of goggles. She raised an eyebrow. "What is this?"

"You have heard of parasailing? You cast a levitation spell on the board, Amber stirs up the wind and we're off. We should get to the treasury long before Frederick. Hurry up!"

Taryn did as instructed and with a little coaching, felt she had a decent understanding of the apparatus.

The boards were strapped to their feet and hovered a few feet off the sandy desert. They laid the parachute-looking kites out in front of them.

"I know you're tired, but you can do this." Cyrus was trying to be encouraging to his sister as he put his goggles in place, but he also knew that her control over the air was erratic at best.

Amber nodded and looked out across the desert. They could still see Frederick's dust trail. She took a deep breath and looked to the sky. The winds began picking up and soon the kites were aloft. With an abrupt tug, the winds carried the kites away with surfers pulled behind. The blowing dry desert air kicked up sand, making their approach look more like a sand storm.

Amber guided them by directing the wind to the south and then southeast. The parachutes caught the wind and pulled the trio across the desert as if surfing on water, but much drier. The levitation spells kept them from digging into the sand and wiping out.

The wind was at their backs and visibility poor, but that didn't prevent Cyrus from enjoying himself. He jumped over sand dunes and swerved around temples and ruins like a surfer tied to a parachute. He almost forgot about his injury until he swerved around a pillar and glanced against a stone wall. The pain shot back into his side, but it did little to dampen his spirits. He was having fun.

Taryn, on the other hand, was hanging on for dear life. She was a fire elemental sorceress. She had never been close enough to water to even think about surfing or sailing—let alone something as crazy as parasailing.

"Isn't this awesome?" Cyrus yelled to Taryn.

Practically spitting to clear her mouth, Taryn yelled, "I'd rather be eatin' haggis than all this sand."

Cyrus smiled even more when he noticed a camel and rider in the distance. He figured the rider had spotted the kites when he started urging his mount to go faster and faster. The rider raised a fist and let out what was probably a barely audible curse in German.

At the southern end of Petra, they navigated through a series of passageways in the rock to arrive at the Khazneh—the Treasury of Petra. In a way it looked similar to the monastery, but it was down in a narrow valley.

No sooner did they approach the entrance than they felt an invisible force send them flying backward about ten feet.

"Either Frederick found a way to get here before us or this place is magically protected," commented Cyrus.

"But there are tours here every week," added Amber. "I've never heard of anyone having problems getting in before. It must only be protected from sorcerers."

"There has to be a way in," said Taryn. "We just need to find it before Frederick gets here."

"What do we know about Marduk?" inquired Cyrus.

"He was a Babylonian sorcerer who defeated Tiamat," said Taryn. "Some thought of him as a creator god, others described him as a storm god. It was said he brought order out of chaos. After defeatin' Tiamat, he used the Tablets of Destiny to rule over the other gods or sorcerers. Accordin' to Veena, one of his descendants may have brought the tablets here to Petra to keep them out of the hands of those who would free Tiamat."

The three of them stood there thinking for a while until Cyrus had an idea.

"Amber, if this Marduk was a storm god, then maybe what we need is a storm. Maybe a bolt of lightning can break through the magical barrier," suggested Cyrus.

Amber looked concerned. "Cyrus, you know how I feel about that. Controlling the winds is one thing, but to intentionally stir up an electrical storm powerful enough to break through a magical barrier? Even if I could do it, I doubt I could control it. It could kill us just as easily as break through the barrier."

"It's a risk we'll have to take," said Cyrus. "Taryn, take cover."

Cyrus and Taryn went back down the rock passageway as Amber prepared. With her hands outstretched, she looked to the sky above. Smaller clouds coalesced, dark and menacing, like they were building up such power as to destroy the world. The winds began to blow fiercely, whipping through the passageway like a giant wind tunnel. Amber could barely maintain her balance.

A minute later, thunder and lightning cracked across the sky and rain poured down with such torrential force it made visibility difficult. Cyrus knew Amber was less than thirty feet from his position, but he could not see his sister. Taryn was next to him and he could barely see her.

Suddenly lightning hit the mountaintops near their position. The thunderous boom was deafening. Cyrus knew a storm of this power was already beyond Amber's control. She would not be able to stop it. He left his protective spot in the passageway and headed to where Amber was still standing.

"Amber, shut it down!" called Cyrus.

"I can't, it's too powerful," replied Amber.

Another lightning bolt struck, this time hitting the treasury. The barrier exploded in a wave of force so powerful it propelled both Amber and Cyrus backward like a couple of bowling pins. They bounced off the sandstone walls of the passage and collapsed to the ground.

Cyrus crawled over to Amber who was cringing in pain and holding her left wrist. He placed a gentle hand on her head. *"Semo nigh free,"* said Cyrus and Amber fell gently asleep.

No sooner did Amber fall asleep than the storm weakened. Within minutes it had dissipated and the sun shone.

Taryn rushed to Amber's side. "Is she okay?"

"I think she may have sprained her wrist, but she'll be alright. She's taking a little nap," replied Cyrus. "See what you can find inside. I'm not sure how far in it goes, so don't go too far ahead."

He then picked up Amber in his arms and carried her to the treasury's entrance. Setting her down under what little protection the structure provided, he gently brushed a few strands of wet hair from her face. *"Dim-tar mai secul,"* said Cyrus to remove the sleep spell.

Amber awoke groggily to see Cyrus hovering over her. "Did it work?"

"Yes," replied Cyrus happily. "Taryn is taking a look inside right now. Can you stand?"

Amber nodded as she slowly stood up, bracing herself against her brother.

"I'm tired. When we get back to the castle, I'm going to sleep for a week," commented Amber.

With assistance, the two of them made their way inside. The central room was similar to that of the monastery, a few alcoves, but for the most part just one big room. There appeared to be a smaller room at the back of the treasury, but it too was empty. The space was solid stone carved right into the side of the rock face. Taryn examined a section of wall along the back of the smaller room.

"Have you found anything?" inquired Cyrus.

"Yes and no," responded Taryn. "There obviously doesn't appear to be anythin' in the treasury, but for some reason this section of wall is botherin' me. It's almost like I'm drawn to it for some reason."

"I feel it too," added Cyrus. "Like a magical source is pulling me that way. Any chance of a secret passageway?"

"Something doesn't feel right," commented Amber. "If Marduk or his descendant was trying to hide the tablets, then why lead us right to them?"

"*Dim-tar mai secul,*" said Taryn casting a spell. The section of wall Taryn had been examining faded to reveal a stairway leading up.

As Taryn was about to take the first step up the stairs, Cyrus called, "Wait!" Taryn turned her head to look back at him. "It could be a trap," he cautioned.

"Or it could just be the magic from the tablets that we feel," added Taryn.

"Stand back," instructed Cyrus. After making sure Amber could stand on her own, Cyrus reached down and picked up a small stone from the floor and tossed it up the stairs. The stairs filled with a blast of electricity.

"Okay, trap," comment Taryn. "Thanks, but now how do we get to the tablets?"

"I'll leave that up to the two of you," said a voice from behind them.

Cyrus and Taryn turned around to find a soaking wet Frederick Von Woonst standing behind Amber with his left arm around her waist, his right holding a long blade at Amber's throat.

"I assume I have you to thank for the dousing I received on my way here, *Fraulein,*" said Frederick in his thick German accent, glancing sideways at Amber. "Sorry for the knife. I know it's a bit old school for sorcerers, but it's just as effective." Turning back to Cyrus and Taryn, he continued, "Well? Shall we proceed?"

"If you hurt her in any way, there will be no place on this planet where you can hide from me," said Cyrus with a look of pure hate.

"I would expect no less," replied Frederick.

"Any ideas how to get past the lightning?" asked Cyrus.

"No," said Frederick simply.

Cyrus just rolled his eyes then turned back to Taryn. "How about you? Any ideas?"

"I'm beginnin' to wonder if ye weren't on the right track," said Taryn. "What if this is just a trap and the tablets are somewhere else in the room?"

"Okay, where?" questioned Cyrus.

"Uh, guys," said Amber.

As the others turned to look at her, they realized that because of the knife at her throat, she was looking up. They all raised their line of sight up to see a circular opening in the ceiling a few feet in diameter.

Cyrus walked to the center of the room, and pointing at the ceiling, cast a spell. *"Alecto orona na-see."*

A little ball of light appeared right below the hole in the ceiling, but then was sucked up into the hole. The hole started to shimmer and a minute later, glowing symbols began to float downward. They floated around the room, but never up the stairs or out the main entrance. More and more symbols entered the room until they were everywhere.

Taryn attempted to touch one of them, but her hand passed right through it. After a few minutes, they stopped dropping and the glowing hole went dark.

"What are they?" inquired Frederick.

"Ancient cuneiform used in Babylon," replied Taryn.

Frederick's eyebrows scrunched together while his jaw hung loose. Amber and Cyrus looked equally confused.

"Are ye daft? They're words."

"And what do they say, Fraulein?" asked Frederick angrily.

"After defeatin' Tiamat, the other sorcerers gave Marduk fifty names," said Taryn. "I count fifty symbols. My guess is these symbols are his names."

"So, say his names, girl," ordered Frederick.

"I'm not sure if I remember them all, and I'm not sure I want to know what happens if I don't," replied Taryn.

Frederick tightened his grip around Amber, pushing the blade firm against her pale throat.

"Give it a try or this one dies," commanded Frederick.

Taryn looked around at the floating symbols. She knew she could not read cuneiform so she hoped just calling the names was good enough and that they didn't have to be in any particular order.

"Marduk," called Taryn loudly. Instantly one of the symbols disappeared. Taking this as a good sign, she continued. "Marukka." Another symbol disappeared. "Marutukku. Barashakushu."

Taryn continued to say the names of Marduk. She thought to herself, *I'm glad Cyrus had me research Marduk before comin' here.*

As she said the last name, the final symbol disappeared. The hole in the ceiling began to glow again and this time, a set of clay tablets began floating down from the hole. They were about two feet long and a foot across and covered in a layer of dust that must have collected for over a thousand years. The tablets gradually touched down on the stone floor and lay there in the center of the room.

Frederick and Amber backed out of the treasury and he instructed Taryn to carefully load the tablets into saddlebags on his camel and then return inside to Cyrus.

"If you don't want your friend here to die, don't follow me." He then looked up, and using the appropriate hand movements, cast a spell, *"Destra assor rectu."*

As Frederick finished the spell, the handcut stone of the treasury exploded, crashing down around the entrance. The stonework that had lasted thousands of years was destroyed in mere seconds by Frederick. Amber watched helplessly as her brother and Taryn were trapped within the now destroyed treasury.

"Semo nigh free," said Frederick casting a sleep spell on Amber. The last thing she saw was Frederick's smiling face.

The air was filled with dust and sand from the rubble of the collapse. Even as it began to settle, no light returned to the space. This alone was a bad sign for escape. Cyrus and Taryn were sealed in the rock tomb as firmly as the light was sealed out.

The creaking and crunching of rock made it obvious the rest of the chamber could come crashing down at any moment. Shifting the rubble at the entrance could loosen what little support was still left. The only remaining direction to go was through the electrified stairway.

Cyrus got to his feet first, casting a spell to create light once again. He then helped Taryn to her feet as well. After pointlessly dusting the dirt off his clothes, he looked around the room.

"Any suggestions?" inquired Cyrus. "That won't bring the room down on us?"

Taryn scanned the space for any new cracks or secret passages, but found none.

"That ceilin' won't last much longer and the only exit I see is the trapped stairway," replied Taryn.

Cyrus picked up a rock and approached the stairway. He threw it up the stairs and to his surprise there was no electrical discharge. He quickly turned to Taryn and asked, "Is it dead?"

Taryn also approached the stairway, but stopped short. Crouching down, she tried to look up the passage as best possible. There appeared to be another room at the top, but no sign of what had created the electrical discharge.

"Only one way to know for sure," replied Taryn.

Cyrus nodded then started up the stairs. To his relief there was no lightning. He continued upward to the room with Taryn following close behind. Upon entering, they discovered another empty room. However, to the one side, a spell was apparently failing. Another doorway flickered in and out of view.

Cyrus and Taryn looked at each other and then Cyrus led the way into the next room. Upon entering, they discovered why this was called the Treasury of Petra.

In the center of the room, a ray of light from a small shaft in the ceiling lit the chamber. Gold and jewels, weapons and shields, scrolls and relics all reflected with a warm glow.

As Taryn examined the treasure, Cyrus pondered the hole in the ceiling.

"How far up do you think the surface is?" he inquired of Taryn. "Do you think we could find some way to blast through and get out of here?"

"We should check out some of this stuff before we try blastin' our way out of here," said Taryn as she looked at him and then looked at the ceiling. "We could damage or destroy some or all of this..."

"I'm not concerned about treasure! He has my sister!" Cyrus cut her off abruptly.

Taryn set her jaw. "I realize that. But if we get out of here, how do ye suggest we follow?"

Cyrus opened his mouth, but didn't respond.

"We need another form of transportation. A mirror would be nice, but I doubt we'll find one of those here. Unfortunately, Frederick took our wind power and left me with a bag of hot air!"

"Sorry," said Cyrus as he lowered his gaze. "I was just concerned about Amber."

Taryn relaxed her posture a bit and began looking around the room. Cyrus picked up a golden sword, but realized it would not provide much help against a sorcerer.

"*Searo te-yon maku,*" said Taryn as she cast a spell while raising her left hand. She held her palm perpendicular to the floor as she turned around in place with her eyes closed.

"What are you doing?" inquired Cyrus.

Taryn didn't respond right away as she continued turning in place. After one complete revolution, she lowered her hand and replied, "Lookin' for magical energies. It seems whoever left this stuff here left a few other magical items in the treasury."

Taryn walked across the room and grabbed a spear then tossed it to Cyrus.

"Be careful with this," she said. "It radiates magic, but I have no idea what it does."

She continued to a table with a pile of scrolls and picked one up and carefully placed it in her backpack.

"What good will that do in a fight against a sorcerer?"

"Knowledge is power. Why do you think there are so many scrolls in here?" Taryn retorted.

In the far corner, she moved some gold treasure aside and grabbed a large rolled-up carpet. With the rug in one arm, she turned back to Cyrus.

"Okay, now we're ready to go."

"You wanted a piece of paper and a carpet?" asked Cyrus.

"The scroll is magical, most likely a spell book," replied Taryn. "The carpet is also magical and I'm hopin' for an Aladdin moment."

"Unless you know the proper way to undo the spell Frederick used to trap us here, I don't see any way out," said Cyrus.

"Not well enough to use in close quarters, but give yer new toy a try," suggested Taryn.

Cyrus looked at the spear then the ceiling.

"Well, here goes nothing," as he rammed the spear upward. The blade just made a loud clinking noise as it bounced off the ceiling.

"That worked really well," said Cyrus.

Clearly disappointed, Taryn looked at the spear and asked, "Is there any writin' on it?"

Cyrus examined the blade and hilt and found a small inscription he could not read. He crossed the room to Taryn and showed her the symbols.

"That's probably the one of the few cuneiform symbols I do recognize. It was the second symbol to disappear when I was callin' out Marduk's names. Call the name 'Marukka' when you use it again. See if that does anythin'."

"You do realize this makes me nervous," said Cyrus. "Using a magical weapon with no idea what it does, how to use it or how to control it?"

Taryn just smiled and walked to the other side of the room. "Why do ye think I gave it to ye?"

Cyrus sighed and lowered his head. "Thanks."

Once again, he raised the spear toward the ceiling and this time called, "Marukka." As it struck, the spearhead exploded, taking out a section of the ceiling with it. Cyrus dove out of the way as the ceiling caved in around the center of the room, burying much of the treasure in more rubble, but the small hole filled with light in the center of the room and was now large enough to climb through to the surface.

Cyrus noticed the spearhead was destroyed so he dropped it and started climbing up and out of the chamber. Once on the surface, he reached down for Taryn's hand. He felt instead the scratchy nap of the carpet, and had to use both hands to pull it out. Taryn then proceeded to climb out herself.

"Okay, now what?" asked Cyrus.

"Unroll the carpet," she instructed.

As he did so, Taryn proceeded to sit in the middle. It was about six feet across and ten feet long. It was obviously of ancient Mesopotamian origin based on its patterns.

Cyrus looked confused, but as Taryn did not seem to be moving from the center of the carpet, he slowly sat down next to her.

"Okay, now what?" he asked. "We sit here and wait for the sun to bake us alive?"

Taryn did not respond, she continued to sit there with her eyes closed. In the bright sunlight Cyrus had a momentary flash of how beautiful she was, her long bright red hair gently blowing in the light breeze. The smell of her perfume made him forget everything else that was going on. Then he reminded himself, *I still don't completely trust her.*

Suddenly, the carpet jerked and snapped Cyrus back to his senses. He looked around, realizing the carpet was no longer on the sandy desert. It was quickly rising in the late morning sun. Staying as far from the edge as he could, he stretched his neck to look over the side of the carpet to see they were heading east.

"It's a magic carpet... ye think about where ye want to go and it takes ye there!" stated Taryn smugly. "It'll take us to Babylon. Dependin' on how Frederick and Amber are travellin', we might even beat them there."

"Great," said Cyrus. "So we can get our butts kicked by Vincent's automatons. Even though you claim your master is doing this against his will, he's still working for the enemy."

26 CERBERUS AND THE UNDERWORLD

Max, Meagan and Hank stood before the entrance to Hades, but their way was blocked by the very creature they were there to prevent from escaping. Cerberus, the massive three-headed hellhound stood forty feet tall and crimson in color. Its dark red muscular flesh gave it more the appearance of a dragon's hide than a dog's coat. All six of its glowing yellow eyes stared at the three intruders. Each head bared razor-sharp teeth and its growls echoed throughout the cavern. The saliva dripping from its mouths sizzled as it hit the ground like acid eating through solid rock. Max figured it had not tasted human flesh in a very long time.

Hank's dim magical orb, hovering above their heads, provided the only light.

As the three of them stood there, Max noticed that no one took a step forward to challenge Cerberus. Their mission was to prevent Malcolm from getting Hades' Helm of Darkness from the Underworld fortress. Removing the helm would break the spell binding Cerberus, who would be free to roam the world—in which case there would be plenty of people for each of his three heads to devour.

"Maybe we should just wait and let Cerberus eat Malcolm," Hank suggested.

"Interesting thought," commented Max, "but my guess is Malcolm already has a plan for getting past that three-headed beast." The idea sounded good to all of them, but they couldn't underestimate Malcolm's desire to release Cerberus. If there was even a chance Malcolm could accomplish his goal, they had to be ready to stop him.

"I just wish we had a plan," added Meagan as she stared up at the enormous three-headed monster standing before them.

"He isn't coming out after us," said Hank, "which means the circular formation must be a boundary."

Max took this as a good sign for two reasons. First it meant they wouldn't get eaten, at least not yet; and second, it meant Malcolm had not yet removed the Helm of Darkness from the underworld.

"Any ideas?" inquired Max hopefully.

"In Greek mythology, there were two cases where someone went into the Underworld," said Meagan trying to remember her history lessons. "When Orpheus tried to save his wife he put Cerberus to sleep with music—and then used his music again to convince Hades to let her follow him home. The other time was one of Hercules' twelve labors. He was to capture Cerberus by overpowering the beast."

"I don't know about you two," responded Max, "but I'm pretty sure I'm not going to sing him to sleep... and there is no way I have a chance at overpowering him." The other two shook their heads offering no other ideas.

"We can't just wait for Malcolm," pointed out Hank. "We have a head start. We need to stay ahead of him if we're going to find the Helm of Darkness first."

"Well, if we can't put it to sleep and we can't overpower it, then we need to find another way," suggested Max.

Hank raised a single eyebrow. "What did you have in mind?"

"Do you know any illusion or shape-shifting spells?"

"Illusion and shape-shifting aren't my strengths when it comes to magic," admitted Hank with some reluctance, "but I might know one or two spells. Why?"

Max led them back to the river Styx so they were out of sight of Cerberus. "If I can make Cerberus believe I'm Hades, he might let us pass."

"There's just one problem with your plan, Max," said Hank. "We have no idea what Hades really looked like. Just crude paintings and sculptures, and we don't even know if any of them are accurate."

"Teach me the spell. I remember what Hades used to look like," said Max trying to relieve Hank's concerns about the plan.

"I can see his image in my mind. If I can duplicate it, we should be able to get past Cerberus."

Meagan had been keeping an eye out for the massive creature, but now snapped her attention to Max. "Hades lived thousands of years ago. He wasn't an immortal god, he was a sorcerer like us. What makes you think you know what he looked like?"

Hank pursed his lips and looked at the ground, then up to meet Max's eyes. "You haven't told her yet, have you?"

Max cocked his head and shrugged. "I'm still trying to deal with it myself."

"What?" demanded Meagan.

"We don't really have time for a long explanation," said Max. "It seems that my real name is Chronos. As in King of the Titans, Master of Time and one of the three sorcerers who created the magical barrier between our world and the Nightmare Realm. I'm one of the three immortals."

Meagan stared at Max wide eyed. "Oh... If anyone else would have told me that, I'd think they were nuts. Coming from you, that almost makes sense. I think."

Hank spent the next few minutes teaching Max the illusion spell. Confident in his ability to use the spell, he cast it on himself, *"Mimno alt tru-viso."* In a second his appearance changed. Max now had long black oily hair, a black beard and wore black robes. His evil sneer gave Meagan chills down her spine.

"This is just a basic illusion—if Cerberus touches you, it will break the spell," Hank warned.

The three of them approached the entrance to the Underworld again. Once more, Cerberus came running to the circular opening, roaring and growling. When he saw Hades though, the giant dog lowered his heads and backed away.

Max led the other two through the entrance. Cerberus tried to sniff at "Hades." Max put up his hand to pet the giant dog, but Hank cleared his throat as if to say, "Don't do it!"

Max quickly drew back his hand then continued with Hank and Meagan following close behind. Cerberus continued to sniff at the air, but made no attempt to follow the trio.

The Underworld appeared to be an enormous underground cavern. Its roof was so far up in the gloomy darkness it was impossible to tell how high it was. The ground was still covered in the red dirt they had been following since the sea caves. As they made their way across the wide open expanse, they noticed ghostly shapes fade in and out of existence. The figures seemed not to even notice them as they walked along.

Max cast the spell, *"Dim-tar mai secul."* When the illusion faded, he looked at the others. "Sorry, I couldn't stand walking around the underworld looking like that. It was kind of creepy."

They did their best to avoid walking through the ghosts, but every once in a while, it was unavoidable.

A ghost passed through Meagan and the cold sense of dread sent a shiver up her spine. "Oh! That was gross."

Max avoided another apparition. "These are the Fields of Asphodel, the land of the dead."

As they continued to walk with no sense of direction, they noticed three things on the horizon. Off to their right the cavern floor dropped out of sight into an enormous black pit. The ghostly apparitions seemed to avoid the pit. They made no attempt at getting closer to the blackness.

"That must be Tartarus," suggested Meagan, "the pit where evil souls were cast into for all eternity."

Off to their left they saw a lake. In its center was an island. At this distance, there was no way to tell how large the island might have been.

"That must be the Elysium Fields," suggested Hank, "the eternal home of all the heroic and good souls of virtue."

"And that must be Hades' fortress," indicated Max pointing directly ahead. The fortress was a tall black castle with many spires. It looked decrepit at this distance and did not improve as they got closer. The black surface made the castle difficult to see in the gloomy heights of the Underworld. Clad in black granite its gates were rotten and shredded... yet the ghosts did not approach it.

"Well, the doors are open, I guess we just walk on in," suggested Max.

The sheer size of the building was immense. Once they entered, they realized it was like the castle back in Baltimore. Corridors didn't always take you where you expected to go. It was a maze of rooms and hallways all made of the same black granite. There were torches that lit each hallway and room as they entered, obviously some leftover spell from when Hades really did live there.

They had wandered the fortress for an hour. As they rounded a corner, a smell partway between vomit and spoiled meat smacked them in the face. They realized they had entered what must have one time been the kitchen, but all of the food had rotted and decayed long ago, yet the stench remained. Thousands of years of mold and mildew covered surfaces with dark-colored stains in the food prep areas.

Meagan commented, "Ugh, no wonder they call this place the Underworld, the gross factor keeps rising."

They quickly left the room only to enter an enormous hall. At one end sat Hades' great throne, a second smaller one at its side. Black granite columns lined both sides. Paintings of Persephone hung interspersed with shields and swords. The floor was covered in thousands of years of dust and cobwebs. It had the dark and eerie feel of a haunted mansion—which in a way it was. Sitting on Hades' throne was a dome of black metal the size of a human head. Though everything else in the room was covered in dust, the helm was as bright and clean as the day it was made.

"You three are more trouble than you're worth," said an unexpected voice from behind. They turned in unison to see a middle-aged man of African descent standing in the doorway. The left sleeve of his black shirt was shredded near the elbow and blood streaks stained the left leg of his black pants. At this distance, they could see he had a little grey in his otherwise dark goatee. He leaned against the door with his right arm and wore an angry expression on his face.

"You've looked better," commented Hank, obviously happy to see Malcolm's discomfort.

"I don't know how you three got past Cerberus unscathed, but he obviously saw through my illusion of Hades," stated Malcolm angrily.

Meagan and Max tried to hold back a chuckle. Obviously Cerberus wasn't dumb enough to fall for the same trick twice. Max then realized it also meant they would need another way out.

"I'm taking the Helm of Darkness," demanded Malcolm. "If you want to live, you'll stay out of my way."

He started walking with a slight limp. He was making his way around the trio toward the throne when Hank moved to block his path. Malcolm stopped mid-stride with a look of disgust.

"You couldn't make this easy, could you?" snarled Malcolm. "You always have to stick your nose where it doesn't belong. I'd hoped spending time in my dungeon would have taught you a lesson. This time, there will be no dungeon. This time, none of you will leave here alive." Malcolm had a glint of satisfaction in his eyes as he smiled. "It's fitting you're already in the Underworld."

"I haven't picked out a room quite yet. I was thinking of this as more of a summer vacation spot," joked Hank.

"You avoided the megalodon," said Malcolm displeased. "Let's see how you do with my newest followers."

Max heard a fluttering of wings and looked up into the shadows of the high-vaulted ceiling. He could tell something was up there, but he couldn't make out what.

From behind one of the columns stepped the massive Minotaur. The creature stood nearly ten feet tall and carried a huge spiked club. It wore a leather loin cloth and was covered in short hair from head to hoof. His horns extended to either side of its bull head, almost two feet each. He snarled and growled and stomped his hoofs to display anger.

"I'll take care of Malcolm," ordered Hank. "You two get the Minotaur and the Harpies."

Max quickly looked to the ceiling again. If what he saw were the harpies, they were staying within the shadows waiting to strike. "Keep bull-boy busy, I'll see what I can do about Aello, Celaeno, and Ocypete," suggested Max to Meagan.

"Who?"

"The harpies," replied Max. "They're flying around up there." Max continued to strain his neck as he looked up. He ran between two columns to the wall and grabbed a pair of swords then returned to Meagan's side. He offered her one, but she refused. They stood back to back as she prepared to magically engage the Minotaur.

Max took a quick glance out of a barred window, catching a glimpse of the lake surrounding the Elysium Fields. Silently he concentrated on the water in the lake. Distracted, he didn't notice the buzz of wingbeats until one of the harpies dove at him. She was humanoid in form, a thin girl about Meagan's size, but with bird talons for hands and feet. Wings sprouted from her shoulder blades and fully extended, her wingspan must have been close to ten feet. She had feathers for hair, a nasty grin on her face and loose fitting rags for clothes.

She dove at Max, talons first, but met the blade of his sword before returning to the safety of the shadows. Two more dove at him from the opposite direction. He deflected the first attack with his other sword, but the second harpy raked him across the back. Max clenched his teeth and tried to bury the pain coursing through his torn muscles.

Meagan attempted to stay focused on the Minotaur's charge. She threw her hands up and a wall of black granite shot up from the floor, just in time for the Minotaur to slam into it. Cracks like a spider web formed on Meagan's side of the wall. If the Minotaur had been up to full speed, he might have broken straight through.

Dark brown, fur-covered hands became visible on either side of the wall. The upper half of the granite barrier creaked and cracked until it was ripped away from the lower half. The remaining wall segment crumbled at the point of impact. The Minotaur casually tossed the wall section aside and stepped closer.

Meagan noticed its bloody nose and broken horn... and the even angrier look on its face. With clenched fists she coaxed the granite floor to reach up, encasing the Minotaur's feet in blocks of black stone.

He looked down and pounded the floor with his fists. He reared back his head and let out the yell of an angry bull with steam emanating from his nostrils. Returning his gaze to Meagan, he quickly grabbed for her, but she retreated into Max, slamming into his already injured back. Max staggered, but regained his balance.

"Sorry," she said.

Two more harpies swooped down at Max and Meagan this time. Meagan threw her arms up over her head and two pillars of granite formed up out of the floor, one to either side of her and Max. The two harpies bounced from the granite and flew off again. As Meagan lowered her arms, the granite returned to the floor.

Hank was having his own issues.

"Magna fir-tor loma," commanded Malcolm. As he flicked his right hand a fireball appeared in his palm. Hank narrowly dodged the fiery blast by diving behind a pillar. The heat from the fireball scorched the black granite column.

"Magna fir-tor loma," Hank cast his own spell from the safety of the pillar. He lobbed the fireball toward where Malcolm had been, but as soon as he threw it, he saw the dark sorcerer making a mad dash for the helm.

"Stop him!" Hank called to Max.

Max turned. "Where's that blasted ice?"

Without turning around, Meagan questioned, "What?"

Malcolm was nearing the throne, but he never made it to the helm. With a loud crack and crumbling of granite, a large chunk of ice flew in through the wall and crashed on top of the throne. The impact sent Malcolm flying backward and landing on his already injured left arm. Malcolm let out a silent curse and glared at Max with clenched teeth.

"I pulled that ice from the lake, but it took longer than I expected to get here."

Struggling to stand, a fireball exploded at Malcolm's feet, knocking him back down again.

Hank already had another ball of flame in hand and was preparing to throw when a harpy swooped down from the shadows, grabbing him by the arm and lifting him into the air. The sudden shock and pain of being lifted by his arm caused the fireball to fall from his loose hand. It harmlessly exploded on the floor below. She lifted Hank halfway to the ceiling as he flailed his free arm at the winged creature. With a good swat from Hank, it dropped him. He landed in a crumpled pile on the granite floor and the others heard a crunch. Max knew it was not the granite that had crunched. It was the sound of bone breaking on stone. Hank curled into a ball, clinging to his right leg.

Malcolm stood and started limping toward Hank, another fireball held in his right hand.

Max's thoughts whirred as he tried to assess the situation. Hank was obviously in trouble, Meagan was having difficulty keeping the Minotaur at bay and he wasn't doing much better against the harpies. The helm was lying on the floor next to the broken throne, but there was no way Max could get to it without leaving Meagan alone to fight both the harpies and the Minotaur.

In a desperate move, he threw one of the swords at Malcolm. While the sword did hit him, it merely glanced off his injured arm. Malcolm turned to Max with anger in his eyes.

"You are the most bothersome, insolent and aggravating whelp I've ever met." Malcolm then threw the fireball at Max.

For a split second Max thought, *Good, Max. Save Hank only to get yourself killed.*

With a rumble, the floor in front of Max shot up in another column just before the fireball could reach him. It detonated against the surprise column. "You need to work on your defense," Meagan teased.

"Look out!" yelled Max back at her.

The Minotaur grabbed for Meagan's left arm. The pressure from his grip forced her to one knee as he clamped down, almost breaking it. She held in a scream of pain as she averted her gaze from the Minotaur's foul breath.

Meagan clenched her free fist and swung it in an uppercut. As she did, a narrow stone pillar shot up out of the floor and slammed into the Minotaur's jaw. It released Meagan, stunned and staggering backward. The monster's head shook slightly and he glared and growled through clenched teeth.

Tired of the battle, Meagan clapped her hands together and then quickly spread them apart. The floor beneath the Minotaur opened into a gaping hole. The surprised Minotaur fell to the next level below and landed with a loud thud. With a motion of her hands, the hole in the floor then closed.

"The Minotaur is unavailable right now, he had to drop out for a while," she said as she turned to help Max.

Max peered around the column that had blocked Malcolm's fireball to find the dark sorcerer was nowhere to be seen. He quickly looked to the throne, but Hades' Helm of Darkness was still there among the ice fragments.

"Get the helm and Hank and get out of here," instructed Max. "I'll take care of the harpies." As he said it he was still wondering how he was actually going to accomplish his task.

Meagan opened her mouth to protest, but Max emphasized his instructions this time, "Go!"

Reluctantly Meagan made her way to the throne with Max following close behind to give her protection. Max kept his eyes and sword pointed upward in anticipation.

The harpy screams could be heard from above as they approached the throne. Meagan spotted it amongst the ice fragments and broken throne. As she reached for it, her hand hit something solid. "Max, it's encased in ice. I'd need a chisel to break it free."

Max took a quick glance and waved his hand. The ice surrounding the helm instantly released its prize and it splashed into a puddle of water. Meagan reached in and picked up the helm still beaded with droplets of water. The two of them then ran to Hank's side. Hank was still lying on the floor clinging to his right leg.

"It's broken," he said with a strain of pain in his voice. "Go on without me, I'll only slow you down."

"Not gonna happen," replied Max. Then looking to Meagan, he asked, "Do you know a levitation spell? We can float him out of here."

Meagan nodded, *"Levas mon see-tor."* Hank gradually raised inch by inch until he floated two feet off the ground, his clothing drooping from his elevated body.

"Get him out of here," said Max. "I'll take care of the harpies and be right behind you."

Meagan wanted to argue again, but Max had a determined look in his eyes. There was no dissuading him. She leaned over and gently kissed him on the cheek. He snapped his head around to look at her wide eyed and saw the concern in her eyes.

Meagan then began pushing Hank on the shoulders as he continued to float above the floor. Better than a stretcher, there were no bumps or bounces along the way. They quickly exited the room the same way they'd come in.

"Watch out for Malcolm," Hank called back to Max. "He hasn't given up yet."

Max returned to the center of the room and looked to the darkened ceiling.

"Okay, Aello, Calaeno and Ocypete. I'm here. Let's get this over with!"

The three harpies all screeched and squealed as they came diving out of the shadows. Max dropped the remaining sword to the floor and wrapped his arms around himself, forming an energy shield. He cast a spell, *"Crono mon tra-ton,"* and flung his arms wide open. The energy shield expanded at blinding speed, knocking his attackers in all directions. Aello crashed into the pile of ice still covering most of the throne. Celaeno slammed into a pillar that was already in bad shape which shattered under the impact. The debris came crashing down upon the harpy. Ocypete was blown out one of the windows with bars on it. The force destroyed the bars and the framing around the window.

Max collapsed in fatigue, but knew the harpies would not bother him again for some time. After a few minutes to catch his breath, he slowly stood and staggered out of the room. *Note to self. Use that spell as a last resort.*

27 BABYLON AND THE RETURN OF TIAMAT

The carpet ride from Petra to Babylon was fairly uneventful and very quiet as neither Cyrus nor Taryn made any attempt at conversation. Neither one wanted to completely trust the other. Cyrus was focused on Amber, but Taryn had started feeling concern for Cyrus, especially now that he was injured and poisoned.

Before they landed near ancient Babylon, Taryn offered, "Let me see yer wound. I need to make sure it isn't infected."

"I'm fine," replied Cyrus, pushing her hand away from his side.

"Ye pig-headed centaur," exclaimed Taryn. "I just saved your life by slowin' the poison, I saved yer sister after she cast that strength spell twice and I found this magic carpet in order to get us to Babylon before Frederick and Amber," she spat indignantly, "and ye still don't trust me?"

"I'm sorry, but you did attack us in Miami," pointed out Cyrus.

"I told ye, we were bein' watched," said Taryn. "It had to be convincin'. Besides, now that Frederick knows I'm helping ye, it won't be long before Malcolm finds out and then Master Vincent will be in even greater danger."

"Yeah, that's right," said Cyrus a little angrily, "the guy who's trying to open the Babylonian prison."

"Not by choice."

"So you say."

"I should have left ye buried in that treasury!" screamed Taryn.

"I should..." started Cyrus, but was abruptly stopped when Taryn raised her hand, palm facing Cyrus and placed it a few inches from his face. Confused by the gesture, Cyrus refrained from any further conversation.

A few minutes later, the carpet landed about a half-mile south of the ancient palace in Babylon. To the south of their position, they could see the remains of the Etemenanki Ziggurat. The sun was high in the midday sky. There was a gentle breeze, but the intense heat from the sun made even a gentle breeze feel hotter.

After disembarking from the carpet, Taryn turned back toward it. *"Mino zor-ti redu,"* said Taryn. The carpet shrank down to the size of a napkin. Taryn gently rolled it up and placed it in her backpack. She then turned toward Cyrus who was scanning the northern and southern horizons.

"Any sign of them?" she asked.

"No."

"She'll be alright," said Taryn as she placed a hand on his shoulder.

Cyrus said nothing, but gave a little sigh.

"So, the palace or the ziggurat?" asked Taryn.

Cyrus looked from one to the other then decided, "The ziggurat. At the top of the Etemenanki Ziggurat there was once a temple to Marduk. Since he was the one who imprisoned Tiamat, I'd say that would be the place to start."

Cyrus immediately started walking south toward the ruins with Taryn following close behind. About halfway, Cyrus stumbled and fell to one knee. Taryn could see sweat running down his face and figured it was the heat, but then feeling his forehead, realized he was burning up.

"Cyrus, how are you feelin'?"

"Apparently your spell to slow the poison didn't work," replied Cyrus.

"It worked, otherwise ye would've been dead over an hour ago," replied Taryn. "It must be this heat. The poison is still movin' through yer system. We need to get ye back to the castle for some help."

"No. They still have Amber and I won't leave her here alone," stated Cyrus as Taryn helped him to his feet again.

"Ye really are a pig-headed centaur," said Taryn more calmly this time. She then re-cast the spell to slow the poison, *"Sempi tro-serp amond."* Within seconds, Taryn could see Cyrus relaxing a little. "That won't last long. Each time I use that spell it will wear off faster. Eventually, it won't work at all."

Cyrus nodded his understanding and motioned for them to move on.

All that remained of the ziggurat was the square-shaped base. It was mostly in ruins now. Few features of the great pyramid still remained. As they approached, they spotted two of Vincent's guards patrolling the ruins. A shot from one of the automaton's rings blasted the sand nearby.

Cyrus called to Taryn, "Follow me," as he charged the ziggurat. Taryn hesitated then followed.

The guards continued to fire at them, but missed at such a distance. As they neared the ruins, a blast finally hit Cyrus, but deflected off him and hit the sand nearby. He looked down at the ring Elisa had given him and smiled.

With a furrowed brow, Taryn looked at the charred depression where the blast hit the sand. She didn't have time to question, but continued to follow Cyrus.

Once they reached their destination, they took cover behind a mound of dirt and sand.

A guard leapt over their cover and landed on Taryn. The automaton was in his black security guard uniform and black sunglasses with a black cap.

Cyrus thought to himself, *If these guys are made of water, they've got to be boiling wearing all black like that.* He raised his right arm and lobbed a fireball at Taryn and the guard. It hit them about shoulder height. The guard exploded on impact, instantly turning to steam. The fire seemed to have little effect on Taryn other than making her mad.

"Ye did that intentionally!" she screamed.

"What?" said Cyrus defensively. "You're a fire elemental sorceress, it didn't hurt you."

"And because I'm a fire elemental sorceress, that makes it okay to just throw fireballs at me?" replied Taryn.

"He was attacking you and he had a ring," said Cyrus still on the defensive. "He could have hurt you or even stunned you!"

"Speakin' of which, how did ye deflect those blasts earlier?" demanded Taryn. "Somethin' else ye didn't trust me with knowin'?"

"You two argue like an old married couple," said a voice from above them. They looked up to the top of the mound to find Frederick holding Amber gagged, hands tied behind her back. On either side of them were four more automatons all with rings pointed at Cyrus and Taryn. "And if you were trying to sneak up on us, you did a very poor job of it."

Cyrus immediately held up his right arm as if he were about to throw another fireball.

"Cyrus, my boy," said Frederick trying to sound pleasant with his German accent, "you may have found a way to protect yourself from the rings of Vincent's automatons, but your friend and sister are not protected. I suggest you surrender now. I'd really hate for this to get unpleasant."

Cyrus and Taryn looked at each other in disgust then raised their hands above their heads as a sign of surrender.

After stripping their gear, they were bound and gagged like Amber. Automatons led Cyrus and Taryn onto the remains of the great ziggurat. Near the center stood two more guards, on either side of a freshly dug hole about twenty feet deep. They peered down to find a ladder leading into a secret chamber. The warm glow of torchlight flickered below. The three of them were carefully helped down the ladder. The room was square and in fair condition, protected over the years inside the ancient ruins. One wall held a doorway with a set of stone stairs leading down.

Frederick led the way, followed by Cyrus, Amber, Taryn and four guards. As they descended, the walls became smoother and in better condition. Obviously this part of the ziggurat was rarely seen even in ancient times. They descended more than a hundred feet until arriving in a room over a hundred feet long.

There at the bottom of the stairs was Vincent still in his business outfit minus his tie and jacket. His vest hung open and he looked like he needed a shave as he leaned on his left hand against the wall, his back to the stairs.

Cyrus scanned the room to find one more guard standing with Vincent. Down the length of the room were dark spots on the floor. Obviously something had happened to the other guards who had been there. The floor was covered in a layer of dust, but otherwise in good shape. Torches lined the wall on either side every ten feet for the length of the room.

Frederick approached Vincent with his three captives in tow.

"We have guests," announced Frederick, "and I think you know one of them. The redhead was until recently your apprentice, I believe."

Vincent turned his head toward Taryn, but gave no indication of acknowledgment or recognition. Cyrus guessed Frederick already suspected Vincent of betrayal.

"We have more important matters than your guests," said Vincent with disgust.

Frederick glanced from Taryn to Vincent. He continued to watch Vincent as he took a few steps further into the room.

"Where's Malcolm?" asked Frederick smugly. "I'd like to present him with my prize," he said indicating the teenagers.

"He left yesterday on an urgent matter," replied Vincent. "Something about information on another prison. His instructions, before he left, were to release Tiamat before midnight or we're both dead." Vincent looked over his shoulder at Frederick as he spoke. Frederick gave no indication of concern.

"I count six spots on the floor. I take it your automatons didn't fare so well?" asked Frederick as he looked down the length of the room.

"No, and what's puzzling is they just exploded for no reason," said Vincent studying the situation. "I've detected protective magic in the room, but I can't seem to identify what kind. There isn't even enough water nearby for me to strengthen or recreate my automatons. With the five here and the two up top, that's all I have left."

Frederick looked at the captives then returned his gaze to Vincent. "Perhaps it's a good thing I brought some more volunteers." Vincent snapped his head toward Frederick who merely smiled.

"Ah, so the stoic Vincent does have feelings," said Frederick gloating. "My intention was not to sacrifice them, but merely present them to Malcolm. However, if it is a matter of life and death for us, I would rather risk their lives first."

"I will not permit it and as the automatons obey me..." started Vincent.

"Not so fast, my friend," interrupted Frederick as he held up an amulet. A gold disk with a coiled snake dangled from a gold chain in Frederick's right hand.

Vincent said nothing, but just stared at the amulet. Frederick continued to smile as he placed the chain around his neck. The others realized the amulet obviously held some significance for Vincent. Frederick then turned to the three captives.

"So, who would like to go first? Oh, don't worry; you'll all get a chance."

Vincent said nothing, he just stared down the length of the room steaming.

Gagged and unable to speak, Cyrus took a step forward.

"Wait. Send the traitor of an apprentice first as punishment for leaving," suggested Vincent.

Frederick looked at Vincent for a moment, fondling the amulet around his neck. "Send the redhead," he ordered.

"Release her bonds first," interjected Vincent. "She may need what magic she has to make it through."

Frederick pulled a knife from his belt and walked around behind Amber. Placing the knife at her throat, he instructed the guard to release Taryn. "Try anything funny and she dies. Do we understand one another?"

Taryn nodded. As she turned to face Vincent, she caught Cyrus' gaze and winked at him. She then faced Vincent, but said nothing. After only a second's hesitation she started walking toward the other end of the room.

"The automatons failed because of the temperature," she called back. "It has to be over two hundred degrees and risin'. My fire elemental powers are protectin' me so far."

As she continued forward, the temperature increased further. She hurried her pace, hoping that reaching the other end of the room would alleviate the elevated heat. At the far side however, the temperature was near two hundred and fifty degrees, but it did not subside.

She could see a stone door inset into the wall with no visible hinges or lock. On either side of it stood short, square pillars about three feet tall. She tried pressing on the stone, but it did not budge.

"I'm startin' to feel the effects of the heat," said Taryn as she looked back to the others. "I won't be able to take much more of this. The door won't open and I don't see a lock. Any ideas?"

"Are there any symbols or writing on the walls?" asked Vincent.

"The pillars each have a symbol on them, but I have no idea what it means. I'm not familiar with this writin'." The heat started to affect her vision.

"Describe the symbols," called Vincent.

Cyrus quietly struggled with his bonds. He watched and listened as Taryn described each of the two symbols to Vincent.

"The symbol on your left is for Marduk. The symbol on your right is for Tiamat. Is there any other writing?" inquired Vincent.

"Yeah, but it's in cuneiform. I've no idea what it says. There are bowl-like indentations on top of each pillar," responded Taryn.

Cyrus tried saying something through his gag, but it came out as a mumble. One of the guards punched him in the stomach to keep him quiet.

Frederick admonished the guard then said, "Perhaps I should put these two to sleep. That way they won't bother us for now."

Vincent stopped him as he was about to cast the sleep spell, "Wait, undo his gag."

"What? Why?" questioned Frederick with a single raised brow.

"Just do it," ordered Vincent.

Frederick reluctantly did as Vincent had suggested, but placed his knife at Cyrus' throat. "Cast a spell and you'll be dead before you finish."

Cyrus shot Frederick a nasty look, but then turned his attention to Vincent. "The tablets, maybe there's something in the tablets explaining what to do."

"Nonsense, the tablets contain a spell to release Tiamat," replied Frederick.

"Not true," corrected Vincent. "According to myth, the tablets were created for seeing the future. They are also a spell book that contains the necessary incantation to release Tiamat, but there is other information on them as well. Give them to me."

Frederick's eyes darted around as he considered the instructions. Cyrus could tell the German was growing more and more uncomfortable with the situation. If Vincent broke free of the amulet's power, Frederick wouldn't stand a chance against them and the automatons.

Frederick removed the backpack containing the tablets from his shoulder, but hesitated, holding Vincent's gaze. Wordlessly he handed the pack to Vincent who quickly took the tablets and starting reading.

At the other end of the room, the intense heat was getting to Taryn. She dropped to one knee, resting her right arm on the pillar of Marduk. "Guys, I could really use some help here. What do I need to do?"

"Hurry up, she's dying over there," insisted Cyrus. "If you can't figure it out, have her come back and try again later."

"No good," replied Taryn. "I don't have the strength to make it back at this point. If I don't move on soon, I'll die here."

"What about a cold spell? Or Amber could stir up the wind," suggested Cyrus.

"I suggest you save your strength," said Frederick, "because if the redhead doesn't make it... you're next. Oh, and at that temperature, a cold spell would just make a lot of steam. And stirring up the wind would roast her like an oven's fan."

"It's a lock!" shouted Vincent looking up from the tablets. "The two pillars are a lock. You must place water into one of them—but there's a catch. You can only try one pillar. If you choose wrong, the heat will become so intense not even a master fire sorcerer could withstand it."

"And where exactly do I get water?" questioned Taryn. "Even your automatons couldn't make it this far."

Vincent pulled a bottle of water out of one of the backpacks and tried to throw it the length of the room to Taryn. Before it made it halfway across, the bottle exploded into steam.

This time it was Amber who tried to speak. Vincent untied her gag to Frederick's dislike.

"Tears," suggested Amber. "You have to cry. Using your power over fire should keep them from evaporating."

Taryn pulled herself up to the pillar of Marduk. She stood there for a moment, trying to think about all the worst times of her life. She remembered watching as her parents died in a car crash when she was young. She remembered being teased at school when her fire power got out of control. She thought about wandering the streets alone and hungry after she'd run away from her foster family. Slowly she could feel the tears welling up in her eyes.

Before the first drop fell, Cyrus called out, "Taryn, the Tiamat pillar. Make sure to use the Tiamat pillar."

Without asking why, Taryn stepped away from the Marduk pillar and leaned over the Tiamat pillar just as the first tear fell. A second tear dropped in the bowl-shaped indentation in the pillar, followed by a third. As the fourth tear splashed down, the stone slab of a door started to rise. The heat in the room dissipated. Taryn collapsed to the floor.

"Good call," said Vincent as he glanced at Cyrus, "but how did you know?"

"I did a little research myself before we came here. Marduk was considered a storm god—which means he was probably an air elemental sorcerer," replied Cyrus. "Tiamat was the Babylonian goddess of saltwater and the primordial oceans. It only made sense."

With a pat on the shoulder, Vincent led Cyrus and Amber down the length of the room to where Taryn lay on the floor. Frederick and the five remaining guards followed closely behind. After reaching Taryn, Vincent pulled out another bottle of water and held it to Taryn's lips. She looked tired and dehydrated.

Frederick lifted her up from the floor and made sure she could stand on her own, then proceeded to bind her hands again.

"Is that really necessary?" asked Vincent. "She barely has the strength to stand let alone put up a fight." Frederick didn't reply, but continued his task.

Cyrus edged over to her. "You trusted me without even knowing why I chose the Tiamat pillar."

With dry lips and a hoarse throat she replied, "I've always trusted ye. Ye were the one havin' trouble trustin' me." She smiled slightly as Vincent tipped one last drink from the bottled water into her mouth, then Frederick gagged her once again.

Frederick looked through the newly open door and saw nothing besides a set of stairs leading down. There were twenty or so steps, but then nothing. No walls on either side, no ceiling and no floor. They could see nothing in the room. Frederick cast a light spell, but it quickly faded.

"Okay, so what do the tablets say about this room?" asked Frederick gruffly.

Vincent pulled them out again and started reading. He read for many minutes without saying a word.

"There is a darkness spell on the room," said Vincent finally. "Its dimensions and contents are intentionally concealed except to say Tiamat herself is in that room. There is a spell here to free her, but first we have to find her. No other magic will work in there until we do. Somehow Marduk found a way to block magic."

"And exactly how do we do that?" questioned Frederick.

Vincent turned to one of the automatons and ordered it to go into the room. The automaton did so, but as it stepped off the last visible step, it fell into nothingness.

"There isn't even a floor in there!" exclaimed Frederick as he watched in horror. "How are we supposed to find Tiamat if there's no floor to stand on?"

"Well, I guess we can't go any further here," commented Cyrus who was still able to speak at this point. "We might as well head back."

The security guard slapped him alongside the head then gagged him too. Frederick looked at him with annoyance. Then his expression turned to a smile.

"We can't find Tiamat," said Frederick pivoting to Amber, "but you can."

"How?" asked Vincent.

"She's an air elemental sorceress," announced Frederick. "She can use the air to keep her aloft."

"Didn't you just hear what I said?" asked Vincent. "No magic will work in there."

Frederick grinned as he regarded Vincent. "Marduk was considered by the locals to be a storm god, right? That means he was probably an air elemental sorcerer. If he was, then maybe that's the *only* magic that might work in there." He gave an evil grin. "If it doesn't, then she falls to her death and we have one less captive to worry about."

Cyrus became agitated by this turn of events and tried to speak and free himself. This time it took two security guards to restrain him.

Frederick turned back to Cyrus, "Unless you'd like to volunteer to go first?"

Cyrus nodded. He wouldn't let his sister die without a fight.

Frederick then returned his attention to Amber. "No, you have the best chance of survival, my dear. If you find Tiamat, I promise your brother will live. If you fail, you will all die, understood?"

Amber quickly nodded with wide eyes. Frederick released her then led her to the stairs as she took one last look at her brother.

Vincent approached, "If you want my opinion..." but he did not get the opportunity to speak his mind.

"I'm sorry, my friend, but I did not ask for, nor do I want your opinion," said Frederick. "At this point, I'm willing to risk their lives to save my own."

* * *

Amber moved down each of the steps until she reached the last one. She lifted her arms, but nothing happened. Her knees and hands shook and she knew her nerves were getting the better of her. *What would Cyrus tell me to do? Calm down, breathe and relax.*

She stood there on the last step with her arms at her sides and closed her eyes. She took a few long deep breaths and did her best to relax. When she re-opened her eyes, she raised her arms. Wind in the dark chamber started blowing, eventually lifting her off the step and out into midair.

Amber was relieved to see her air elemental powers did in fact work in this chamber, but without sight or a sense of direction she was blind to the size and dimensions of the chamber. She also realized she was in there with a dragon. This last thought shook her nerves again. The wind calmed and Amber started to drop, but then closed her eyes and concentrated on her breathing again. Her flight stabilized.

Amber knew she was moving around, but couldn't tell if she was anywhere close to the dragon. *I wonder if Tiamat can see me?*

Once again her nerves were shaken, but she did her best to maintain her breathing and stay aloft. Her mind was racing now, thinking about the dragon. *How big is it? Can it see me? Is it stalking me? Will it eat me if it finds me?*

The darkness and lack of a floor was starting to get to her as well. She couldn't touch anything, she couldn't see anything—not even herself—and the only smell was old and musty. The dark was suffocating. She lost focus and to her sudden surprise, the wind died down around her. Like a heavy object tossed from a window, she dropped. Panic flooded through her. But then her feet hit a solid surface after falling only a few inches. The darkness spell lifted and she was able to see. Amber was relieved to be standing on a solid surface. She looked down to gain her bearings.

An ear-piercing scream echoed back up to the entrance.

Amber was not standing on the floor, but on the nose of Tiamat. The dragon's head was the size of a large yacht, large enough for the dragon to swallow her whole. Its huge grey eyes were staring right at her. She didn't notice much else before she fell from its nose and started plunging into what looked like a bottomless pit.

Amber flung her arms out to her sides and closed her eyes. The winds once again caught her and she started to rise. She looked up to see the enormous dragon also floating in midair. It wasn't flapping its wings or moving at all. As Amber used the winds to lift her up to the dragon, she realized Tiamat was a giant stone statue.

The dragon appeared to be frozen in a fighting stance, its mouth open displaying huge teeth. Amber realized just one tooth was as big as she was. The dragon's arms were raised with claws spread for a sweeping attack. Tiamat's outstretched wings were over a hundred yards from tip to tip. Its hind legs were over a hundred yards away with its tail ever further curling down and away from where Amber floated. The enormous body was long and muscular.

She looked around, but couldn't find the stairs to exit the chamber until she looked up and realized just how far she had descended. The entrance was so tiny and far above her Amber had trouble judging the distance. As she concentrated on floating up, she raised higher and higher until she reached the last of the stairs.

No sooner did she reach the long room than she collapsed to the floor shaking and sobbing.

* * *

The guards held Cyrus still.

Frederick pulled a blanket from a backpack and placed it around Amber. "Well done," he whispered softly. "Rest now, your part is over."

Even as Frederick consoled Amber, Taryn was feeling better. She might not be able to cast spells, but she still had other skills. She was stretching and twisting the ropes that bound her hands.

"There's no point in freeing Tiamat," said Vincent from the doorway. "She's too big to go out the way we came in."

"It doesn't matter. Malcolm wants her freed, so we free her, one way or another. Cast the releasing spell," said Frederick. As he gave his instruction, he made sure Vincent could see the amulet he fondled in his hand.

Vincent set his jaw and with a look of disdain he held up the Tablets of Destiny. *"Orkrum est min-vue cora non-tue mae ceiva don Tiamat."*

The now calm winds of the chamber rose to hurricane force. The ceiling started spinning and began to open up like an upside-down whirlpool. Then it ripped away entirely.

As the light of the afternoon sun shone down into the chamber, the grey colorless stone statue of Tiamat changed to shades of dark brown and tan. The enormous creature began flapping its wings as the spell holding her in place was released. She breathed a huge blast of fire from her mouth before ascending into the air.

Frederick stepped out onto the third step and held up his hands. The four remaining guards lined the doorway.

"Tiamat, we are the ones who freed you," called Frederick.

The enormous dragon flapped her wings to bring her face level with the small entrance to the massive chamber.

"Where is Marduk?" asked the massive head of the dragon.

"Marduk died thousands of years ago," replied Frederick. "It was my master Malcolm who ordered your release. In exchange, he commands you help him defeat his enemies and..." But Frederick never got the chance to finish his statement.

"He commands!" roared Tiamat. "No human may command me. I care not for the lives of mortals."

She then breathed a huge blast of fire, frying Frederick to a cinder in a matter of seconds. The fire of her breath entered the chamber, but Taryn had already wiggled free of her bonds. She held up her hands, blocking the fire from all but the four guards at the entrance.

"My captor is dead. My only wish now is to be left alone," commanded Tiamat. She then flapped her wings more vigorously and flew to the surface and freedom.

The hole above Tiamat's chamber opened up right next to the ziggurat ruins where she landed temporarily, crushing the remaining guards. She let out a loud dragon roar and breathed fire once again. Squinting her eyes in the bright afternoon sun, she ripped part of the rubble away from the foundation and hurled it at the remains of the ancient palace about a mile away. The huge chunk landed on the southern edge of the ruins smashing many walls. Tiamat let out one more loud roar and lifted off into the air, circling the step-pyramid a few times before flying south.

Down below, Taryn looked to Vincent as she stood beside him at the prison chamber entrance. "Tiamat is free, now what do we do?" she asked.

"I have no idea," replied Vincent. "No modern-day weapon is going to stop her. But she was heading south. Even in ancient times, there was a peaceful dragon colony in Antarctica. If she wants nothing to do with humanity then maybe that's where she's heading, hopefully."

Vincent descended the few steps into the prison chamber and picked up the amulet out of the ashes of what was once Frederick Von Woonst. After looking at it for a few seconds, he placed it in his pocket.

Taryn and Vincent then freed Cyrus and Amber. As Cyrus' bonds were removed, he collapsed to the floor. His sweating had returned and he looked pale. Amber rushed to his side.

"It's the poison, isn't it?" she asked Taryn.

"I tried gettin' him to return to the castle," said Taryn as she nodded, "but he wouldn't leave ye here alone. He's not doin' well. I've already used the spell to slow the poison twice. We have to find a mirror back to the castle fast."

"There's a town not far from here," stated Amber.

"I've got transportation in my backpack," added Taryn.

Max found himself stumbling along through the castle looking for the way out and back to Hank and Meagan. He knew Malcolm was still on the loose and so was the Minotaur. Malcolm would not give up so easily—he wanted the helm and would stop at nothing to obtain it.

Max had gone up and down stairs and around corners he thought he'd recognized only to find it was a new corridor or room. He realized after a while he was lost. *It wasn't this hard getting in. So why am I having such difficulty getting out?* Hoping the other two were not in a similar situation, he continued on, desperately searching for an exit... or at least a window.

As Max wandered through the corridors, he heard a sound. He stopped quickly to listen. Who was it? Or worse, what was it? The sound was moving up ahead, but it was hard to make out the source. The echo in the castle's corridors distorted it to the point it was unidentifiable. He could call out, but if it wasn't Hank or Meagan, then he didn't want to attract attention. However, if it was Hank or Meagan, then he needed to find them as quickly as possible. He decided it was worth the risk to find the others.

"Hank? Meagan? Is that you?" called Max cautiously.

The sound stopped briefly, but then started again. This time, it was definitely moving in his direction. Since neither of them replied, he had to assume it was not friendly. Max took a tentative step backward when the Minotaur came into view at the end of the corridor ahead of him. The monster was definitely not happy, gritting his teeth and blowing steam from his nostrils. The angry expression confirmed to Max he did not want to face this creature again.

Max turned and ran. The Minotaur charged down the corridor after him, but Max knew the Minotaur was not a sorcerer; the creature was all about brute strength. Max had to find a way to use that to his advantage.

He rounded a corner and then turned and held out his hands palms up. As he rotated his hands palm side down, the floor of the intersection froze over in a thick sheet of ice and the temperature dropped fifty degrees in a matter of seconds. Max turned and ran once again.

Looking back, Max saw the Minotaur hit the icy floor and slide right past the intersection where Max had turned. The creature slammed into another wall. Max continued running, but he could hear the monster make multiple attempts to recover before it continued pursuit. By this point, Max had put a good distance between himself and the half-man half-bull.

Max rounded another corner and found himself near an exit. It didn't look like the way he had come in, but any exit at this point was a good thing. He dashed out to find himself in an area that might once have been a garden, though he had no idea what kind of vegetation could grow down there. He ran through dead vines and rotted trees. The plants might have been dead for thousands of years, but the stench of the place lingered on. It smelled like rotted and decaying meat. As he exited the garden, he realized the stench was not coming from the garden, but the gigantic pit just outside—Tartarus.

As he stood there near the pit, he had a strange sense there was something familiar about this place. Like he had been there before. The sound of the Minotaur's roar snapped him back to the present. He looked over his shoulder to see if the beast was approaching, but saw no sign of the creature yet. He decided not to stick around to wait for it to show up.

From this point, he had a fair idea where the entrance to the Underworld should be. He ran around the castle to his right. It took a while as the exterior was larger than he had expected, but eventually he came to the doorway where he, Hank and Meagan had passed earlier. From this point, he sprinted back to the entrance of the Underworld and back to Cerberus.

He ran across the fields of Asphodel trying his best to avoid the ghostly shapes shimmering in and out of sight. He could only hope Hank and Meagan had made it this far, but Cerberus was up ahead. He hoped they would not try to take on the monster without him. Hank was badly injured and Meagan could not protect him and defeat Cerberus all with Malcolm still on the loose.

As he neared the entrance, he heard a voice from behind. Max quickly turned to find Meagan still pushing Hank as he floated along. Max was relieved to see them, but concerned about how they would all escape the Underworld.

Meagan wore a big smile at seeing Max once again, but her expression turned from joy to terror in a split second. They could hear the *thump, thump* of Cerberus's approach before they saw the hellhound.

Meagan pointed past Max and called, "Cerberus!"

Max's relief in seeing Hank and Meagan also turned from joy to terror as he pointed past Meagan and called, "Malcolm!" Just as Max called Malcolm's name, they heard another sound—the Minotaur. They couldn't yet see the monster, but knew it was nearby and heading in their direction.

Cerberus was closing on Max's position quickly so he cast a spell, *"Magna fir-tor loma."* He threw his fireball at Cerberus who just ran right through like it wasn't even there. Max then thought to himself, *A hellhound is a creature of fire. I need a new tactic. But the lake around the Elysium Fields is too far away.*

Max glanced at Meagan to find Malcolm charging her position with a fireball already in hand. He flung the fireball directly at Meagan. Max calculated at that distance she could just jump out of the way, but that would leave Hank in the line of fire. Instead she stood between Hank and Malcolm and placed her forearms together. A green shield appeared around her. The fireball slammed into the shield and dissipated. Hank was safe for the moment.

Max had a plan to immobilize Cerberus but needed the beast to follow him back to the Underworld's entrance. Max ran straight at the beast as it charged. With only a few feet left till impact, the huge three-headed dog leapt at Max who dove under its feet. The massive creature landed on all fours and skidded to a stop. It then turned around and growled at Max.

Max was already up on his feet again and running for the entrance. Cerberus went charging after him. As they neared the entrance, Max could feel the water from the river Styx. Before

Max could make it through the circular entrance out of the
Underworld, Cerberus caught up to him and knocked him aside,
preventing his escape.

Max flew through the air for a good twenty feet and landed
hard on his back, aggravating the earlier injury from the harpies.
He winced in pain and stood up once more. Cerberus had turned
and was coming back around. Max was now close enough to the
water that he reached out to it and it came flying through the
entrance just as Cerberus was about to pounce. The water column
knocked the three-headed hellhound to the side, avoiding impact
with Max.

Max then used the water column to pin Cerberus to the
ground by forming ice blocks around its front and back paws. He
also used it to place an icy muzzle on each head. Cerberus was
obviously angered by his capture and fought harder and harder
to break free.

Max ran back to find Meagan still fending off Malcolm by
using stone walls to block his attacks. Max was a long distance off,
but he knew time was against her. A dome of earth was beside
her, but there was no sign of Hank. Max figured she'd covered
Hank with the dome to protect him, but he wasn't sure how much
air Hank would have. He witnessed her block another attack from
Malcolm, but a not so distant roar let them know the Minotaur
had arrived.

She turned to face the charging Minotaur and raised her
arms, forming a stone wall. Once again, just like in the castle, the
Minotaur ran head first into it, the stone cracking in a spider web
pattern.

Max continued to run hard as Malcolm flanked Meagan. She
turned to find him standing next to her. Malcolm began casting a
spell, but she elbowed him in the gut to break his concentration.
As he recovered from the punch, he grabbed Meagan's backpack
and pulled it from her shoulders. He then slammed her head into
her own stone wall she'd used to block the Minotaur.

Malcolm ran off as the Minotaur let out another loud roar and
ripped through the stone barrier. It came tumbling down on top
of Meagan. One of the stones caught her on the left side of her
head and she fell face down on the ground, dazed by the impact.

Max was still too far away. He knew what was coming, but felt helpless to do anything.

Meagan made a feeble attempt to crawl away, but a hoof to her right ankle pinned her in place and prevented her escape. She struggled against the immense pressure then looked up in terror. The Minotaur stood over her. Lifting a large stone over his head, his muscles bulged from the enormous weight of the rock. Steam shot from his nostrils as his brow furrowed. With a mighty effort he slammed it down square in the middle of Meagan's back, crushing her into the ground. She lay there motionless as the monster raised his arms in victory and let out a loud roar.

"NO!" cried Max, rushing to her aide. In an instant, time froze. Max was the only one still able to move as he gazed down at the large stone covering Meagan's dead body. He looked around as he took in the motionless scene. With one wave of his arm, time began to rewind itself. The Minotaur's arms lowered and the stone slab raised to his hands. He raised the stone above his head as steam retreated into his nostrils. A chunk of rock flew from the ground past Meagan's head and back up to the stone above. The monster took a step back and lowered the rock onto the barrier Meagan had created. To Max's surprise, Meagan was once again alive, but dazed.

The Minotaur stood over Meagan with a large stone wall section in its hands. As he was about to slam it down on Meagan, Max cast a fireball spell, slamming it into the monster's chest. The Minotaur staggered backward a few steps and dropped the stone on his own head. Falling to its knees, it was only stunned. Meagan shook her head to clear her thoughts then turned to find Max standing next to her. She took a step back wide eyed at Max's sudden appearance.

"How?" said Meagan. Then immediately remembered, "Malcolm has the helm. He's going for the exit. I got this guy."

Max hesitated for a brief moment as he realized the import of what he had just done. Meagan snapped her fingers, bringing Max back to the moment. He took off with a sprint and headed back toward Cerberus and the exit to the Underworld.

Max watched at a distance as Malcolm arrived at the exit to the Underworld only to find it blocked. He'd anticipated

Malcolm's escape and sealed the exit with a large sheet of ice several feet thick. Malcolm's fireballs did little more than melt a few inches of ice in an area about five feet in diameter.

Max arrived as Malcolm threw another fireball to no effect. Malcolm turned to Max, just as Max reformed the melted ice into a water tentacle which snagged the helm out of Malcolm's hand. The helm flew through the air, landing right in Max's own hand. Malcolm's immediate anger turned to a laugh as he looked above Max.

Max could feel the hot breath on his neck. He turned to see Cerberus standing over him. Just as Cerberus attempted to engulf him, Max tossed the Helm of Darkness into one of the three-headed monster's mouths. The helm dissolved on contact with the creature's acidic saliva. The metallic goo disappeared down the gullet of the gigantic hellhound who let out a long, loud cry.

Cerberus could not leave until the helm was removed from the Underworld. Since the helm was now destroyed, there would be no escape for Cerberus.

"No!" called Malcolm realizing what Max had done.

Cerberus glared down at Max once again. As it did, the ground around its feet rose up and ensnared the four paws of Cerberus. Max looked past the huge hellhound to see Meagan pushing Hank along in midair. Max immediately ran toward Malcolm and out of the range of Cerberus. The older wizard punched Max with a right cross to his jaw and Max fell to his knees.

Malcolm looked around, but there were no other escape routes. He pointed at the icy barrier and spoke the spell, *"Mirtor tolanga se-atum."* The smooth ice acted like a mirror, but its image swirled in erratic patterns.

Hank and Meagan were quickly approaching as Hank called out, "Malcolm, no! It's ice, not a mirror. You have no idea what will happen."

Max moved to block Malcolm's escape and grabbed hold of his right arm with both hands. Malcolm gritted his teeth and furrowed his brow at the teenager's intervention. He reached behind his back with his left hand and pulled a silver dagger from a sheath on his belt. As he raised the dagger above him, Max's eyes widened. Max released his left hand to block, but Malcolm slammed the dagger down into Max's chest, piercing his heart. Instantly the boy felt his strength begin to fade, but he was determined not to allow Malcolm to escape.

As Max slumped to the ground dying, he refused to release his weakening grip on his adversary. Malcolm smiled. In mere seconds he would be gone. With one final lunge from the dark sorcerer, he and Max disappeared into the swirling patterns of the makeshift mirror of ice.

29 MYSTERY REVEALED

Almost twelve hours after the departure of Amber, Cyrus and Taryn, Gollnick was sitting in the library. Worried about his niece and the others, he wanted more than anything to be there to protect them. The throbbing pain in his left leg reminded him he'd only be in the way. He stared at the mirror waiting for a message or someone to return with news.

Elisa entered the room after only a couple hours of sleep. Gollnick could tell by the bags under her eyes and the drained look on her face she was still tired. She walked up behind him and placed her arms around him.

"You're not in any better shape than I am," said Elisa. "We'd both be a hindrance to the others. You need your rest."

"I can rest here," replied Gollnick softly. He appreciated her presence, but needed to wait by the mirror in case there was a call for help.

Elisa noticed a piece of paper in Gollnick's hand and took it from him. It contained the same symbol that had appeared above Max's name on his door in the new circle room. "What's this?"

"I'm not sure," replied Gollnick. "I think it has something to do with Max's true identity."

"Perhaps we could ask that muse Meagan mentioned, the descendant of Clio."

Gollnick thought about it for a moment then reached out to the mirror and cast the spell, *"Mirtor a mirtor tong-la."*

A few seconds later, the mirror showed a beautiful garden with birds and butterflies and flowers of all colors and sizes.

"Hello? Is anyone there," called Gollnick.

A beautiful young girl wearing a white dress danced into view.

"Hello!" she said politely.

"I need to speak with the descendant of Clio. Is she available?" asked Gollnick.

"I will summon her," said the girl and she danced off down the path and out of sight.

Gollnick turned to Elisa. "That must be Emma, Terpsichore's descendant."

A moment later, the communication shifted to a mirror at Veena's desk. "I don't mean to be rude, but I'm very busy right now. Who are you?"

"I'm Gollnick Strom, leader of the old Circle," he said in an official manner. "I believe you met my niece and her friends recently."

"Ah, yes. I know of you," replied Veena. "They are no longer here. They went to the Underworld to prevent the release of Cerberus."

Gollnick wanted to ask if they were alright, but realized she wouldn't know any more than he did.

"Actually I need some information. Do you know this symbol?" asked Gollnick as he held up the piece of paper bearing the ancient design. "We think it has something to do with Max."

Veena studied the symbol for a few seconds then shuffled though some papers on her desk.

"That is the symbol for Chronos of Greek mythology," she said. "Based on that symbol and what Max has told me about his identity, I think your Max may be one of the three immortals. According to legend, the three original sorcerers who closed the portal to the nightmare realm became immortal after doing so."

"Chronos?" questioned Gollnick. "You mean Chronos, as in leader of the Titans and father of the Olympian gods, sorcerers, whatever? That Chronos? Is that even possible? Max has no memory of who he is, and what little he does remember are brief flashes of ancient times. But how could he be the original Chronos?"

"You are correct, Chronos was a Titan and the father of many of the Olympian sorcerers of Greek mythology," said Veena, "and the only sorcerer in all of history to master the power of time. I have found brief references to such a person showing up all throughout recorded history. It's almost as if each time, fate brought him back to defend the prisons, but he disappeared shortly afterward. It's possible that Max may actually be Chronos.

If so, I would keep a close watch on your young apprentice. According to ancient Greek mythology, Chronos wasn't always the nicest person. At one point, in order to avoid a prophecy, he tried to kill his own children."

"But if Max is Chronos..." said Gollnick, and he let his words drift off without ending the sentence.

"Then he is quite possibly the most powerful sorcerer alive today," said Veena. "However, he may also be destined to disappear again once the prisons are safe, which may not be a bad thing. He has the potential for doing great good, but he could also represent great evil. Be careful."

30 AFTERMATH

Hours after speaking with Veena, the mirror began to swirl. Amber and Taryn stepped through while supporting Cyrus who immediately collapsed to the floor. To Gollnick's surprise, Vincent also emerged from the mirror. Cyrus was having trouble breathing and could not stand on his own.

"Cyrus has been poisoned by the spikes from the tail of a manticore. He needs help," said Amber, panic straining her voice. She knelt beside Cyrus and held his hand.

Gollnick stooped to examine the wound while Elisa ran from the room. "I'll get a healing potion."

"You bandaged it well," commented Gollnick, "but the poison is spreading quickly now. I take it you used a spell to slow its progress?"

Taryn nodded, but said nothing.

Within minutes, Elisa returned with a vial of blue liquid. "This should take care of the poison if it hasn't been in his system too long. Otherwise, he may be in for a rough night."

She poured the potion in his mouth and Cyrus swallowed. No sooner had he taken the medicine than he passed out. Elisa checked to make sure he was still breathing then sat next to him to wait.

Gollnick faced his former friend turned enemy, "Vincent?"

"I'm free of Malcolm's influence," said Vincent, pulling the amulet from his pocket and holding it up for Gollnick to see.

The lines on Gollnick's face wrinkled as he broke into a smile. He took a few steps forward then the two old friends embraced. After a few seconds, they returned their attention to Cyrus.

Amber and Taryn brought everyone up to speed on the events of the past twelve hours. As they were relaying the details of Tiamat's escape, Cyrus chimed in with, "What does someone have to do to get some food around here?"

Relief washed over the group as they helped Cyrus to his feet. He could barely stand, but they were able to get him down to the infirmary and into a bed.

Elisa examined him while they all gathered around. "He'll be alright, but he needs to rest. Actually, I think we all need some rest." She then shooed them out of the infirmary.

Before she could leave, Cyrus grabbed Taryn by the hand. She turned back to look at him. With drooping eyelids and a weak grasp, he quietly said, "Thanks." Then he fell asleep. Taryn just smiled and placed his hand on the bed next to him and left the room.

The others went their separate ways, heading back to their rooms. Gollnick placed his arm on Vincent's shoulder as they were leaving the room. "It seems the crystal has changed its mind about you. Welcome to the old circle, my friend."

* * *

Taryn entered the kitchen. She was tired but also dehydrated from the intense heat in the ziggurat. She pulled a gallon of water from the refrigerator and poured herself a glass. As she sat down to drink, the mysterious cat jumped up on the table.

It sniffed around a bit then stretched out across the table like it owned the place.

"I heard what ye did to help Max and Cyrus," Taryn spoke directly to the cat while holding its gaze, "so ye can't be all that bad. Thanks."

The feline's penetrating eyes shone brightly. The cat blinked, licked its lips, then jumped down from the table and departed the room. Taryn was left to wonder if it actually understood her at all. She shook her head and continued to drink.

A few minutes later, the cat returned and stood at the kitchen entrance, meowing continuously. Taryn just looked, wondering why it wouldn't stop meowing. When she stood, the cat turned and ran a few paces out of the room, pausing to look back and make sure she was following.

One more meow and Taryn decided to see what the cat was up to. She followed it into the library where Hank and Meagan lay collapsed at the base of the mirror. Neither appeared to be conscious.

Taryn ran to their sides and called to the cat, "Find Elisa!"

In un-catlike fashion, the cat darted from the room as if to follow her instructions.

Taryn paused before going to Meagan's side. *I just told a cat to go get Elisa and it obeyed. Definitely somethin' strange about that cat.*

She examined Meagan and Hank and found they were both in bad shape. Hank had a broken leg and looked pale and weak. Meagan was bleeding from a gash on the side of her head and had numerous cuts and scrapes all over. Taryn made sure both were still alive and tried to rouse them.

Elisa came running into the room behind the cat which disappeared behind some books. She lost interest in the feline when she spotted the new arrivals. "Where's Max?"

"I haven't seen him," replied Taryn.

"Let's get these two down to the infirmary," instructed Elisa.

Taryn cast the levitation spell and they carefully guided their wounded friends down to beds.

* * *

No sooner did they get them into bed than Vincent rushed in chasing after the cat. Gollnick was close behind hobbling along with a cane as best he could. A wisp of black tail could be seen slipping underneath one of the beds. Wide eyed, Gollnick forgot about the feline and hurried to Meagan's side.

"Meagan, can you hear me?" he said frantically. "Are you all right?"

Meagan made only the slightest mumbling noises, but no cohesive speech.

While Elisa was examining Hank, she had Taryn hold him down. It was necessary to set his broken leg. The painful sting woke Hank immediately. He almost jumped out of bed, but was too weak to move that fast.

Gollnick turned to steady his friend and make sure he didn't hurt himself further. "Hank, what happened? Where's Max?" he demanded.

Hank settled, but was still pensive as Elisa began wrapping his broken leg. "Max tried to block Malcolm's escape, but Malcolm stabbed him through the heart with a dagger. He died right in front of us."

Gollnick raised a single eyebrow. "Are you sure he died?"

"His body went limp, but was pulled into an ice mirror Malcolm used to flee the Underworld."

"An ice mirror? Even Malcolm is smarter than that," pointed out Gollnick. "Who knows where in the world you could end up?"

"He was cornered and desperate," said Hank still wincing in pain. "The Helm of Darkness was destroyed, but the Minotaur was approaching. We had no choice but to follow. We ended up falling out of some clouds high above the Painted Desert in Arizona."

"From that altitude, how is it you're not dead?"

"Lucky for me I already had a levitation spell upon me and was spared the worst part of the fall. My leg was previously broken. Meagan held onto me to avoid falling as well. At least we made it partway to the ground before she lost her grip and fell. Of course when she passed out, the levitation spell gave out and I fell too."

"Don't worry," said Elisa as she placed a hand on his head, "you may have some internal bleeding, but we'll take good care of you. You'll be fine."

"Where's Meagan?" asked Hank. He paused when he spotted Vincent.

"She's resting in the next bed, but she's unconscious," replied Gollnick. He turned to follow Hank's gaze and said, "It's a long story, I'll explain later. What about Max?"

"I don't know," replied Hank. "They apparently didn't come through the same cloud we fell out of. With a dagger in his chest and a fall from the clouds, he couldn't have survived. We were thousands of feet in the air when we started to fall," said Hank hanging his head, tears welling up in his eyes. "Meagan must have found a way to get us back to Ravenicon Castle."

"Could you find the spot where you fell out of the sky?" asked Gollnick.

"I doubt it," said Hank looking a little confused. "It was dark and we had no sense of direction. Why?"

"I'll explain in the morning, my friend. Rest now," instructed Gollnick.

The next day with the help of Elisa's magic, everyone was alive and recovering. Meagan had regained consciousness, the poison was gone from Cyrus' system, Hank's leg was in a cast and the others had gotten at least a little sleep. But the loss of Max weighed heavily on everyone in the room. All but Gollnick, Elisa and Hank.

Gollnick started with a loud sigh to get everyone's attention. "The good news is, Cerberus was prevented from escaping. And while Tiamat did get away, we've had a report that she appears to be heading south to the dragon colony in Antarctica. We've also recovered the Tablets of Destiny. Hopefully, examining them may help us find other prisons or even ways to re-imprison Tiamat, if it becomes necessary."

He looked around at the sad faces before continuing.

"You've all heard Max is dead," Gollnick paused as everyone hung their heads. "This may not be completely accurate."

All eyes snapped up to focus on Gollnick.

"When Max came to us, two names appeared on his door in the new circle room—Max's own name, along with a symbol we could not identify until recently. Max's name has now been scratched out on his door, however the symbol has not. Even the crystal can't seem to make up its mind if he's dead or alive. His Scorpio sign continues to flicker."

Everyone looked at him with wide eyes, their attention locked on Gollnick's every word.

Meagan was the first to speak, "Hank and I saw Malcolm stab him through the heart with a dagger. He must be dead."

"I understand that," replied Gollnick with a kind smile, "but I also have reason to believe Max may be hard to kill. Based on information from Veena of the Muses and a chat I had earlier with Hank, we have reason to believe Max may be one of the original sorcerers who closed the portal between our world and the nightmare realm." The others exchanged brief glances before Gollnick continued. "His real name is Chronos, the Titan and master of time."

"What?" exclaimed Cyrus.

Gollnick understood his confusion. "We think that's why he can remember events from ancient times. We're still not quite sure what's causing his amnesia."

"Even if Max has power over time, how is it possible he isn't dead?" asked Cyrus. "A dagger to the heart would kill anybody." He looked around the room at everyone's faces. "Don't get me wrong here. It's not that I'm upset he'll live, but I'd like to know how."

"According to legend," stated Elisa, "the three original sorcerers became immortal. Veena has found references to Chronos showing up throughout history to help protect the prisons, but then he disappears again. Each time, he goes by a different name because he doesn't remember who he is, but the symbol of Chronos has always been associated with this stranger."

"Taryn and Vincent will go to Arizona tomorrow, to the Painted Desert. They're going to try and locate Max," said Gollnick. "We've identified the gas station where Hank and Meagan found a mirror to get home. They'll start there and see what they can find. Once they have some leads, and you're feeling up to it, the rest of you can join the search."

* * *

In the Arizona desert, the sun was rising on a new day. A gentle wind blew as a tumbleweed rolled on by. The painted hills gave a colorful backdrop to the arid landscape.

In the middle of a barren space, a sizeable impact crater twenty feet in diameter could be found. From its pattern, it appeared as though an explosion had taken place.

Near the edge of the crater, footprints could be seen emerging from the pit, headed west. A silver blood-stained dagger was all that remained.

About the Author

Edward Eck lives in Pennsylvania and works as a network administrator and computer programmer. His love of fantasy emanates from stories such as *Star Wars*, *Lord of the Rings* and the mythology of various cultures. His hobbies include dancing, reading and writing.

In high school he lost his interest in reading, finding it boring. It wasn't until later in life that his love of reading was rekindled when he discovered fantasy and sci-fi novels. He realized that he hadn't grown bored with reading, he just wasn't interested in the same material he had been required to read in school. Since then he has read many books and found a love for writing as well.

"Reading is an escape from the boring and mundane. Let your imagination soar!"

www.ingramcontent.com/pod-product-compliance
Lightning Source LLC
Chambersburg PA
CBHW071252250626
47159CB00004B/1155